**A RETIRED ATTORNEY'S ADVENTURES
TAKE ON HOMICIDAL INTENT**

JUSTICE DELAYED

JUSTICE DENIED

PRESTON HOWARD
ANNE HOWARD

COPYRIGHT

Contents

DEDICATION

**To the memory of Buster and the rest of the
clan hangin' out in The Olde Irish Cemetery,
lamenting the extinction of the Republican party
of Abe, TR, Ike, and The Gipper**

AUTHOR'S NOTE

The three police officers who are central to this story—Willie Banks, Jimmy Buhl, and Ted Williams—are fictional and based on no persons, living or dead. The same is true with Sergeant Sam Evans. I make sincere apologies to the Austin Police Department and anyone in that department who is dismayed by the characterization that the agency is rife with criminal activity. The fact is, the APD leadership and its officers are persons of the highest integrity and should be applauded by the citizens of Austin for the top-flight services provided by the department.

Donald Trump and his cabal of lackeys, along with many other public figures who are skewered in this book, are all the real thing; albeit, their depictions are solely the author's often sardonic opinion. People in the public eye become involved in all kinds of misconduct, peccadilloes, or foolishness that is just open to all kinds of mockery.

The only factual setting that has been changed is the cigar bar where the author hung out in the book. Sadly, the Heroes and Legacies cigar shop in Northwest Austin closed a few years back, but using my magic literary wand, I resuscitated it, only because of my fond memories of the place.

"Anyone can become president. That's the problem."
George Carlin

"The dead cannot cry out for justice. It is the duty of the living to do so for them."
Lois McMaster Bujold

-1-

EMAIL FROM ANNE HOWARD December 3, 2018

Dear family and friends,

I want to first apologize for keeping all of you at arm's length for the past few months. But I know that you will cut me some slack: Between the allegations made against my dad, his untimely death, and my duties as his executor, I simply did not have the time or energy to reflect on recent events.

Now that life has slowed down a bit, I have had some time to consider why my dad went down such a dark path and the reasons for his actions and motives. I am not so blind to the reality that my dad has *probably* done some unspeakable things. I have carefully emphasized the word "probably" because no court in the land has found him guilty of anything other than innuendo and conjecture. Although, sitting back and objectively looking at the facts, if any of you determine that a compelling argument can be made against him, I will not be the one to condemn you.

However, I refuse to pass judgment or denounce him; he is, after all, my dad. And in spite of what he did—or *perhaps* did—I will always love him and appreciate the many pearls of wisdom that he provided over the years.

One thing has troubled me more than anything else. As my dad headed toward retirement, he wrote his well-received memoir, *The Sheltering Palms*, which I thought boded well for his future. The last chapter sounded so positive where he mentioned adventures and achievements that he would look forward to as he had during his remarkable career.

Somehow, though, he fell off the tracks and apparently into a morass of criminality. I still pinch myself from time-to-time, hoping all of the events surrounding my dad's acts of irrationality were just a nightmare that didn't really happen, and his murderous rage—make that alleged acts of irrationality, *alleged* rage—were never plastered across the front page of the *Austin American Statesman* and every other major city newspaper not only in Texas but throughout the country.

It would be exhausting and time consuming for me to telephone each of you. There are simply too many facts and nuances surrounding the entire episode. Therefore I have just mailed each of you a USB drive that contains a large number of files that should go a long way toward explaining what took place.

The items include a transcript of my dad's retirement party, personal letters, many excerpts from his journal, relevant newspaper articles and blogs, emails, doctor reports, a copy of the Banks legal file, several commentaries by me along the way, and some other miscellaneous items. Everything in the flash drive is set out in chronological order except for the Banks legal file and accompanying articles/blogs from the *Statesman,* so don't get jarred by the sudden regression from the recent past backward to 2008 and 2009.

My dad and I are both writers, but he is a novelist—quite good at it, I must add—while I am a computer dudette for an AI software company, working as a scrum product owner which is a fancy way of describing my job as herding cats (employee scamps who tend to veer off-course and must constantly be reminded of the right path and goals). My dad frequently chided me that this work would ultimately result in the loss of workers' employment and in his usual acerbic way asked if I could sleep at night knowing how I will be taking food off the table of so many people who will be caught in the crosshairs of the AI revolution.

But as Dad often said, I digress. So to the point I made before, please don't condemn me for the placement of the Banks file and any other errors in this tale. Being a linear woman, my first inclination was to place the Banks file front and center—get it out of the way in the interest of getting to the gist of the story. However, after much agonizing and confusion over where to place this file in the narrative, I decided to begin with my dad's retirement party for a little background on him and some of the other characters pertinent to this story, followed by a painful letter written by my mom, and my dad's first journal entry. Then I'll go backward to the Bank's case. Just sayin.'

A word about the Banks file. I requested a copy of the file from Conrad Diamond, my Dad's law partner and my longtime friend. But after much agonizing by Conrad, he decided against turning over the file to me, citing confidentiality and attorney-client privilege. But lo and behold, the file showed up anonymously on my doorstep; someone in my dad's office apparently felt differently than Conrad. By the end of this narrative, you will likely figure out who the transgressor was.

I felt torn like Scylla and Charybdis about including the file on the USB drive. Conrad and my dad were exceptionally close, and Conrad has extended me so many courtesies over the years. On the one hand, Conrad will become enraged at me for publicizing it; on the other hand, the file is central to the narrative, and I will feel like I let down my dad if it isn't included. So in the end, as Admiral Farragut said, "Damn the torpedoes, full speed ahead." Sorry Conrad.

One other note. Some of the emails between principals in this narrative have not been included due to security and personal reasons. My apologies for these omissions, but the reasons will hopefully become clear further along.

If after reading through the drive, you still have unanswered questions, then feel free to call me. Hold on folks because as the old saying goes, this tale has many twists and turns, and it's gonna be a bumpy, wild, and crazy ride!

Sincerely,

Anne Howard

-2-

TRANSCRIPT OF THE PRESTON HOWARD RETIREMENT PARTY PROVIDED COURTESY OF HOWARD, DIAMOND, AND MCGOWAN LAW FIRM
December 20, 2015

CONRAD DIAMOND: Good evening y'all. I hope that everyone has enjoyed our superb dinner and liquor provided by the Austin Club. Also, I appreciate so many of you coming here tonight since we're fixin' to honor our good friend, colleague, and law partner, Preston Howard. If anyone in the room doesn't know who *I* am, then you're probably at the wrong event, so make yourself scarce, go downstairs to the main desk, and let them help you find the right location.

SMATTERING OF LAUGHTER

CD: First, a few housekeeping items. As you came in tonight, some of you signed a form committing to be designated drivers at the end of the night. I expect those of you who agreed to this important task to live up to it. Our law firm doesn't need any lawsuits arising out of this party. And second, and I really mean it, *cell phones off! No calls, no texting, and no Googling!*

BOOS THROUGHOUT THE ROOM

UNRECOGNIZED VOICE: Enough all right, Conrad! Get on with it.

CD: I hope whoever said that isn't one of the designated drivers. He sounds already well on his way to a hangover tomorrow.

MORE LIGHT LAUGHTER

CD: What an auspicious time to celebrate Preston's career, a few days before his retirement and the upcoming holidays. I didn't need to make any notes for my talk tonight. I've known Preston Howard for more than forty years and been his partner for more than thirty, so other than his wife and children, I am more qualified than anyone else in this room to talk about the real Preston Howard. I'm going to talk about the many highlights and a few of the lowlights of Preston's career. I will try to keep the talk PG with maybe a tiny bit of R-rated along the way. But due to the sensitivities of Preston's lovely wife, Donna, other ladies in the audience, and his three wonderful kids—Kyle, Preston Junior, and Anne, all grown up now—there won't be any X-rated material about Preston's exploits. And believe me, I could blackmail Preston over his many salacious adventures.

LAUGHTER

CD: Speaking of his family, Donna Howard, the better half—make that *way* better half of the marriage—Preston's long suffering wife, please stand up. And his three kids stand up too.

INTERMITTENT CLAPPING

CD: Preston and I have spent much time over the years arguing over the relative credentials of our higher education. I, of course, attended the elite UT just up the street from here, for both my undergraduate and law degrees. Preston claims that *his* UT—that would be the second-rate university where he spent seven years in Knoxville—is the Harvard of the South...the *real* UT and *real* orange and white. Preston has been so sadly deluded over these many years, in large part due to his inferior education. Beyond the fact that Tennessee's football uniforms are a hideous shade of orange, as opposed to the gorgeous Texas burnt orange, only one out of ten graduates of the law school in Knoxville pass the bar. That's why there are so few attorneys practicing in the state of Tennessee. I don't even know how he passed the Texas bar his first time out. His law degree is such a feeble excuse of a school that Preston shouldn't even include his higher education on his resume.

LAUGHTER

CD: Preston's highlights could go on for hours, but to save time, I will cover his greatest successes, the many contracts he has negotiated for cops not only in Texas but also over the width and breadth of the country and the score of police officers he saved from termination or criminal conviction. He has developed a well-deserved, nationwide reputation as one of the premier labor lawyers. He was often sought out to speak not only around the country, but even internationally, about labor issues of the day. He once went to a press conference in the media room of the Capitol and screamed at an arrogant Fort Worth police chief for his misleading statements about the arbitration process: "You are a liar! I am telling you in front of the media and all the citizens of Texas, *you are a complete liar!* The police chief got so flustered that he walked out of the room; Preston took over the press conference and told the assembled media the truth about arbitration.

SUSTAINED APPLAUSE

CD: Of course, one of his most famous victories was over Ice-T's "Cop Killer" song in 1992. Preston insisted that we get involved in what eventually became a nationwide story—even the president, vice-president, and *The Wall Street Journal* spoke against the song. Against my better judgment, our firm took on the fight against Time Warner and Ice-T. We, and most of all, Preston, took them out to the woodshed for a real whippin'. The climax came at the Time Warner shareholders meeting in Beverly Hills Hilton where Moses, AKA Charlton Heston, read in his melodious voice the lyrics to *Cop Killer*, shocking the shareholders and embarrassing CEO Ira Levin. I want to publicly apologize in front of the entire office staff, and to Preston, for my objections to this project; he was right and gave our firm much terrific publicity that further advanced our firm's profile nationwide. Sit down Preston, and quit looking so damn smug. I'm not done talking yet.

LAUGHTER

CD: But the pinnacle of Preston's career has to be what we refer to as the Banks case in 2007 and 2008. I convinced him some years before to get more involved in our criminal practice, and he turned out to be one of the finest criminal lawyers not only in Texas but throughout the country. Preston represented three Austin cops indicted for murder and their subsequent termination case. Those three officers were Willie Banks, Jimmy Buhl, and Ted Williams; folks in the office refer to Ted as the Splendid Splinter. For those of you who don't know who the Splendid Splinter is…absolutely do not Google his name right now! Wait until you get home. Willie, Jimmy, and the Splendid Splinter are all here tonight, so guys, stand up and be recognized.

THUNDEROUS APPLAUSE

CD: Preston did such a great job at the their criminal trial that the three officers walked out of the courtroom free men, avoiding guilty verdicts for murder; then he later represented them in the city's termination case; the City of Austin capitulated, declined to arbitrate the case, and reinstated Banks, Buhl, and Williams with full back pay. Having been out of work for almost two years, it was quite a payday for the three officers. Preston's representation of those officers was as skillful as any

I have ever seen in my career. I still get goose bumps when I recall Preston's work on their case.

MORE APPLAUSE

CD: But let's not let Preston get off without talking about another side of him, so I'm gonna let you in on a few lowlights and also some examples of Preston's truly wicked humor. I picked Preston up one late afternoon from the airport in Corpus Christi, and we drove right away to a dinner meeting with the local union president and vice-president. As we were wont to do back in our more unsettled days, one drink led to another, and suddenly it was closin' time. I somehow drove to our hotel in violation of any number of Texas laws concerning open carry and alcohol consumption. The next morning, Preston and I met for breakfast, both feeling the queasy ill effects of our previous, injudicious night of carousing. Preston informed me that he had been so under the influence that he apparently left his overnight bag outside his room, and the bag was nowhere to be found in the morning. Preston was less worried about the bag and more concerned that when he returned home without his luggage, Donna would suspect him of some scandalous adventure flouting his marriage vows.

SUSTAINED LAUGHTER

CD: Donna, I swear on a stack of Bibles that if you still have any suspicion about the night in question, I can assure you that your husband was as righteous as rain.

MORE LAUGHTER

CD: And then there was the time that Preston and I were driving along a byway coming out of Brownwood—by the way, a good place to be driving away from. There had been a great deal of rain during the week, and we came across a cow that had become stuck in a culvert filled with rain and mud alongside the road. Preston, always a sucker for the downtrodden, insisted that we stop to get the cow out of the culvert. So we slogged down into the rain and goop, trying to push that stupid-ass cow out, but being a stupid-ass cow, she didn't move so much as an inch and just started bellowing.

INCREASED LAUGHTER

CD: At this point, I was damned well determined to get the cow out of the culvert, so I told Preston to get a rope in the back of my Ford F-150 and tie it to the cow so I could tie it up to my winch and pull this brainless animal out of the culvert. But Preston's shoes and pants were soaked with water and covered with mud at this point, so he didn't have as much concern with the downtrodden as before and said to hell with the cow. But he used a different word that due to the PG nature of my talk can't be spoken. After some disagreement between us, Preston reluctantly got back down into the culvert and roped up the cow, getting wetter and muddier than before and cussing the whole time. I tied the rope to the truck winch and slowly pulled the cow, still bellowing, all the way up to the road.

MORE LAUGHTER

CD: As Preston began to pull the rope off the cow, we discussed what to do next with the animal. But the cow had a mind of its own and suddenly started running off down the road in a direction opposite to the way we were headed. Preston and I then concluded that we had done our good deed for the day and that the future of the cow was no longer in our hands but instead in the hands of the Bovine God. We drove on back to Austin, so full of dirt and water from the experience that it took me two days to clean out the inside of my truck. I have wondered from time-to-time whether the cow's owner ever recovered that pathetic animal.

ROARING LAUGHTER THROUGHOUT THE ROOM

CD: And now a few examples of Preston's famous, or maybe I should say, roguish humor. Since I received these accounts secondhand, I can't absolutely verify the truth of what I'm about to tell you, but the events certainly sound like the Preston I know. He was negotiating a contract for the Corpus Christi cops, and during a lull in the talks, Preston was approached by a television reporter named Lola, along with her cameraman. Preston had been smoking one of his monster cigars, a seven-inch-by-seventy ring, and the reporter asked with the camera rolling: "Why do you keep pulling the cigar out of your mouth when my cameraman tries to catch you while you're smoking? And why do you smoke such a monstrous cigar?" Preston considered the questions for a moment, apparently finding both of the lady's questions beyond ridiculous, so he said, "First off, why would I let the media portray me as some kind of northern union goon smoking a cigar? And second, I've concluded that I'm a latent homosexual and sometimes think that I might want something else in my mouth other than a cigar." The cameraman began laughing so hard that his camera began bobbing up and down. But Lola didn't let Preston's comment faze her in the least; she simply said, "Preston, would you like to answer that again." Good going, Lola the TV reporter! Needless to say, Preston's first take of his comments didn't make the six o'clock news.

LAUGHTER

CD: In 1981, Preston was negotiating a new contract for the San Antonio police officers. As these talks were going on, the baseball union and owners were having a major conflict in their negotiations over free agency. During a break from the San Antonio talks, a newbie woman, and as it turns out very naïve radio reporter, asked Preston about the major issues in negotiations. Preston went into a windy and convoluted explanation to the sweet, young lady about the one huge issue—free agency for San Antonio police officers. He explained that when a cop from there resigned and took a job with, say, the Houston police department, the question became how much the city of Houston would have to reimburse the city of San Antonio. The reporter furiously wrote down notes about this major development. Then the city's negotiator sat down at the table, and the reporter breathlessly asked him what his position was on free agency. The city negotiator gave Preston a quizzical look but then got the joke and said, "No comment at this time." So as to not embarrass the reporter, Preston cautioned her to not publish anything about this vital issue until he told her otherwise. She kept bugging Preston throughout negotiations, so toward the end, he told her that the issue had been dropped. She never figured out that she had been pranked—fortunate for both Preston's credibility with the press and her continued employment with the radio station.

BREAK IN TRANSCRIPT

CD: As I look at the Preston of today, he's not much different than when I first met him, except that he's got some faint crow's feet around his eyes and speckles of gray in his goatee and hair, or at least what's left of his hair. Preston, please cover your head so when you turn to the light, I'm not blinded like the Greek dude Tiresias.

LAUGHTER

CD: But he still has that one…*prominent* feature on his face. Preston and I went down to Corpus once with our families and spent some time on the beach. Preston jumped into the Gulf and started swimming a backstroke, quite ably I might add. Suddenly I heard people screaming "Shark! Shark!" and they were running from the water onto the beach. It was like a reenactment of *Jaws*!

MORE LAUGHTER

CD: Sorry, Preston, but I had to knock you down a peg or two before you get up to speak; otherwise, your ego will get so swollen that your head won't squeeze out of the room when we're done. Ladies and gentlemen, may I present my longtime good friend and law partner, Preston Howard!

DEAFENING APPLAUSE

PRESTON HOWARD: Thanks, Conrad. I'm not sure whether I should be appreciative of your introduction or thankful that I will no longer have to see you at the office, listening to your rather sardonic wit that often drove me to distraction. But then again, I might have to come down to the office every now and again just to listen to your insipid stories at my expense. Actually, Conrad, I will, in truth, miss you and the rest of the staff. It's been one helluva ride through these many years of doing the right thing for police officers around the country. While on the subject of the staff, I want to recognize one man in particular—Tony Nelson. Tony, please stand up and be recognized.

SMATTERING OF APPLAUSE

PH: I met Tony when he served on the Austin police union negotiating team back in the nineties when I represented the union in contract talks. Tony and I hit it off from the get-go, and his retirement from the department coincided with our firm's need for a new investigator. Tony's extensive experience in the special investigations unit made him an immediate fit for our law firm. Plus, I would no longer be the baldest guy in the firm. So I scooped him up in a New York minute, thus starting a long and close friendship. Thank you so much, Tony, for all your efforts on my behalf over the years and for saving my ass from many potential screw-ups.

LIGHT APPLAUSE

PH: I promised Donna earlier today that I would take it easy on the wine tonight, but it's one of several promises I have not kept to her over the years. This pinot noir is superb; thanks Conrad for at least once not acting like a cheapskate and suppling an excellent wine. It tastes damned good. I developed quite an affinity for this particular red when Donna and I spent time in Buellton, California, during the *Sideways* movie tour. So honey, I'm sorry, as I have been so many times before, but my alcohol level is way beyond .08, so you will be driving home tonight.

MUTED LAUGHTER

PH: Speaking of Donna, I want to do that hackneyed routine that everyone does when they give a retirement speech and at some point give a shout out to their family. So Donna, Preston Junior, Kyle, and Anne, please stand up again.

RESPECTFUL APPLAUSE

PH: Holy cow, how 'bout them kids! Junior was an all-star goalie in the MLS and now coaches for the Red Bulls. Kyle is a professor at West Point, the head of the History Department. And Anne works on AI software. She has explained it to me numerous times, and all I ever hear from her explanations is gibberish. I still have no idea what she's talking about except that it's going to put a lot of hard-working folks out of work. My kids have become so accomplished in their various fields—probably due more to Donna and her genes than anything I had to do with it.

TAPE GOES SILENT FOR MORE THAN A MINUTE

PH: Sorry, I've become a little verklempt. My emotions have gotten the better of me. One day I was a young fella starting my law practice and then suddenly I'm an old man going out to pasture. Who knows what the future will hold? How did I get from there to here in just the blink of an eye? How did the time go by so fast without realizing, until this very moment, that the life and work I love so much has come to such an abrupt end?

TAPE GOES SILENT AGAIN FOR SEVERAL MINUTES

PH: I'm sorry folks, but I just can't continue without breaking down. So all I can say is thanks to all of you who have worked with me loyally for so many years. It has…been my pleasure…. We have…sorry again. I just can't continue.

SILENCE, FOLLOWED BY INTERMITTENT APPLAUSE

CD: Okay, let's all give Preston the recognition he so deserved for his many years of service with our law firm. Show your appreciation by giving him a great sendoff!

DEAFENING APPLAUSE

CD: One other thing before the festivities end: Preston, I know that you've always thought I'm a skinflint when it comes to the firm's money, but just to show that I don't have a total heart of stone, please accept this eighteen-carat-gold watch as a gesture of how much we all care for you. On the back of the watch, the inscription says "Best Labor Lawyer in the World." Also, considering how much you love to travel, we are giving Donna and you two open, first-class tickets to Australia. I know, Preston, that

Australia is one place you've never been and that it's on your bucket list.

APPLAUSE

CD: Finally, I know how much Donna and you love those two grandkids up there at West Point. So we're also giving you both another two open first-class tickets to Disney World—and for your grandkids as well. So Preston, I don't ever want you to say again that I'm such a cheap bastard. And bon voyage!

LAUGHTER AND APPLAUSE

CD: So that's the end of the evening ladies and gentlemen. Please be careful driving home.

SCATTERED APPLAUSE, END OF
TRANSCRIPT

-3-
DONNA HOWARD LETTER September 10, 2016

Dear Preston,

So where to begin? Maybe the retirement party at the end of 2015? But both you and I know that things went off the rails a long time before that.

For more than forty years, I have put up with your running around...no idea how many women you have been with. Don't even want to know. Then there's your constant drinking to the point that you have recently been bringing a wine glass to bed every night. And your gallivanting around the country, feeding your ego as you get introduced as The Man. Finally, those stinky cigars—you sit on the patio smoking one after another, then come into the house reeking of tobacco.

I endured all of your imperfections because I, make that *we*, took *our* wedding vows to stay married for better or worse. Since your retirement last year though, your decline—your constant dissatisfaction with life—has become too much to bear. I've come to the conclusion that there's been a great deal more of worse than better—a lot more emotional pain and indifference on your part—and it gets worse by the day. Basically, I have gotten the short end of the stick over these many years, and I am sick and tired of it.

Was the retirement party the culmination of my many frustrations? Well no, not at all. When we flew to Australia for what I hoped would be a way for us to reconnect, you went on a four-week drunkfest from the moment we got on the plane, and sucked down as many glasses of champagne as you could get in your hands. Then the morning to night swilling of Fosters and dirty vodka martinis.

You spent the whole trip pissed off about Trump's nomination. I get that. I am also aghast that this buffoon with hair the color of an orangutan might be our next president. But then you went on and on to any Aussie who would listen. Do you really think the folks down under really gave a shit about Donald Trump? Even worse, when we met some aborigines, you spent at least a half-hour showing off about how they are the fourth classification of human after Caucasians, blacks, and Asians...or something like that. Those poor aborigines seemed perplexed. Do you really think they spend their days reflecting on their different grouping from other humans?

Disney World turned out to be an even worse disaster. When we got on a bus for one of the theme parks, you had the gall when a bunch of blacks walked on the bus to ask whether we were in Soweto...*with our two grandsons listening.* I felt so embarrassed and wanted to shrink away to nothing. At dinner, when you were as usual quite lubricated, you stood up and hollered, "Oh my God, Mickey Mouse was just killed by some terrorists!" If it wasn't bad enough that other kids in the restaurant started bawling, *our grandsons* became so upset that we had to leave the place. *What is wrong with you*?!!!

Now back to the retirement party. It was decent of you to talk about our wonderful children. I know you are as proud as I am about how they have turned out. Although, while I'm venting, you really screwed the pooch on that one too: You conveniently forgot the

21

other kid. You know, the one who is transitioning— who you can't call Dawn rather than Don and can't say her rather than him. Fortunately, she was out of the country undergoing another procedure; not sure if you would otherwise have invited her to the retirement. Get over Dawn's choice to transition from a man to a woman, accept it, and move on.

And what about *me*? Couldn't you have at least said a few words about the wife who spent so many years nursing our babies when they were sick, driving them to and from school, showing up at their various sporting events, guiding them to the right colleges, on and on and on; all the while, you were never home, and always absorbed in your self-important work. Or how about how after they went off to college, I began a career at AISD as a counsellor and have been lauded many times over for *my* work? You don't know how much it hurt when you said not even one thing at the retirement party about me as if I were a nonentity, someone not even worth more than a trifling mention.

Preston, there is still a small part of me that loves you, but unfortunately I don't feel like it's enough for this marriage to survive. There is no way I can spend whatever time is left on this earth listening to you obsessing about our new president or about the Banks case or whatever else you decide to abnormally fixate on as you so often do.

You have many personal issues that need attention, Preston. Your weight has blown up, your drinking is totally out of control, and you have lost your self-identity. You are no longer, and never will again be, The Man who comes in to save the day. I urge you to see your doctor and a psychologist so you can regain some of your physical and mental health and discover something that will make you excited about your life again. Otherwise, I will be reading your obituary in the paper a lot sooner than later, which will devastate our children a lot more than me. I am so sad to make this remark, but it's how I feel.

So it's time to end it. I have met a gentleman who might or might not be someone right for me, but at least he treats me with the respect that you have somehow forgotten about. I know that our finances are in good shape, especially since the firm's buyout of your interest has made us quite flush with cash. You have never been a penny-pincher with me—still one of your better qualities—so let's sit down and reach a reasonable accommodation as to how we split our assets.

Still with a modicum of love,

Donna

NOTE FROM ANNE HOWARD: I wasn't sure whether to include my mom's note. It's a pretty raw picture of my dad and not necessarily the view I have ever had of him. He's always just been Dad to me. But I concluded that my mom's letter is an important prelude to at least some of the events that took place later.

The memories of my dad are so contrary to the portrayal given by my mom. I realize that my perceptions, both as a child and later as an adult, would be dissimilar from those of my mom....That's a given.

When I was around five years old, I can still vividly recall Dad walking out from a doctor who had conducted a vasectomy on him, and as he painfully and carefully stepped into the car, he said to my mom, "Glad I'll never have my balls cut again." The next morning, my good buddy Marcus from next door walked in the house, saw dad sitting on the living room couch, holding an ice pack down in between his legs, and asked, "What's wrong with your dad." I answered, "He just had his balls cut off."

Every summer, my dad would drive me up to Arlington, plan some work for the next day, and drive me to DFW to fly up to my grandparents' home in Northwest Arkansas. The Texas Rangers had just opened the new, retro-looking ballpark, an excellent imitation of a yesteryear field like Wrigley. Dad suggested that we go to the game the night before I was to leave. As he kept insisting that we go the game, I continued to say no, no, no....I wasn't about to spend dreary hours watching men throw, hit, and run in a game I found too deliberate, with rules that baffled me.

So we passed it up. The next morning, my dad became as agitated as I'd ever seen him; the Rangers' Kenny Rogers pitched a perfect game, the ultimate achievement that would earn Rogers a mention in the Cooperstown Hall of Fame. My dad would rag me over that day so many years ago, and now my husband, Barry, piles it on too, every now and then pulling up Rogers's last out in the game on YouTube and playing it at full volume. When we're all together, their ribbing becomes so out of hand that I have to leave the room.

-4-
PRESTON HOWARD JOURNAL...February 3, 2017

I cackled while watching The Donald in June, 2015, as he descended the elevator at Trump Tower like an Arabian potentate, Melania walking below him in one of her bazillion-dollar outfits (or more...can there be more than a bazillion?). Right off the bat, I figured no rational person would listen to this clown as he ranted about Mexican rapists, recapturing oil in the Mideast, jobs lost to China and Mexico, blah, blah, blah. Right after the Great Bloviator announced his candidacy, Jon Stewart licked his chops and rubbed his hands together in glee but expressed sorrow that he would soon be leaving *The Daily Show*, unable to skewer this phony poohbah in Jon's inimitable style.

Boy oh boy, did Jon and I ever get this one wrong, as did most of the elitist commentators—the FOX reporters impostering as legitimate media excluded, of course. And as well did the multiple Republican candidates, who scorned Trump as a laughable huckster not worthy of consideration. His list of gaffes during the campaign mounted day by day, but the Trumpster shrugged them off like water off a duck's back each time and just kept lying all the way to victory and the White House.

I wonder often how many times after the Republican Convention, Jeb Bush and Marco "Trump has little hands" Rubio asked themselves, "How the fuck did this nimrod beat me?" And Hillary, bless her heart, she must wake up every day thinking "I deserved to win; I was entitled. How could all those deplorables snatch away my victory? How dare they?"

And now we're only a little over a month into the Trumper's first year; it's clear that he is a liar, a bully, and for sure, a windbag. How can our republic survive one year, much less a full term, with this kind of offensive behavior?

I smell all kinds of foul play by this guy, but what exactly it is hasn't yet emerged. Like the All Knowing and Magnificent Carnac, I predict dark days ahead for our Republic. Jesus, I don't even have to be Carnac to see an unmanned train roaring down the tracks, headed for a collision like our country has never encountered before. Well okay, maybe excluding the Civil War. Rein it in a bit, Preston!

My kids got all worked up when I didn't vote last November. I figured out before the election that Trump was a sorry piece of shit. Couldn't vote for Hillary either; she was carrying more baggage around than a redcap hauling six huge pieces of luggage.

And anyway, my vote would have been meaningless in Texas. This state has been redder than a Junagold apple going back to the eighties. It's the same anti-union, Bible-thumping, pro-business tax slashers; they just changed affiliation from D to R.

The only bright moment came in 1992 when Ann Richards beat Claytie Williams in the governor's race. Claytie—the guy who said rape was just like the rain; you just have to wait 'til it's over. Now that's a turn of phrase I'd never heard before or since.

Claytie stands in a long line of oddball Texas politicos. Congressman Charlie Wilson could throw out some droll comments as well as anyone; when asked about his attractive, well-endowed secretaries, he said, "You can teach 'em to type, but you can't teach 'em to grow tits." And then there's Congressman Louie Gohmert. Applying the old saw about not being the sharpest knife in the drawer, Louie's knife is so blunt that it's not even allowed in the drawer.

The governor's mansion sat just two blocks from our office, so Ann would drop by every now and again just to chat and thank us for our financial and other support during that exciting campaign. Having an interest in my on-going bout with alcohol, I once asked her how she got off the sauce. She told me it was AA and will power. Not that her counsel helped me at that particular time with my weakness.

The arc of my life has turned on a dime. One moment I was living out in Rob Roy in a fancy-pants kind of house, hanging out with some of the Austin elites until Donna pulled the rug right out from under me. Not that I'm bitter. Our marriage had been on a downhill slope for many years. I intuitively knew that the end would come sooner or later to a skidding halt, either in a conversation or, as it turned out, a letter. It's just I never did have the will to deal with it, and at this point, the buzzer has sounded, and the game is over.

Donna's letter pretty much said it all. I did feel a twinge of guilt over her remarks about Dawn/Don...her/him. I love the...guy/gal as much as the others. It's just been a major rethinking of how

I see her/him from a college football player, then police officer, manly man to a pretty attractive woman with boobs and a higher pitched feminine voice. I read somewhere, probably the *NY Times,* my normal repository of all factual information, that forty-plus percent of all transitioned men and women commit suicide…probably because when they get to the other side, there's nothing but disappointment. The change doesn't make you feel any better about yourself. I worry more than a little about that disheartening outcome for my kid.

Now I live alone in a condo; at least I can walk outside and look down on the 360 bridge and out further to the downtown skyline. Breathtaking views for sure! At night, the coyotes howl and yip below a ridge outside my wraparound deck, a pack sounding like at least ten or more of them. The unsettling sound is like death coming up the ridge toward me.

I sometimes pull out my extravagant gold pocket watch and feel the hollow thrill of being the greatest labor lawyer in the world as if that means a whole lot at this point. Who gives a rat's fuck about a has-been attorney who sits around the condo soused half the time? Make that most of the time.

A rock group in the eighties called Whitesnake sang this one song…trying to recall what it was that seems so apt right now. Oh, now I remember: "Here I go again." It was something about being alone, which pretty much, no, exactly describes my current status.

It's not all bad living alone. I'm not lonely; it just feels different walking into a house that feels as quiet as a graveyard at midnight with no one to talk to other than myself. My granddaddy Buster used to say it was okay to talk to yourself so long as you don't answer. Buster would tell me that if you're answering yourself, some kind of derangement might be at work. I'll have to pay better attention to my speaking habits.

I think about Buster frequently. I wrote about him fondly in my memoir, the father-figure who mentored me, and I suppose, turned me into a cynic in so many different ways, whether religion, politics, or history. Every now and then, he inhabits my dreams, and we have intimate conversations about…damn it, I can never remember what we talked about when I wake up.

Been doing some research lately on presidential assassins: John Wilkes Booth, Charles Guiteau, Leon Czolgosz, Harvey Lee Oswald. Their bullets all hit the mark, but none of them got away with it. Guiteau and Czolgosz were crazy as mad hatters. Booth—not so much. He just raged over the Confederacy's defeat a few days before Lincoln's assassination.

Now Oswald was in a category by himself. The Warren Commission ascribed a number of possible motives, but in the end, they always seemed obscure, hidden from the view of the countless Monday morning quarterbacks.

I'm wondering if it's at all possible to pull off something so dramatic and escape undetected. Probably not, but who knows?

Annual physical next week. I look forward to my appointment with Doctor Ghazini; she is only one of two physicians I've ever had who has a sense of humor. She referred me to the urologist, Doctor

Chaudhry—the other witty doctor—who snatched out my cancer-ridden prostate and turned me into a Viagra-popping dude. Not that I've been taking the blue pill anytime recently. How the hell did I wind up with two Pakistani, Muslim women for my doctors?

Most doctors have such an inflated sense of self-importance as if the Hippocratic God appointed them as the Second Coming. Doctor Ghazini, on the other hand, has always acted like a down-to-earth, good ol' boy—make that gal. But her exam will be just like the *Groundhog Day* movie with the same recommendation every year—lose weight, give up the cigars, stop drinking, *ad nauseum*. This visit will be like cheating on a midterm test by getting the answers in advance. Maybe I'll cancel it.

-5-

THE BANKS FILE

Austin American Statesman…May 15, 2007…State and Local Section

Three Austin narcotic officers conducted a raid on East 17th Street in East Austin last night around ten p.m. Gunfire was exchanged between the three officers and residents of the house. There was no more information available at press time, but as more facts become available, you can read them at *The Statesman* on-line.

***

Austin American Statesman…May 16, 2007…State and Local Section

Three Austin narcotic officers executed a search warrant at East 17th Street in East Austin last night at 9:48 p.m. Gunfire was exchanged between the three officers and residents of the house. The three officers have been identified as Detective Sergeant Wilfred D. Banks and Detectives James X. Buhl and Theodore L. Williams, all assigned to the Organized Crime Unit, working narcotics cases.

The residents of the house have been identified as Leroy Wallace, 42; Shanice Wallace, 38; Jazmine Wallace, 10; DeShawn Wallace, 8; and Tyrone Wallace, 7. Four members of the Wallace family were pronounced dead at the scene. Shanice Wallace was transported to Brackenridge Hospital where she died shortly afterward. The police department's public information officer, Randall Van Houten, stated that the Wallaces were all shot inside the living room of their home.

One neighbor of the Wallace family, Narvia Hornsby, said she was stunned by the shooting. She stated that the family attended St. James Missionary Church every Sunday and that the three Wallace children attended Magnolia Montessori for All. Ms. Hornsby noted that Jazmine Wallace was apparently so intelligent that her mother was considering whether to enroll her in high school next year.

A police department source indicated that Leroy and Shanice Wallace were allegedly known drug dealers not only in Austin but throughout Central Texas. According to the source, both of the Wallaces have convictions and incarceration for cocaine drug sales.

The scene at the Wallace house on 17th Street was inundated with Austin police officers and civilians from the Special Investigations Unit, Internal Affairs, the Crime Scene Unit, and Ballistics Unit. Assistant Police Chief Wayne Schmidt and Assistant District Attorney Oliver Baird were also present at the crime scene.

Austin attorney, Preston Howard, arrived at the scene shortly after the shooting and was observed talking to officers Banks, Buhl, and Williams. Officer Van Houten further stated that the three officers have been placed on administrative leave pending investigation of the shooting.

***

PRESTON HOWARD NOTES, BANKS
FILE…May 16, 2007

Detective Sergeant Willy Banks and detectives Jimmy Buhl and Ted Williams visited me at the office following their shootout in East Austin yesterday. Being a real fan of 50s and 60s baseball, I renamed Williams the Splendid Splinter. None of them knew anything about Ted Williams, but it seemed to break the ice with the officers.

I asked Teddy if he knew that the Splendid Splinter had been sent to a cryonics facility and that the Splinter's head had been lopped off and now sits in a bottle that looks like a lobster pot. Teddy shrugged; I suppose he had more important things floating around in his mind than Ted William's head.

Client Banks stated that the three of them wanted me to represent them. I told them that I could do so temporarily, but if the case received intense scrutiny from the district attorney and indictments resulted from their conduct, we might have to do a severance and find separate attorneys for each of them.

I explained that there might possibly be conflicts of interest between them that would require a severance; in fact, whatever judge would preside over the case might insist on it. They all chimed in, objecting to this idea. Client Buhl stated that they did nothing wrong and had their stories straight. (NOTE: the words "had their stories straight" set my lawyer-antenna aquiver!) I decided to just let the idea fester for a bit.

We briefly discussed the scene of the shooting yesterday. Buhl referred to it as a cluster fuck, and after looking around the scene, that surely was how I saw it as well. I have never seen such a mob of cops and civilians tromping inside and outside the residence; don't know how such confusion could result in anything other than contaminated evidence.

Clients Banks, Buhl, and Williams are assigned to the Organized Crime Unit, specializing in narcotics investigations. Banks has held this position for almost seven years, Buhl and Williams for about five years. They normally work as a team. Client Banks stated that a CI provided information that Leroy Wallace, AKA "Black," and/or his wife, Shanice Wallace, AKA "the Vamp," were holding a large supply of cocaine in their possession.

When client Sergeant Banks drafted a search warrant, he sought a no-knock provision in the warrant since the Wallace couple were known to be armed and dangerous and would likely attempt to destroy evidence. The warrant, including the no-knock, was thereafter submitted to Municipal Judge Felipe Garcia, who approved the warrant for a search of the Wallace premises. Sergeant Banks stressed that as a supervisor, he was permitted by department procedures to approve and draft a search warrant.

On May 15, the officers proceeded to the Wallace residence. When asked if they wore balaclavas when they approached the house, they said no. All three carried their service weapon and AR-15s. Client Buhl noted that they took the AR-15s as a safety measure. The Splendid Splinter indicated that the lights were totally off, both outside and inside the house. Clients seemed to have trouble recollecting their respective positions prior to the entry. After some discussion, they concluded that Banks and Williams entered by the front door, Buhl the back door.

Client Banks used a metal battering ram to open the front door without prior notice, per the no-knock warrant. Banks and Williams asserted that as soon as they entered the premises, someone fired at them. Both clients returned fire toward where the shots originated, which they approximated to be from a downward location, later verified to be from a sofa. Their AR-15s both discharged all 30 rounds. Client Buhl stated that being at the back of the house, he was never in a position to fire.

Client Banks noted that Shanice Wallace was apparently still alive, appeared close to death but trying to talk, and was transported, likely to Brack.

I reminded them at the scene the previous night and again this a.m. to keep tight-lipped with everyone about this case: IA, DA, police colleagues, friends, etc. They acknowledged my warning. I told them what to expect: IA won't interview them until any question of the circumstances surrounding the deaths is cleared up. The shooting will go to the grand jury for review. My clients seemed concerned about the grand jury. I advised them that normally the grand jury no-bills police shootings. I told them that after more information had been gathered, we could discuss their grand jury testimony and whether they should take the Fifth. I told them that unless some negative facts develop, they normally would testify before the grand jury without any concerns.

Follow-ups for Tony Nelson

1. Wallaces' criminal records

2. Clients' personnel files
3. Witnesses at or near the scene?
4. Any statements by Shanice Wallace?

***

BANKS FILE – TONY NELSON NOTES June 6, 2007

Preston,

Per your request, I have looked into the matters you requested. As both your long-time investigator and close friend, I have to note at the outset that based on my initial work, this case will be an uphill climb.

Both Leroy and Shanice Wallace have extensive criminal records. Both have arrests for various drug-related offenses and one conviction. L. Wallace spent 8 years up in Huntsville for selling cocaine; S. Wallace, 6 years for the same offense. While they were in Huntsville, the children were apparently cared for by their maternal grandmother. A stash of cocaine was found at the residence; I will find out the amount shortly. That's about the only good news.

Internal Affairs officers have been busy beavers when it comes to your clients. Their personnel files are littered with excessive force complaints, racially tinged remarks toward African-Americans, and suspicion of money and/or drugs not making it into the evidence room. Several of their superiors have sought numerous times to move them out of narcotics, but Banks *et al* seem to have a rabbi further up the chain of command. The Austin PD has always been perceived as a pretty clean operation, but apparently there have been some going-ons below the surface that don't meet the smell test.

And now for some really bad news. You would have gotten these tidbits from the DA's office anyway after the grand jury proceeding when, not if, true bill indictments are brought against your clients. My source inside the PD slipped the following items to me *sub rosa*, as were the internal affairs files.

One special investigations unit detective interviewed a gentleman by the name of Maurice Holloway who lives directly across the street from the Wallace house. In the detective's report, the witness asserts that he just happened to be looking out on the street when he saw the three officers approach the Wallace house. The lights were on in the house, and the officers all wore balaclavas. When the three officers stood by the door, one of them used some kind of ramming device to open it, and once opened, two of the officers immediately began shooting their rifles (i.e.; AR-15s). Mr. Holloway states that prior to and during the AR-15s opening up, he heard no other shots. Then within thirty seconds, Mr. Holloway heard further shots inside the house that didn't have the same loud resonance as the AR-15s. He believed he heard four shots of this type. Mr. Holloway also observed the third officer, who stood behind the other two, run into the house after the AR-15s discharged, and this officer appeared to disappear somewhere further inside the residence.

My source provided me with the preliminary forensic firearm examination by the Ballistics Unit of the bullets and cartridges discharged at the scene. One set of the striations on the bullets and cartridges was determined to be made by .223 Remingtons, the rounds typically used by the APD for AR-15s. Sixty such cartridges were located near the living room area, meaning that Banks and Williams had expended all their rounds. Sixty rounds seems a little excessive under any circumstances, if you ask me, but according to your clients, the house was dark inside so maybe some leeway for the discharges was acceptable.

A .38 special handgun was found alongside Leroy Wallace's body. Four bullets and cartridges were recovered from the scene; the striations for these were from TilAmmo rounds consistent with the .38. The striation images recovered from the .38 were uploaded to both the Texas and FBI databases, and no comparison was found. The .38 was found alongside Mr. Wallace's right hand. Have to follow up on gun residue on Wallace's hand. Also, the four bullets were found on the right side of the front door, lodged in the door jamb.

I took a chance and went to Mr. Holloway's house on 17th Street. He was an African- American, probably in his mid-to-late sixties. He didn't appear intimidated by me or my involvement in the case. He was comfortable talking about the events on May 15th.

Mr. Holloway seemed to be quite the street busybody, always alert to the comings and goings in the neighborhood. He noted the constant traffic in and out of the Wallace residence, referring to those people as scumbags, meaning both the visitors and the Wallaces. When I asked him to relate the events on May 15th, he stuck almost verbatim to the detective's interview. When I pressed him a bit, he simply said, "I saw what I saw and heard what I heard." In my opinion, he will be a difficult witness to confuse on cross-examination. He's one of those guys who sees himself as a righteous Christian who believes in telling the truth.

And the hits just keep on comin'! A night detective, Sergeant Sam Evans, was working an overtime job at Brackenridge in the ER and saw the ambulance coming in with Shanice Wallace. Evans somehow either had the foresight to carry a mini tape recorder, or he asked one of the Brack staff to give him one (have to follow up on this fact). As Ms. Wallace was waiting to be wheeled into the operating room, Sergeant Evans talked to her.

Although apparently on the brink of death, Ms. Wallace was able to somehow divulge the following: Three officers barged into her house. They were wearing ski masks (balaclavas). Her whole family was sitting in the front living room watching television. Two of the officers began shooting right away, and another detective ran past the family toward the back bedrooms. Her husband had stowed three kilos of cocaine and more than five million dollars inside a closet in the master bedroom. She said that she and her husband had told only one person about the money, a nephew by the name of Janard Coleman.

I am projecting here, but it might be possible that Coleman tipped off your clients in return for a get-out-of-jail card. By the time the trauma surgeons got to the operating room, Ms. Wallace had expired.

You're the lawyer, not me. But if you ask me, Ms. Wallace's statement is a classic dying declaration.

Although you didn't ask for this information, I took it upon myself to drive out to the Magnolia Montessori for All and speak to the head of school, Maureen Reagan, about the Wallace children. She stated that all three of the kids were exceptionally bright, but the oldest, ten-year-old Jazmine, was in the Mensa stratosphere, so brilliant that Ms. Reagan and Ms. Wallace had discussed whether the girl should go right into high school or even skip it and start attending college classes. I'm glad I made the visit because if I were the DA's office, I would call Ms. Reagan simply to demonstrate how much was lost by the death of the three children.

Please let me know if you want any more information, Preston. I sure hope you can spin your usual magic on this one! Good luck—make that ten truckloads of luck—because you're really going to need it. As the Warren Zevon song goes, you'd better grab onto a whole bunch of "Lawyers, Guns, and Money." For sure, the fit has hit the shan.

Tony

***

BANKS FILE June 8-9, 2007

Partner Conrad Diamond and I met today for several hours to discuss Tony Nelson's report, first agreeing that Tony has been the best hire we ever made for an investigator. He always brings the goods, and then some.

If Tony's information is even remotely correct, our clients Banks, Buhl, and Williams have weaved complete fabrications out of whole cloth. These guys are Pinnochios times one hundred.

Based on Tony's information, we project that the DA's office will submit the case to a grand jury and likely seek capital homicide charges against them which will put our clients' execution in play. This scenario raises ethical issues for our firm and for the impact on our clients' financial interests.

Our firm will have to separate the case so that three different attorneys represent Banks, Buhl, and Williams. No judge will permit one lawyer to represent all of them in a capital murder case. Then our three clients will have to decide whether they want their trial conducted together or separately. Since client Buhl's version of events is somewhat different than the other two officers, he might decide on a trial by himself. If our firm handles all the cases, there will have to be a "wall" between each attorney; we won't be able to confer about the specifics of our respective clients' positions with each other. The Texas Bar ethics rules so impede free-wheeling behavior by attorneys; what an annoyance!

A capital case will require a great deal more time than normally expected...by three different attorneys plus a second lawyer for each client—another requirement in this kind of trial. A jury consultant will also be needed, so our clients can't later claim inadequate assistance of counsel based on the lack of one. The point being...*ching-caching, ching-*

caching. I told Conrad that our clients will have to dip into their money jars and grab out a whole lot of Benjamins. Conrad and I agreed we'd require each of them to pay fifty grand up front as a retainer.

Conrad and I discussed one other facet of the case: We would recommend that our clients take the Fifth, the privilege against self-incrimination, when called into the grand jury—no sense putting themselves in more jeopardy by perjuring themselves. I drew up a document for each of them to sign, demonstrating that they had been advised against testifying at the grand jury. If they were convicted later on, we could demonstrate that we had provided our best advice.

I requested my clients to come in tomorrow, at which time I will deliver the bad news like a subordinate of Robert E. Lee telling the general that he had an appointment at the Appomattox Court House.

The next day, Conrad and I sat with our three clients and laid on the successive explosions to them like the firebombing of Dresden. As we covered the need for three lawyers, seconds, possible separate trials, a jury consultant, and an ass-puckering retainer, our clients, both separately and together, screamed, cussed, whined, and pissed and moaned, expressing their great displeasure in many inventive ways. Typical penny-pinching cops, looking for another freebie, like some coffee, a meal, or discounted goods, only exorbitantly more expensive—our clients had probably never once counted up to fifty-thousand, much less laid their hands on that much money...but then, maybe they had.

In the end, Banks, Buhl, and Williams, each of their faces now having turned as grim as an IRS letter in the mail announcing an audit, came to the sudden realization that they were in deep doo-doo. They asked to step outside and discuss their predicament. A few minutes later, they returned, and a subdued client Banks said, "Okay, we don't at all like the vise you've squeezed us with, but we don't seem to have any choice. We'll each bring in fifty thousand to your office by the end of the day."

After they left, Conrad said cynically, "I guess they have a whole lot of pennies in their money jars and maybe even a few nickels, dimes, and quarters as well."

***

BANKS FILE September 11, 2007

Very grim meeting and news today. I met with Willie, Jimmy, and the Splendid Splinter at the office. Conrad and another partner, Alma Viles, sat in as well. Conrad, Alma, and I had spoken beforehand and agreed that since we had to split up our clients' representation three ways, our meeting the clients all together pushed up to the edge of a visit from the Texas Bar Association's Professional Ethics Committee. But we needed at least this last time to make sure everyone was on the same page.

Yessiree, my friends! Howard, Diamond, and McGowan roared into the twenty-first century by promoting a woman to partner, breaking the glass ceiling so loudly that it could be heard way down in

New Braunfels. Being a politically correct firm—well, in the middle of the night I might have to snort balderdash at this observation—we hired Alma in spite of her predilections that leaned toward the fairer sex. Once our male staff figured it out, they didn't bother to hit on her (plus, that would be so not PC…no dipping your pen in the office inkwell!). One lawyer did believe that his smooth charms dazzled any woman, whether hetero or otherwise, and that any lady would jump into the sack with him faster than Superman outrunning a bullet. Alma ignored the lawyer's supplications and mocked him once by saying that unless his dick shriveled down to a clit, he was not desirable material for her; thus, his lesbian-fuck fantasy ended.

The three of us agreed that I'd represent Banks, Conrad would handle Buhl, and Alma would deal with Williams. We could have left the decision up to our clients, but we decided that Banks appeared to be the ringleader of the other two, and my special attributes included controlling clients with strong personalities. The three second lawyers from our firm would be determined later.

In the end, splitting up the representation between the three clients would be a façade played on the judge but not necessarily the DA's office which had a long history of legal battles with our firm. Conrad and Alma knew that I specialized on and understood cops better than they did, so in the end, they would defer to my decisions and instincts throughout the trial.

They would be akin to a movie where their speaking roles were limited to just a few lines. The star of the show—of course, yours truly—would hog the spotlight throughout the movie. Think Rose (Joyce Jameson) and Kelly (Matt Clark) sitting around in the Santa Rio bar lamenting about their miserable lives in *The Outlaw Josey Wales* starring Clint "Make My Day" Eastwood. Is that a little too egocentric?

The grand jury just returned a true bill indictment against the three clients: five charges of capital murder against each detective and seven charges of perjury against each of them. They were stunned by the verdict, and even worse, the district attorney's office had decided to seek the death penalty. So obviously, they were most concerned that if convicted, they could face execution and become dead men walking.

The perjury charges faded in significance to a capital murder conviction and a verdict of death. While incarcerated up in Huntsville, they would await the sluggish appeals through the Texas court system and hope they wouldn't ultimately lie down on the Grim Reaper's bed, waiting for the three vials of death to wend into their bodies (we're walking, we're walking, down the highway of hell!). They would have the obvious fear that any incarcerated cops encounter—other inmates, most of whom detest the police. The only upside would be that prisoners facing execution get segregated away from the other inmates, housed in single cells along with other felons convicted of a capital crime.

I felt compelled to walk our clients through the steps that would immediately take place. First, they would be arrested and processed at the police department (i.e. fingerprinted and photographed, just like they used to do with suspects). I would phone the DA's office and let someone there know that I would present the suspects at the back door of the PD, where we might avoid the press—the "perp walk" has always been an ignominious experience for arrestees, and being cops, they would find it especially distasteful.

After that, they would be transported to the Travis County Jail. Jimmy Buhl asked, "Can't we get out on bail immediately?" I told him that due to the seriousness of the charge, there was a chance that they guys wouldn't get bail at all. We would seek a bail hearing at the earliest possible time. All three of our clients screamed like crazed baboons at this development. "We're the police," Banks howled. "We deserve special treatment." All I could do was shrug my shoulders.

I advised the three clients that following the bail hearing, a judge would set an arraignment hearing where they would enter a plea. Obviously, I said they will each plead "not guilty" and then wait for a trial date, likely sometime early to mid-year. Once again, collective carping rose from the cheap seats about the possibility of staying in jail for this length of time. What a bitch, being on the other side of the law.

I reminded Banks, Buhl, and Williams that I had urged them to take the Fifth during their grand jury testimony, and that they had signed statements to that effect, although the only result would have been no perjury charges against them. The murder charges would still have resulted. I have worked with cops going back more years then I can remember, and many of them thought they were smarter than I, which definitely was the case here.

Banks insisted they had done nothing wrong at the Wallace house; they had just wanted to tell their stories to the grand jury. Banks said that he spoke for the other two as well and that they were absolutely not lying. They wanted to tell their story to a jury when the case came to trial.

These guys are as clueless as a priest giving penance to a rapist. Or maybe a pedophile, but wait, then the priest might be atoning for his own transgressions. Jesus weeps.

I told them that since they are now stuck with their stories as a result of the grand jury record, we could discuss later whether they should testify, but if they did, their testimony at trial would have to be absolutely consistent with their grand jury testimony.

I then turned to how we could develop a winning strategy that gave our clients at least a shot at a not-guilty verdict.

Four-pronged defense:

1. Impeach the testimony of Maurice Holloway. He undoubtedly testified before the grand jury, and will testify at trial. I cautioned the clients that Holloway would be a difficult witness to cross-exam, and that my investigator had found the old man's recollections truthful. The best result would be if Holloway got a sudden heart attack or a pulmonary embolism that killed him, but what were the chances of that? Or maybe he gets the itch to leave Austin for greener pastures

somewhere out west. I did admonish my clients to stay away from Mr. Holloway; otherwise, they could face witness tampering charges on top of everything else they were facing.

2. Impeach Shanice Wallace's dying declaration at Brack. I explained to the clients that a dying declaration means that Ms. Wallace's testimony, while hearsay evidence normally not admissible at trial, could be admitted through the dying declaration exception to the hearsay rule. Since she was in imminent danger of expiring, her words may be heard by the jury. We can attack Ms. Wallace's declaration first, based on her prior felony conviction for cocaine sales. Second, the DA's office allowed me to listen to the tape; it is so garbled as to be almost inaudible. I will first hire a sound engineering expert to determine if the tape can be enhanced; hopefully, it can't. If not audible, I will move to have it excluded from evidence. However, Sergeant Evans can still testify based on his recollections of the conversation with Ms. Wallace under the same hearsay rule. I am certain that he testified before the grand jury, and he will for sure turn up at trial.

3. I asked clients questions about Sergeant Evans, whether there is anything we can use to impeach him over his dying

declaration testimony. Client Buhl said that Evans had been their supervisor around two years ago; he had consistently tried to get them transferred out of narcotics. All three clients agreed that Evans had animus toward them. Client Banks noted that their CI for the search warrant on the Wallace information was Janard Coleman, who was also Shanice Wallace's nephew. Banks stated that Janard Coleman would probably testify on their behalf as to giving them the information about the cocaine in the Wallaces' possession. Client Banks emphasized that Janard Coleman had no knowledge about the Wallaces' money (Wait, didn't Shanice Wallace's dying declaration contradict Banks' assertion!). Also, Coleman had a prior relationship with Sergeant Evans that might have included Coleman alerting Evans to known drug dealers who held money and/or drugs; Banks suspected that Evans would shake the dealers down.

4. Hire a jury consultant who can assist us with selecting the best jurors for their case. I let them now that our firm has used a gentleman out of Chicago by the name of Hal Leffew, who I have always found irritating like a stone painfully rubbing inside my sock, but Conrad swears by the man. "Will he charge an arm and a leg?" Jimmy Buhl asked with rancor. "I'll work

on it," I told Jimmy, "and see if Mr. Leffew will give you guys the super-duper police discount worth more than a Dunkin' Doughnuts cup of free coffee and a few crullers." Jimmy's face reddened, his hands clenched, and I suspected he might jump off his chair and lay me out, but he thought better of it. Most cops have an oversized sense of entitlement like a man who lives in a mansion, drives a BMW X7, and hangs out at the country club, parading his over-sized pecs bulging underneath his Peter Millar shirt. Jimmy probably developed one early in his career, although without all the lavish accouterments.

5. Follow-up for Tony Nelson: Contact Hal Leffew and interview Janard Coleman

PS: [copy and paste to my journal] Conrad convinced me in the eighties to start handling criminal cases, and I was damn good at, representing cops on all kinds of criminal matters—aggravated assault, robbery, even rape. But never anything this grave. My clients have every reason to be terrified. Hell, I'm terrified, not only for my clients, but for me. I don't cotton losing a case—any case. I have a ninety-nine percent batting average in these criminal cases. Some of these sleazebags deserved a guilty verdict, but I was able to get them off, so they're walking free today. Not that I feel any pride over several of those victories.

The only reason the percentage isn't any lower is because of the very first case I handled, a *pro bono* assignment by the court that Conrad urged me to take simply because it was a total loser that my partner thought would be a good way to ease me into the world of criminal representation. My client was a black guy by the name of Charlie Little who lived on the east side of Austin. He had been drinking in a bar where mostly folks of his color hung out; he shot another fellow during an argument. When the cops brought him into the station and Mirandized him, Charlie waived his rights and then was asked what happened. He said, 'Well, I didn't mean to kill nobody. I just meant to shoot the son-of-a-bitch in the head. Him dyin' was between him and the Lord."

When we met in the Travis County jail, he told me the same story, and it was so fuckin' comical the way he told the story that I couldn't help but laugh right in front of the dude. Anyway, the DA's office was willing to reduce the charge from capital murder down to manslaughter. Charlie figured two to twenty sounded much better than the alternative of life or a lethal injection courtesy of Pfizer, so he signed off on the deal. But Charlie stroked out a few days later in his jail cell, dead as dead could be. So I never had to put this loss up on the scorecard.

As it turned out, the only blemish on my record was a Houston cop charged with official oppression. He forced a twenty-two-year-old woman clearly DUI behind the wheel to give him a blowjob on a traffic stop; the *quid pro quo* being that he would let her get off without an arrest. It turned out that the woman's father was a minister. The old man convinced his daughter to do the right thing and report the incident to the HPD internal affairs unit which in turn handed off the case to the Harris County DA.

My client's only defense was that he hadn't cum in the woman's mouth—pretty lame if you ask me. And he told multiple conflicting stories about the traffic stop to criminal investigators, fellow officers, and even to me. As well, the minister's daughter would have made too good a witness; she came across like a cherub with a halo floating over her head. I convinced the cop to take a plea for a ten-year sentence and hoped that he didn't become a little bitch up in Huntsville for some six-four, muscled-up black convict. If I recall, the warden at the Wynne Unit placed the guy in a segregated cell—not that I cared. The guy sickened me to the point that I would have been indifferent if he had been corn-holed by one of the black brothers, plus I never did bother to check up on him.

***

BANKS FILE September 13, 2007

Mixed news today. Professionally, the assignment of Judge P.I. Davis to the Banks case in the 227th District Court feels like music to my ears. Usually, in a ruling that could go either way, Judge Davis will tend to come down on the defense side; his years of representing scumbag drug kingpins and larcenous robber barons hasn't entirely cleansed his hands from the stink of his previous clients. When on the bench, the judge will frequently remark that he drives down the middle of the road when ruling, but he has thrown me way too many bones over the years that show otherwise.

My clients—well technically, *our* clients—have wound up in dire straits, and I'm not speaking about the Mark Knopfler group that entertained fans through the seventies, eighties, and nineties. At the bond hearing, I did a flamboyant routine like Spike Jones in front of Judge Davis, more to impress the three now-indicted cops than the judge. I offered the standard arguments for bail: no prior offenses, ties to the community, and no chance the defendants would commit another offense or flee the jurisdiction.

ADA Oliver Baird had been assigned to the case from beginning to end; when God made pricks—the asswipe kind—Oliver surely was the mold. Oliver laid it on thick with Judge Davis at the bail hearing, stressing the seriousness of the capital murder charges and the innuendoes from Shanice Wallace about missing drug money—lots of moola. I noticed Judge Davis tuning into Oliver's every word. Whenever I spoke, the judge appeared to be reading a magazine. Maybe he was looking over the latest edition of *The Economist* or perhaps more lowbrow like *Hustler*.

The chances of Judge Davis granting bail throughout the hearing appeared slim to none. As it turned out, none.

Conrad, Alma, and I sat with our three clients at the defense table afterward, listening to the three guys scream bloody murder about the injustice of it all. "We're the thin blue line," Willie Banks lamented. "How could we be treated like dirt, three honorable cops like us?" I neglected to tell them that it was better to receive a rotten decision now and hope that Judge Davis would compensate later in the trial with some decisions that go our way.

Jimmy Buhl had been making noises about separating out from his co-defendants since his version put him away from the shooting. But when presented with the fact that the prosecution would likely go after Banks and Williams first, Buhl mewled (like a poet, I can rhyme all the time!) that he couldn't take even more time behind bars and would take his chances with his cohorts.

Conrad, Alma, and I had also agreed in advance, and I advised our clients before they were hauled back off to the county jail, that we would seek a change of venue to another court outside of the Berkeley on the Colorado AKA Austin, preferably to some county north of Travis County where folks thought cops could do no wrong and black drug dealers were presumed to be guilty. I could already hear Judge Davis's comments to my motion arguing that because of the notoriety of the case, potential jurors will be prejudiced against my clients. "Too many logistical issues with moving the case out of Austin...Surely, out of more than a million people in Travis County, we can find twelve fair-minded jurors."

The chances of Judge Davis buying into my argument would be as successful as Harold Stassen ever winning an election for president. "Not gonna happen," he will rule. A real non-starter.

***

55

BANKS FILE – TONY NELSON NOTES
September 24, 2007

Per your request, I first contacted Hal Leffew in Chicago, who agreed to handle jury evaluations for us in the Banks *et al* case. I gave him probable dates over a month's period in May and June, 2008. Mr. Leffew said he would tentatively hold this time, but if another definite offer came in from another firm, he would have to decline.

He sneered at the police discount request. His brother got into some trouble down in Cicero a few years back, hired a lawyer, and faced the music in a criminal trial (probably not an unusual outcome in Cicero). His brother asked Mr. Leffew to cut some slack on the jury consulting fee; he told his brother that he wouldn't consider a reduction even for their mother, so why would he give one to his brother. Not sure I'd want to have Christmas turkey dinner with this family!

I sought to run down and interview possible witness Janard Coleman. Mr. Coleman turned out to be an exceedingly transient fellow with no known permanent residence. He seems to shuffle around, sponging a bed from one friend or another.

I finally located him down at a pool hall in South Austin. He agreed to talk with me only if I'd play a game of pool with him for a $50 bet and also buy him a Bud. After I whittled the amount of the bet down to ten bucks, we spent a short-lived fifteen minutes playing eight ball. I'm grateful to have reduced the bet since the guy cleaned my clock. A bartender told me that Coleman spends many a day at this pool hall scamming other players. Please find attached to this report a receipt for $13.58 for the bet and the Bud. Mr. Coleman agreed to pay for the time played. What a guy.

The gist of my interview with Mr. Coleman—he was in fact the CI who provided the information to Banks *et al* about the cocaine inside the Wallace residence. He stated that he had sat in the Wallace home on many occasions when drug transactions took place. He insisted that he had no knowledge of any money hidden inside the home. He further said that he would be more than happy to testify at the trial and would say anything I needed—for a price, of course. My kinda witness! *Not!*

His relationship with Sam Evans goes back several years when Evans worked in the narcotics unit. Coleman provided him with information about drug dealers in East Austin. On several occasions, he would accompany Evans when the sergeant would go to a drug dealer's house (alone, no other officers along). Sergeant Evans would go into the house, stay for several minutes, and when he returned to the car, give Coleman a wad of cash, or in some instances, some cocaine.

I asked Mr. Coleman why, up until the May 15 raid, he had never ratted out the Wallaces. He said that due to his family ties to Shanice Wallace, he had never before flipped on the Wallaces until last May. His reason for doing so? He had asked the Wallaces for a loan of $100K so he could set himself up as a cocaine distributer. Leroy Wallace screamed at him and told Mr. Coleman that he was a sorry little punk who wouldn't know what to do with the money. Coleman got so upset that he contacted Willie Banks about the Wallaces' drug den.

I asked Mr. Coleman how he figured out to ask the Wallaces about a $100K loan without prior knowledge about their stash of money. He became accusatory, claiming that I was trying to trip him up. He caused such a ruckus at the pool hall that I left immediately.

Here are my conclusions about Mr. Coleman's potential as one of your witnesses. At the outset of him sitting in the witness box, the jurors would see a pomaded, skinny black man wearing a do-rag and tats all over his arms and neck. He speaks Ebonics and displays a perpetual scowl on his face—a typical East Austin punk and not in any way a credit to my race.

He comes across as extremely tense, as if he's trying to hide something. I would worry that even with prior preparation, once tripped up by the prosecutor, he would explode like he did with me. While I believe there is some justification for believing his information about Sergeant Evans, anything he says about the Wallaces, I would take with a grain of salt. In fact, liar, liar, pants on fire. I believe he knew about the Wallaces' stash of money, and once he got mad at Leroy, he decided to tip off the Banks gang in the hopes of getting in on the action and a big payoff.

However, I would recommend including Coleman on your witness list. If anything he said about Sergeant Evans is even remotely true, Evans might get extremely nervous on cross- examination if confronted with prior bad acts carried out by him in his goings-on with Coleman. No telling how Evans might act on the witness stand or what he might say.

***

BANKS FILE April 30 and May 29-30, 2008

Conrad, Alma, and I spent part of April 30th discussing the jury panel for the Banks *et al* trial, allegedly starting next Monday. We didn't spend a whole lot of time going over jury selection and decided not to bring in the high-priced Hal Leffew until necessary. DA Oliver Baird had notified me of his request for a continuance because Maurice Holloway had apparently split for parts unknown. Knowing that Judge Davis would be lenient up to a point and grant the continuance anyway, I told Oliver I wouldn't object.

We also spent time with our clients who were visibly getting nervous as a dog in heat. We're continuing to work through their possible testimony. My team will spend a great deal more time on jury selection before the actual trial date.

Just a side note: Oliver and I really got into it during our phone call—pretty heated call—like two raging lions going after each other for territory or females. I let him know I would oppose a second continuance, and he went ballistic on me. Obviously, he's nervous about Holloway. After a whole lot of bluster by Oliver, I told him to stop acting like an asshole. "Are you calling me an asshole?" he yelled with animosity. I patiently told Oliver that all I was trying to say was he was *acting* like an asshole. But then I said, "But now that I think about it, Oliver, you *are* an asshole." *Click.*

On May 29th and 30th, our office held two full days of preparation for juror selection. So many people sat in on this meeting that we could have adjourned and driven over to the YMCA for a pickup game of basketball. Besides Conrad, Alma, Tony, and me, the three other lawyer seconds from our firm attended (window-dressing, but ethically necessary in this type of case), two secretaries, and finally, our Chicago jury consultant, Hal Leffew.

A few words about Mr. Leffew. He has a lisp and a high voice like a singer in the Vienna Choir Boys. He's rail-thin like someone who has been a vegan for years. He does a comb over in a ridiculous attempt to vainly conceal his thinning hair. He knows his stuff but believes that his opinions are so authoritative, rendered on high like Moses receiving the Ten Commandments on Mount Sinai, that no one should ever question him. Two days of Hal Leffew, plus time during the trial selecting a jury, will be more than a sufficient amount of time to send him packing back to the land of Midwestern twangs and Cubbiesland.

The process of selecting the right jurors takes on paramount significance because the district attorney is seeking the death penalty against my clients—in my opinion an overreach and beyond chicken shit. But that's what's on the table, so I have just have to deal with it.

There is a definite art to this initial part of a trial, and I have become astute—at least as much as a lawyer can—at selecting jurors who will on the one hand have an open mind but on the other, have proclivities toward underdogs and at least a tad of hostility toward government overreach. I look for jurors who know anyone in the criminal justice system (I want them!), who have prior experiences with cops (if positive, select them; if not, get them as far away from the jury as you can), whose religious tendencies are nondenominational (but don't give me one of those Baptist Bible-thumpers who sees iniquity under every rock), who have attitude (jurors with a positive vibe), who are possible leaders on the jury (if they sway the jury my client's way, but then that's impossible to forecast at the front end of a trial), and I observe clothes, hair, and body language (hunched-down jurors with crossed arms, for example, are closed-minded).

Our team discussed the ideal jurors for this case: white, normally men, who are law-and-order types; and given the sleazeball Wallaces, either men or women who feel a strong sense of right and wrong. Mr. Leffew suggested—in fact, insisted—that black, educated men and women who detest drug dealers like the Wallaces would make perfect jurors. We got into quite the rumble over his belief.

Blacks would be an anathema on this jury. So many of them have had negative experiences with cops over on the east side, whether for driving while black or for reading in the paper or hearing in the neighborhood scuttlebutt about the too numerous shootings of black youths by the APD. These kinds of sensationalized incidents are picked up in the local media and read or heard out in the suburbs like Round Rock, Pflugerville, and Cedar Park—

communities where a number of educated blacks live. I told him that he had the sense that God gave a goose. Leffew responded by saying that he was ready to pack his bags and head for the airport. Conrad had to intercede and calm the petulant jury consultant.

There has been considerable disagreement among our group about independent-minded, professional white women, who in my experience could be wild cards. My inclination would be to strike them, except that at some point Oliver Baird would argue to Judge Davis that I have engaged in overt sex discrimination. The judge might very well agree with Baird.

The irony of my jury selection thinking is that personally, I am so much of a left-winger that Gene McCarthy or George McGovern would look like prototypes of moderation by comparison. But I definitely don't want anyone on the jury who smacks of liberalism—generally union members, socialist types, and do-gooders; these folks have an inbred abhorrence to cops. Their bias toward the police is as much an automatic reflex as many white right-wingers who, without even a thought, condemn Muslims, browns, and blacks.

On its surface, this reasoning sounds either hypocritical, racist, callous, or all of the above. But I have an ethical obligation to seek a not-guilty verdict for my clients, which at the moment appears pretty grim. However, if a juror or two will go our clients' way, a mistrial will result, which is about the only positive outcome I foresee at this point. I'll take it in a New York minute!

One line of research that is less of a crapshoot about jury selection is the internet footprint left by jurors. Tony spent numerous hours researching the two-hundred plus jurors on our panel—a helluva lot of work. It's amazing what can be found on political websites, LinkedIn, Facebook, campaign contributions, letters to the editor, and so on. Tony has pinpointed at least forty-four jurors on the panel who belong to fringe radical groups—not uncommon in Austin—have made political contributions to liberal causes, and/or have published LinkedIn posts that reflect anti-police or progressive causes. All are possible bases for bias and disqualification from jury service.

Watching Tony as he dug into juror backgrounds and discussed it with our work group, I reflected on the home run our firm hit when we hired him. His background suited our needs to a tee. He had eight years working for the CIA in postings that he has never divulged to me other than he spent considerable time in the Middle East. He spent twenty-plus years with the APD, where after getting off the street, his first assignment was with the Organized Crime Unit. He has regaled me with stories about prostitution, loan-sharking, and gambling operations that had tentacles leading to cities like New Orleans, Philly, and New York City. He spent considerable time interviewing suspects in those cities with names ending in vowels. The last eight years with the APD, Tony worked as a homicide detective. Quite the illustrious resume.

So off we'll go on Monday, trying to pick the rights jurors and hoping we're not flying by the seat of our pants all the time. Fortunately, Conrad, Alma, Tony, the seconds, and the detestable Hal Leffew, will sit with me during jury selection; these many sets of eyes will always be helpful during this part of the proceedings. I have decided to wear my Panama hat like Buster used to wear to court.

-6-
THE TRIAL

Austin American Statesman...June 2,
2008...*Statesman* reporter Terry Palmer's blog

The trial of the century finally begins today! Austin police detectives Willard Banks, James Buhl, and Theodore Williams have been charged with capital murder and perjury and the district attorney's office is seeking the execution of the three detectives. The *Statesman's* reportage will cover the basic story of the trial; the editor has tasked me with providing blow-by-blow, gavel-to-gavel treatment through my blog so that readers will get the complete lowdown about the trial.

Key state witness, Maurice Holloway, was expected to testify last month in this case but couldn't be located. Assistant District Attorney Oliver Baird made a motion for a continuance, which was granted by Travis County District Court Judge P.I. Davis with the proviso that when the case was reset for June, the trial would continue with or without Mr. Holloway. Mr. Holloway's observations are a key component of the prosecution's case. He is expected to testify as to the comings and goings on the night of May 15, 2007 on 17th Street in Austin when Mr. Leroy Wallace; his wife, Shanice Wallace; and three children, Jasmine, Deshaun, and Tyrone were allegedly murdered by the three detectives.

On the prosecution side of the table, ADA Oliver Baird, two other attorneys from the district attorney's office, and a DA investigator rounded at their team.

The defense included renowned lead attorney, Preston Howard, five other attorneys from the Howard firm, an investigator, and a jury consultant from Chicago named Hal Leffew. There were so many attorneys on the defense side that three tables, one of them perpendicular to the other two, had to be set up in the courtroom.

At the onset of the proceedings, ADA Oliver Baird made a motion for a second continuance, once again based on the absence of Mr. Holloway. Mr. Howard vociferously objected, saying that the state had more than ample time to locate their witness. As an aside, Mr. Howard wore his signature three-piece, light wool, gray suit; a light blue, Ralph Lauren shirt with muted blue tie; and an incongruous Panama hat wrapped with a red and blue hatband.

Attorney Baird accused either Mr. Howard and/or his clients of witness tampering. Mr. Howard said, "Mr. Baird, you he must have been smoking some of the very available doobies in Austin to have made such an unwarranted statement. Perhaps the district attorney's office and police department should call out the bloodhounds, since the dogs would likely have more competence in locating Mr. Holloway." Following considerable laughter in the courtroom, these last remarks by Mr. Howard were met with an admonishment by Judge Davis.

After a further heated exchange between the two lead attorneys, Judge Davis ordered them into his chambers for over a half-hour, and upon their return, the judge ruled that the trial would proceed immediately. ADA Baird slammed a law book down on his table, which resulted in a reproach from the judge. Then Judge Davis placed a gag order on all parties involved in the case and cautioned all attorneys and their staffs that they would face serious sanctions, including contempt, fines, or incarceration if the gag order was violated.

Juror selection began immediately afterward. Judge Davis projected that it would take around two days for jury selection. He noted that since this was a capital murder case in Texas where the three defendants could face execution, each defendant would be allowed eight peremptory challenges, for a total of twenty-four, without showing cause for exclusion of a juror; the prosecution would also be permitted twenty-four.

During the initial *voir dire* conducted by Judge Davis, a number of the empaneled jurors were disqualified for cause. A number of black jurors and white women who appeared to have strong predispositions against the police were automatically excluded by the judge, clearly a victory for the defense. A number of law enforcement types such as police and corrections, and probation officers were also immediately kicked off when they stated in various ways that they would have difficulty finding a guilty verdict against fellow law enforcement officers—a win for the district attorney's office.

It became clear from the outset of *voir dire* that ADA Baird's strategy was to find as many open-minded women on his jury as possible; he invoked preemptory challenges against a number of men who appeared to display "law and order" inclinations. After Mr. Howard issued five preemptory challenges against black jurors—three men and two women—

ADA Baird objected, saying, "The defense is displaying racial bias toward the black community."

Mr. Howard, who clearly seemed to enjoy infuriating ADA Baird, rejoined, "I would change my strategy if Mr. Baird would be more open to white men since apparently, Mr. Baird views men of the Caucasian persuasion as dinosaurs left over from the Mesozoic Era."

After several more intense exchanges between the lawyers, Judge Davis intervened and told the two adversaries that they were both an inch away from contempt citations. He then ordered ADA Baird to state his specific basis for excluding men and Mr. Howard for excluding people of color without a reason. When Mr. Howard asked, "Your Honor, are you referring to people of black, brown, or white color?" Judge Davis picked up his gavel, apparently to admonish Mr. Howard, but then thought better of it and said, "Black or brown color."

When asked to comment on today's development at the end of the hearing, Attorney Preston Howard said that due to the judge's gag order, he could not comment. However, he did smile and give a two thumbs up to several representatives of the media.

June 3, 2008

At the start of proceedings on Tuesday, ADA Baird objected to Attorney Howard's non-verbal reply to the press the previous day when Howard smiled and gave a thumbs up to the press. Mr. Baird said, "His gesture violated the spirit of the gag order." Mr. Howard uttered something that sounded like "touchy, touchy." Mr. Baird then screamed at Mr. Howard. Judge Davis admonished both Mr. Baird and Howard and also warned Mr. Howard to be careful, that he was once again skirting somewhat close to contempt.

The rest of the day was spent with jury selection.

June 4, 2008

By the noon hour, a jury had been selected in the criminal case against the three Austin police officers—Willard Banks, James Buhl, and Theodore Williams. When asked for comment about the composition of the jury, both ADA Oliver Baird and Preston Howard declined comment on the basis of Judge P. I. Davis's gag order.

-7-

BANKS FILE June 4, 2008

The entire defense team huddled up in the firm's conference room to discuss the jurors who would make the final decision on our clients—somber meeting with none of our usual light banter. Baird gloated at me as he walked out of the courtroom. Since I had exercised all the defense peremptory challenges, several additional women made it onto the jury whom I would otherwise have struck.

Six women, three white and three black, of various professional fields or housewives, all open-minded and independent, would have no trouble bringing down the hammer on our cops. The four men were a weird stew of ethnicity. The first three were an Indonesian, a Filipino, and a Chinaman, all of them, naturally in Austin, software types. The one Hispanic guy came across as too cagey and shrouded in mystery, and I would have bumped him but for no more challenges. The other two will be complete unknowns—a Grimm fairy in his mid-fifties and a he/she who transitioned to a woman, had a bellowing voice like James Earl Jones, and was so huge and unfeminine he/she could play right tackle for Notre Dame.

We agreed that the best we could hope for was a mistrial if we could convince one or two of the jurors to vote our way—maybe one of the two wild cards (the Grimm Fairy or transitioned guy/gal), the cagey Mexican, or one of the other three software guys. We concluded that the women were all pretty much lost to our cause.

"We do have one, and I emphasize *only* one thing going for us," Conrad observed, "and it's not going to be Preston sleeping with one of the jurors."

I told Conrad to cool it; my alleged liaison with a juror was the stuff of urban legend. That received a miniscule guffaw from the cheap seats in the room.

After a minute's pause by Conrad, as if for melodramatic effect, Tony said, "Do I need a drum roll with this revelation, Conrad?"

Conrad nodded his head back and forth sideways and answered, "Judge Davis. That's what we have on our side, at least without him appearing too blatant about it. Remember, he came out of the defense bar, we supported him seventeen years ago when he ran, and we've supported him every four years after. In fact, if I recall, we gave him five grand the last time he was up for reelection."

"That's a big stretch, Conrad," I noted. "There will have to be some really strange twists and turns for us to pull the rabbit out of this hat. At least not worrying about Holloway is a lucky break."

"Well, let's hope, or better yet, *say* a prayer or two that there's a whole lot of twistin' and turnin' goin' on. Okay?" Conrad replied.

We agreed to keep our consternation away from the clients. All three of them were already acting like zombies, like the walking dead petrified of the final, devastating result that appeared so close on the horizon.

Naturally, Hal Leffew had to offer the last word. "I don't know why I bothered coming down to Austin," he said venomously. "What kind of hick rodeo are you guys operating down here?"

71

I could have commented that his services had been a waste of our time and money, but why bother. Conrad and Alma agreed with me that while we would normally keep Leffew around for the duration of the trial, he had become such an irritant that we needed to send him packing back to the land of Midwestern articulations. He was now out of our hair.

-8-
THE TRIAL

Austin American Statesman...June 5,
2008...*Statesman* reporter Terry Palmer's blog

The first full day of the actual trial of the century has finally begun! For anyone who hasn't lived under a rock in Travis County for the last year, Detective Sergeant Willard Banks and detectives James Buhl and Theodore Williams have been charged by the district attorney's office with capital murder, and the state is gunning for a verdict of not only guilty, but execution as well. After a continuance last month due to the disappearance of key witness Maurice Holloway, the case will now move forward.

The jury having been empaneled, the proceedings began with ADA Oliver Baird presenting the state's case against APD detectives Banks, Buhl, and Williams. He first outlined the state's case, stating that he would present ballistics and other evidence showing the defendants' guilt as well as a dying declaration from one of the victims, Shanice Wallace, that clearly showed the defendants had murdered Mr. and Mrs. Wallace and their three children. ADA Baird emphasized that this was a capital murder case, and the state would seek the death penalty against the three officers.

Mr. Howard's opening statement was succinct. He stated that detectives Banks, Buhl, and Williams were dedicated police officers and that the evidence would show all of their actions on May 15, 2007, were within the rules and regulations of the Austin

Police Department and that the district attorney's office had rushed to judgment by indicting the officers and bringing this case to trial.

Mr. Baird objected to Mr. Howard speaking for defendants Buhl and Williams since he was purportedly only representing Detective Banks. Mr. Howard's comeback was "You can't even find one of your witnesses, so why are you so worried about how we are presenting our case?"

The spectators cackled at Mr. Howard's statement; ADA Oliver screamed at Mr. Howard and asked the judge to sanction Mr. Howard. Judge Davis seemed amused by the exchange between the attorneys, telling them both to settle down, and instructing the jury to disregard Mr. Howard's comment. Judge Davis sternly counseled Mr. Howard to refrain from commenting on the prosecution's case and in a similar vein, advised ADA Baird that how the defendants' attorneys decide to divvy up their work was their business.

ADA Baird called his first witness, Detective Jaime Elizondo, who was in charge of the Special Investigations Unit that was responsible for handling the shooting of the Wallace family. Detective Elizondo testified that after the first responding officers on the scene determined that a possible homicide had been committed at East 17th Street, the SIU unit went into action.

When Detective Elizondo arrived at the scene, the lights in the residence were off. When he entered the premises and turned on a light, Detective Elizondo observed the five victims, Mr. and Mrs. Wallace and their three children, sprawled out in the living room area on a sofa and two Barcaloungers, all of them except Shanice Wallace deceased. There was blood pooling throughout the living area. He immediately ordered an EMS truck already at the scene to transport Mrs. Wallace to Brackenridge Hospital. He also saw numerous shell casings strewn across the living room.

Detective Elizondo further stated defendants Banks and Williams were standing outside the Wallace residence when he arrived. Elizondo noted that Detective Buhl was not present when he first arrived and didn't appear for at least twenty minutes.

ADA Baird then made a proffer of numerous photographs of the deceased Wallace family. Mr. Howard objected vehemently, "These photographs will undeniably prejudice the jury." After a sidebar between Baird, the three defense attorneys, and Judge Davis, the judge ruled that the photographs could be introduced. As the photographs were passed around to the jury, several jurors were clearly upset at the pictures they observed and stared with considerable hostility toward the defendants.

Through further questioning by ADA Baird, Detective Elizondo walked the jurors through the steps of the investigation at the Wallace residence, including the names of the eleven other Special Investigations Unit detectives and their various duties during the night.

As an aside, Detective Elizondo noted that three kilos of cocaine had been seized at the Wallace residence, later determined to be eighty percent pure with an uncut value of approximately fifty-four thousand dollars. When asked whether any money was located at the Wallace home, Detective Elizondo testified that other than a few dollars found in Leroy Wallace's billfold, no other money had been found.

Following the lunch recess, a parade of SIU detectives testified as to their responsibilities, including a canvas of the neighborhood, interviewing witnesses in the area who had information relevant to the homicide, and collecting and booking various evidence collected at the scene. This testimony took through the end of the day, and upon adjournment, ADA Baird stated that he had many other SIU detectives, Ballistics Unit officers, and a training officer who would testify at least through the following day and possibly beyond.

Mr. Howard was normally silent during this testimony except for a few questions, as were defense attorneys Conrad Diamond and Alma Viles. After adjournment, Mr. Howard was asked about developments during the day. Mr. Howard shrugged his shoulders and said, "I am under a gag order by Judge Davis." But he added, "I fell asleep during the afternoon session because I was bored to death, so I can't comment on the total lack of evidence presented by the state."

June 6, 2008

At the beginning of the second day of testimony in the trial against the three Austin detectives—Willard Banks, James Buhl, and Theodore Williams—ADA Oliver Baird stood up apparently to make some kind of objection; however, Judge P. I. Davis told him to sit down and then ordered Defense Attorney Preston

Howard to approach the bench. The jury had not yet entered the courtroom. Judge Davis then severely admonished Mr. Howard for his comments to the media on Thursday afternoon.

Mr. Howard remarked, "I was asleep during the entire afternoon and hadn't heard anything about the state's evidence. The press must have simply misinterpreted my statement." At the top of his lungs, Judge Davis said that his patience had worn thin with Mr. Howard, that the media had not misinterpreted his statements, and that the lawyer's bank account was now lightened by ten thousand dollars. Mr. Howard complained in a mocking way, "Damnit, Your Honor, my vacation trip to Italy next month will have to be curtailed by two days because of the fine." Judge Davis then said, "Mister Howard, another word and you're going to the hoosegow."

The prosecution's first witness in the morning was Juan Torres, an officer with the APD Ballistics Unit who testified that he found .223 Remington 55 grain bullet casings throughout the living room, used by the APD for AR-15s. He further stated that four TilAmmo bullets, typically used by a .38 special, were located along the jamb on the right side of the front door.

Officer Torres further testified about the likely range of fire of the AR-15s. He stated that all of the .223 Remington shells were centered in the living room area, and the bodies of the five victims lay approximately ten to twelve feet away from the bodies.

On cross-examination, Mr. Howard asked Officer Torres about the four TilAmmo bullets and where they had been fired from. When Officer Torres became evasive about his answer, Mr. Howard asked Judge Davis to order Officer Torres to reply. Officer Torres then testified that the bullets had originated from a .38 special found beside the right side of Leroy Wallace's body. Mr. Howard then asked Officer Torres if he had any knowledge of whether gun residue from the .38 had been found on Mr. Wallace's right hand. Officer Torres reluctantly testified that such residue had been located on Wallace's right hand.

Mr. Howard also asked Torres if, other than the two AR-15s, the three detectives' service guns had been fired during the confrontation. Officer Torres testified in the negative.

On re-examination by ADA Baird, Officer Torres stated that it would have been possible for one of the defendants to hold the gun in Mr. Wallace's hand and fire with Mr. Wallace's fingerprints on the weapon.

Mr. Howard then requested to ask Officer Torres two more questions which Judge Davis permitted over ADA Baird's vociferous objection. Throughout the trial, I have noticed the rancorous back-and-forth between Mr. Baird and Mr. Howard, like two Chinese ping-pong stars violently striking the ball across the net in a kind of death match.

"Officer Torres," Mr. Howard then asked, "do you know whether a gun residue test was conducted on the three detectives?" The officer testified that he had no knowledge that a test had been conducted on the defendants. Mr. Howard then inquired, "Do you know whether Leroy Wallace was right or left-handed?" Once again, the officer didn't know.

A source close to the investigation has told this reporter that there has been distress within the SIU that no residue test had been conducted on the defendants and no determination was made of Mr. Wallace's dominant hand. The source further told this reporter that detectives were scurrying around to find writing samples by Mr. Wallace. SIU supervisors were furious that Mr. Howard had uncovered these blunders on cross-examination. My source stated that Mr. Howard is both hated and feared within SIU.

Officer Ben Stahl from the APD training academy testified that recruits and officers taking in-service classes are taught that when deadly force is used in a shooting scenario, they should only use that amount of force necessary to eliminate the threat. He further testified that the number of rounds fired by Detectives Banks and Williams was, in his opinion, way excessive and against all training and regulations.

On cross-examination, Mr. Howard asked whether the firing of sixty rounds would be excessive when the detectives barged into a totally dark room and someone was shooting at them. Officer Stahl became equivocal when asked this question and would never really offer an opinion.

Following Officer Stahl's testimony and prior to the noon recess, ADA Baird once again sought a continuance for the purpose of locating Maurice Holloway, saying that Mr. Holloway's testimony was one of the linchpins to the state's case. Before Mr. Howard could even stand up clearly to object, Judge Davis stated, "That train has already left the station on this one." The judge's comment resulted in some laughter in the courtroom.

Then Mr. Baird made a motion to introduce Maurice Holloway's recorded interview and written statement which was taken by a Special Investigations Unit detective. He stated that Mr. Holloway could not be located and the state would not otherwise be able to enter his testimony concerning his observations on May 15 of last year. Mr. Howard heatedly objected to this motion, saying that he would have no way to conduct a cross-examination of Mr. Holloway due to his absence and that such a result would violate the defendants' Sixth Amendment right to cross-examination of witnesses.

The bevy of attorneys and Judge Davis then retired again to the judge's chambers. Upon their return, Judge Davis ruled that the detective's interview of Mr. Holloway could not be introduced or read to the jury.

Clearly upset by Judge Davis's ruling, ADA Baird requested that the proceedings end for the day so he could confer with the district attorney about the status of the case. Judge Davis approved the request, and the proceedings were held over until the following week.

June 9, 2008

The testimony continued into the second week. ADA Oliver Baird continued his case this morning by calling Mavis Grizzard. Ms. Grizzard is the mother of Shanice Wallace and grandmother of Leroy and Shanice Wallace's children, Jazmine, 10; DeShawn,

8; and Tyrone, 7. Ms. Grizzard spent time talking about her grandchildren, how she had cared for them when her daughter and son-in-law were in prison, and how polite and intelligent they were.

The witness spent time testifying about Jazmine, saying that she was brilliant and had taken an IQ test with a score of 142. Ms. Grizzard said that this score made her granddaughter eligible for Mensa. After Mr. Howard declined to cross-exam, Ms. Grizzard left the witness box and walked toward Mr. Howard and the three defendants, screaming obscenities and spitting at them. Judge Davis ordered a bailiff to remove Ms. Grizzard from the courtroom. Emotions definitely running high today!

The state then called Maureen Reagan, Head of School at Magnolia Montessori for All. Like Ms. Grizzard, Ms. Reagan also testified as to how wonderful the children were. She spent considerable time discussing Jazmine Wallace, her brilliance, the chance that she might skip high school and go directly to college, and the sadness she felt that such a beautiful child had been snuffed out before her potential could be reached. Mr. Howard declined to cross-exam once again.

APD sergeant, Sam Evans, was then called to testify. Detective Evans first talked about the tape recording of Shanice Wallace he had taken at Brackenridge Hospital before her death. ADA Baird proffered the tape for the jury to hear; Mr. Howard objected on the basis that it was hearsay and inaudible. He noted that his firm had contracted with a sound engineering expert who had made all efforts to enhance the tape to no avail.

Judge Davis ruled that the tape was admissible as an exception to the hearsay rule, saying that it was a dying declaration. But he did want to hear the tape in chamber to determine its quality. Once again, the gaggle of attorneys left with the judge to his chambers.

Upon resuming the hearing, Judge Davis ruled that the tape, while likely authentic, was not audible enough to hear, but he would permit Detective Evans to testify as to what Shanice Wallace said at the hospital under the dying declaration. Mr. Howard's objection was overruled by Judge Davis.

Sergeant Evans then proceeded to testify to his recollections of Ms. Wallace's statements at the hospital where he had been working an off-duty security job. As ADA Baird asked him questions, Evans referenced his notes from time-to-time that he had made while talking to Ms. Wallace.

Going through a long series of questions by Mr. Baird and answers by Detective Evans, the following facts were established by the prosecution: the three detectives (now defendants) barged into the house; although, Ms. Wallace could not identify who was who; they were wearing ski masks, which Detective Evans clarified as balaclavas; Ms. Wallace was sitting with her entire family in the front living room watching television; while two of the officers began shooting, another officer ran past the family toward the back bedrooms; there was more than five million dollars and three kilos of cocaine that she and her husband had stowed away inside a closet in the master bedroom.

She said that only one other person knew about the money, one of her nephews by the name of Janard Coleman. Ms. Wallace thought that Coleman might have tipped off the police. Detective Evans then testified that Ms. Wallace died and provided no other information.

Upon ADA Baird's close, Mr. Howard began his cross-examination. He first asked numerous questions about Ms. Wallace's condition and how coherent she was, meaning could she really have said the things Evans asserted she said. Mr. Howard savagely examined the officer, asking, "Sergeant Evans, it seems quite convenient that you found a tape recorder lying around."

"An attending nurse provided it," the sergeant answered.

"How could you have possibly transposed the recording that was basically inaudible into your notes so easily?" Mr. Howard queried, pointing down toward the sergeant's notes. Sergeant Evans heatedly answered that he took the notes while Ms. Wallace spoke. Mr. Howard then commented, "You, Evans, must be quite the multi-tasker, manipulating a tape recording and writing at the same time." Mr. Howard's comment resulted in laughter throughout the courtroom, a passionate objection from ADA Baird, and a rebuke by Judge Davis toward both Mr. Howard and the audience. Judge Davis upheld the ADA's objection, advising the jury to disregard Mr. Howard's comment.

Mr. Howard next asked Sergeant Evans if he knew Janard Coleman. ADA Baird objected vigorously, saying that Janard Coleman was not relevant to this case. Mr. Howard stated, "Janard Coleman is on the defendants' witness list and will be called when the defense presents its case." Then Mr. Howard observed, "The state has opened the door to questions about Janard Coleman since Mr. Baird brought up Coleman through Sergeant Evans's testimony and Shanice Wallace's dying declaration." Judge Davis ruled that the state had opened the door and directed Detective Evans to answer the question.

When Evans testified that he would not answer this or any other question about Janard Coleman and was going to take the Fifth Amendment privilege against self-incrimination, the courtroom exploded in an uproar. After Judge Davis again reprimanded the audience, Mr. Howard continued asking Evans questions about Coleman: How long had Evans known him? Had Coleman ever been used as an informant? Had Evans ever taken drugs or money from other dealers with Janard Coleman present? And had Evans ever given Coleman money or drugs during their relationship?

It became difficult to determine what then transpired. Between Sergeant Evans invoking the Fifth following every question by Mr. Howard, screaming objections from ADA Baird, and the commotion inside the courtroom, it was difficult to follow the proceedings. Judge Davis continually banged his gavel for order, and only after about five minutes did people in the courtroom calm down.

Judge Davis sat quietly for several minutes, his head slumped down into his chest, massaging his forehead. Then he ordered the jury out of the courtroom and afterward looked directly toward

Sergeant Evans, saying "My first instinct, Sergeant, is to order you to testify, and if you refuse, then jail you for contempt until you agree to testify. This is a sad day," Judge Davis went on, "when a police officer takes the Fifth in my courtroom. But I am going to hold off on that decision because I might just let the case proceed without forcing Sergeant Evans's hand."

Judge Davis continued, saying that if he makes this choice, he will have to hit the books about whether Mr. Howard may, in his closing, comment on Sergeant Evans's refusal to testify. The judge noted that the law clearly states that the prosecution may not comment on a defendant's invocation of the Fifth on summation of its case. But, he continued, the law in Texas is less clear on whether a defense attorney may point out Evans's refusal to testify during summation. "My inclination, if the law is unclear, as I believe it is," Judge Davis went on, "will be to rule that the defense may point out Sergeant Evans's refusal on summation, and the jury can make whatever inferences it wishes, based on Sergeant Evans's refusal to testify.

ADA Baird bolted from his chair and yelled at the top of his lungs, "This is outrageous, Your Honor!!" Judge Davis motioned ADA Baird back toward his chair and said, "Enough with the phony theatrics, Mr. Baird. Here's what is going to happen now. You are going to take the short walk from this courtroom over to the DA's office and have a real heart-to-heart with your superiors."

Judge Davis encouraged ADA Baird to consider whether the state really wanted to continue with this prosecution. Judge Davis stated that because of the absence of Maurice Holloway and the serious questions raised about Sergeant Evans's credibility due to his refusal to answer certain questions posed by the defense, this case had become such a stinker that the state should dismiss it "You understand," Judge Davis said to ADA Baird, "that since the case has already proceeded to this point, double jeopardy will attach, and your dismissal will be with prejudice. The defendants will walk out of this courtroom as free men."

"Stinker?" ADA Baird interrupted querulously. "I believe you are demonstrating total prejudice on behalf of the defense."

Judge Davis took a deep breath as if to control his temper, and then, with a stern tone, said, "Mr. Baird, you are now just one more word away from becoming Sergeant Evans's roommate in the Travis County Jailhouse....If I decide to put him in the slammer. Please continue...if you wish. I understand the cook in the jail makes a sublime lime Jello."

This reporter watched Mr. Howard's reaction to Judge Davis's severe lambasting of ADA Baird. He face moved from a smirk to a wide smile, and then he cupped his hands over his face as he tried to suppress his laughter.

The judge said that if the state foolishly decides to continue, he will likely make some decisions that Mr. Baird will not like, whether it be Sergeant Evans's incarceration or the defense being permitted to comment on his invocation of the Fifth during summation. Judge Davis concluded by advising the parties to be back on Tuesday precisely at nine a.m. Then he adjourned the proceedings.

***

June 10, 2008

As District Court Judge P. I. Davis had dictated the previous day, the proceedings in the Banks *et al* case began promptly at nine a.m. However, ADA Oliver Baird requested a meeting with the judge in chambers; Judge Davis left the bench, directing Preston Howard and the two other defense attorneys to accompany them. The packed audience inside the courtroom seemed more anxious as the minutes passed by, and the attorneys and judge continued to talk behind closed doors. Finally, after almost an hour, the principals to this drama appeared from inside the judge's chambers.

After stepping back behind the prosecutor's table, ADA Oliver Baird continued to stand, and with what appeared to be extreme reluctance, stated that the state was withdrawing all charges against detectives Banks, Buhl, and Williams, understanding that the dismissals would be with prejudice. Once again, pandemonium reigned in the courtroom. Unlike the day before, Judge Davis allowed the uproar to continue until the spectators calmed down.

After the hubbub subsided, ADA Baird continued. "I do want to make it crystal clear that the state is disgusted with this outcome, as the state believes that these three defendants—Banks, Buhl, and Williams—committed heinous crimes. While the long arm of the law has failed to achieve justice in this case, hopefully sometime either on this side or the other, these three men will be severely punished for what they have done."

Judge Davis then said this case is now concluded, and the charges against the defendants are withdrawn with prejudice. "Mr. Banks, Buhl, and Williams," Judge said, turning toward the three men, "you are hereby released from the Travis County Jail and may leave the courtroom as free men."

ADA Oliver Baird avoided the media after the hearing other than to repeatedly say no comment. Preston Howard and the three defendants stood outside the courthouse for more than an hour answering the many questions posed by the media. Following are some of Mr. Howard's more notable remarks. "The state had a weak case going in, and it went downhill from there....The defendants were not guilty from the get-go; this case demonstrated that in the end. justice was served....It was a shame that five people were killed in this shooting that went wrong." Mr. Howard made particular mention of the three Wallace children, saying that he felt especially bad that they would not live to fulfill their potential. When I asked Mr. Howard if anyone ever discovered why James Buhl couldn't be located immediately after the shooting, he stated that he had no idea.

The defendant Willard Banks said that he wanted to especially thank Mr. Howard, saying that Mr. Howard was the best lawyer in Austin, if not all of Texas and the country. Banks further lauded Attorneys Conrad Diamond and Alma Viles for their efforts. When asked about their futures, James Buhl stated that since they had done nothing wrong, they were going to seek full reinstatement with the Austin Police Department, a sentiment seconded by Ted Williams.

As Mr. Howard was leaving the courthouse, one of the television reporters asked him why he always wore the Panama hat which always clashed with his posh-looking suits and Ralph Lauren shirts and ties. "This hat is special," he remarked. "It's a tribute to my long-deceased grandfather, Buster, a one-of-a-kind Tennessee country lawyer who many, including me, have imitated but never duplicated."

***

FOLLOW-UP NEWSPAPER ARTICLES

Austin American Statesman Front Page June 18, 2008 Reporter Terry Palmer's blog

This reporter has spent considerable time after the scandalous finale to the failed prosecution against detectives Banks, Buhl, and Williams, contacting my sources about many different facets of the case. While not commenting for publication, several persons within the Travis County DA's office have stated that prior to the decision to capitulate and withdraw charges against the three officers, a fierce internal debate went on within the DA's office about whether to continue the trial.

Accusations were made within the office against ADA Oliver Baird and also the Austin Police Department for their failure to track down and furnish the key witness, Maurice Holloway.

Apparently, Mr. Baird threatened to resign but was talked out of it by several of his colleagues.

The top brass in the APD exerted heavy pressure on the DA's office to terminate the case. It was perceived by the top dogs in the PD that the reputation of the department had been tarnished to a major extent by Sergeant Sam Evans's refusal to testify on defense cross-examination. This development, along with considerable pointing of fingers between the two agencies, resulted in the final decision by the district attorney to withdraw charges with prejudice.

Outside the courthouse after the final decision in the case, the three defendants—Messrs. Banks, Buhl, and Williams—could be observed laughing and doing high-fives with each other. Mr. Howard's attempt to calm them down had no effect on their boisterous behavior. When this reporter asked officer Buhl what he was going to do now, he stated that he was going to beat the living s*** out me. It was at this point that Mr. Howard guided the three officers away from the courthouse and toward his office.

A few hours after the case ended, I telephoned Mr. Howard, seeking an interview. He stated that he would stand by his comments outside the courtroom and that anything else he said would be superfluous. When I asked him to elaborate on the injustice to the Wallace children, Mr. Howard slammed the phone in my ear—quite unprofessional behavior for such a famous, or maybe now it's infamous, lawyer.

Mavis Grizzard, mother of the deceased Shanice Wallace spoke out after the trial. Ms. Grizzard told several media representatives that the defendant's attorney, Preston Howard, was the sleaziest human being she had ever seen and hoped the man went to the bowels of hell along with the three detectives.

She stated that she would be contacting an attorney immediately to file suit against the corrupt cops. Ms. Grizzard then followed Mr. Howard and detectives Banks, Buhl, and Williams as they left the courthouse and walked back to Mr. Howard's office, cussing and spitting at them. Unfortunately, Ms. Grizzard had a stroke two days after the end of the trial and died. This reporter has been unable to determine whether the Wallace family had any other family members who would be eligible to file suit.

***

Austin American Statesman Editorial Page June 22, 2008
Justice Delayed is Justice Denied

The Statesman Editorial Board has closely followed the trial of Austin detectives Willard Banks, James Buhl, and Theodore Williams for several reasons. Our own top-flight reporter, Terry Palmer, covered the trial through his blog and wrote an excellent recap afterward exposing many of the behind-the-scenes events during the trial.

First, the district attorney's office completely botched this case, both in not keeping track of the key witness, Maurice Holloway, and not adequately prepping Detective Sam Evans. Speaking of Detective Evans, what does the police department intend to do with him after he invoked his privilege against self-incrimination?

Second, the case appeared to raise the specter of grave misconduct within the police department. How were three narcotics detectives with tarnished personnel records permitted to continue working in this unit? What really happened on East 17th Street last May 15, 2007? Was there any witness tampering prior to the criminal case? How deep was Detective Evans's involvement in illegal activities?

These are the questions we have, and we demand answers. In fact, we are sure that the public would like to know as well. In any event, it is our decided judgment that, unlike Attorney Preston Howard's post-trial hollow statement that justice was served, in fact, justice was not served. While the editorial board ordinarily doesn't comment on jury decisions, this case screams for a different result. A guilty verdict should not only have been expected, it should have been delivered. As the old adage goes, "justice delayed is justice denied."

***

Austin American Statesman State and Local section, July 4, 2008

As fireworks exploded over Lady Bird Lake last night, the body of Janard Coleman was found in an alley between 15th and 16th Streets in East Austin. He was apparently killed with a handgun. Mr. Coleman was on the defendant witness list during the high-profile criminal case involving detectives Willard Banks, James Buhl, and Theodore Williams. At this time, the make of the handgun has not been determined. There are no witnesses to the shooting, and there are no suspects at this time.

***

Austin American Statesman State and Local section, August 20, 2008

The Austin Police Department Public Information office released the following today: Detective Sam Evans, a 14-year officer, has tendered his resignation. Detective Evans was embroiled in the well-publicized criminal case last May and June against narcotics detectives Willard Banks, James Buhl, and Theodore Williams for allegedly killing five people in a house on East 17th Street. Detective Evans invoked the privilege against self-incrimination during the trial, which was one of the reasons that all charges against the three officers were dropped. The release states that Detective Evans was offered the option of accepting the resignation or being fired and possibly facing perjury charges, and he accepted the resignation.

***

Austin American Statesman State and Local section, September 18, 2008

The Austin Police Department Public Information Office issued the following release today. Detectives Willard Banks, James Buhl, and Theodore Williams have been reinstated to the department with full pay going back to May, 2007. The department decided against seeking termination through the arbitration process. Effective this date, once the three detectives have received their back pay, they will immediately retire from the police department.

NOTE FROM ANNE HOWARD: Now that wasn't so hard, was it Conrad?

-9-

MEDICAL REPORT FROM DOCTOR
GHAZINI FEBRUARY 15, 2017

Preston Howard
Austin, TX 78730

From the Austin Internal Medicine Practice
Dear ~~Mr. Howard:~~ *Preston,*
I don't understand why my nurse continues to refer to you as Mister Howard. Since I have been your physician for almost thirty years, surely we can be and have been on a first name basis for a long time.

I have always looked forward to our appointments because of your wit, even though it sometimes borders on the obscene. But you really need to get some new material when you show up at my office; otherwise, I am going to get bored with your visits. For example, every year I admonish you to give up cigars since there will be that one that will kill you, and you always say, "But think of all the great cigars I've had before that." Or when I check your prostate for growths, you always ask me to do it again to remember me by until we meet again. Doctor Chaudhry told me once that you used that line on her too. Come on...please show a little bit more creativity.

Anyway, about the results from your blood work taken on February 10—your liver enzymes and enlarged blood cells indicate excessive alcohol intake. I want to do a follow-up with an ultrasound to check if you have a fatty liver. You are also overweight, some of which is the result of your drinking, but you already know that.

I would therefore recommend the same things as last year—daily aerobic exercise, cessation of alcohol, cessation of cigars, and eating a heart-healthy diet. Although your cholesterol and blood pressure are under control through various medicines, your sugar count is pre-diabetes and close to diabetes. You must absolutely follow these recommendations; otherwise, your health and life are greatly threatened.

One other note. I noticed during my exam that you seem agitated and depressed. I would surmise that due to your retirement and, from one of your comments, a pending divorce, your mental state is unstable. You are at the highest dosage of Cymbalta, so before I look at other alternatives, I would encourage you to see a psychologist as soon as possible. I will refer an excellent lady who will hopefully be able to assist you.

Please contact my nurse or me if you have any questions, and best of luck to you. You are one of my most enjoyable patients!

Regards,

Faiza Ghazini

-10-

PH JOURNAL...February 23, 2017

No surprises from Doctor G. Seeing a head doc won't change anything either; I know I'm fucked up in the head.

I miss my work so badly and don't know why I retired, for God's sake. Conrad and the other partners gave me not-so-subtle hints that it was time to go. Why would these ungrateful bastards push out the guy who made the law firm what it has become today?

I am drinking red wine by the vat these days. At some point, my skin will start turning carmine, or maybe it'll look purple like a grape.

What to do when you live alone and have way too much time on your hands? That is the burning question these days. What the hell. Will I just sit around twiddling my thumbs 'til the Judgment Day? Surely not.

Started watching some of the Great Courses. First up to bat—the Etruscans. I learned so much about those folks that the next time I'm at a party, it'll be a real conversation starter: "Hey, how 'bout dem 'Truscans? Did you know that they pre-dated the Romans by 700 years? And that's BC by the way?" What an impression on the fellow listening to me who wants nothing better than to get away as soon as possible from this oddball guy.

Next up—the Roman Empire, the obvious next inquiry after the Etruscans. I can learn about Augustus, Nero, Tiberius, and other emperors who have long gone to dust. Maybe the guest lecturer will make comparisons between the fall of the Roman Empire and what some historians now observe as the decline of our more than two-hundred-forty-plus-year-old country—things like corruption, inequality, and inability to integrate outside people. One thing can be concluded before even diving into the Roman experience: Civilizations all ultimately rise and fall, and the US of A will, without a doubt at some point, either near or far away, face its own collapse. So anyone who yells at me, "Love it or leave it," I say, "Bah, humbug!"

Speaking of parties, I got to talking once with some guy at a get-together years go. As people tend to invariably do at parties, he asked what I did for a living. "I represent unions and union members," I responded. The guy literally took a full step back from me, as if I had AIDS, leprosy, or some other malignant disease. When I then inquired about his line of work, he responded with excessive pride, "I sell copper wiring." I couldn't help myself, so with a little too much sarcasm, I responded, "That must be the most fulfilling work ever in the history of time." He must have been terribly offended because he walked off in a huff and avoided me through the remainder of the party...gee, like I was some kind of party-pooper.

Another time-filler has been reading. During the many years of practicing law, I mainly stuck to historical biographies. My knowledge in this genre has become so humongous that I'm a walking fount of Wikipedia knowledge. Anything you want to know about most presidents, exclusive of Millard Fillmore and those successive presidents after Grant that I always confuse (wasn't it a bunch of Republicans with one Democrat stuck in there somewhere?), I've got a ready answer. Or, as they say over in East Austin, jus' aks me.

Without trying to sound too racist, why can't black people say the word the right way, like my good buddy and former investigator, Tony? Back in the day, we were like Batman and Robin, the Lone Ranger and Tonto, or the Three Musketeers, less Aramis—the awesome duo out to right the wrongs of the American judicial system.

With so much leisure time now, I have expanded my selections, reading thriller books by Nelson DeMillle, George Pelecanos, and James Finder, and a terrific memoir by Katherine Graham. I found some biographies about obscure World War II heroes like Betty Pack and the FBI agent and cryptologist who uncovered the theft of US atomic secrets by Julius Rosenberg and his unholy den of Russian agents. What those two government agency employees accomplished by uncovering the Rosenberg spy ring was amazing. Stephen King chastises authors who use "amazing;" he says there are multiple words that writers can use other than that one. I say, "Fuck you, Stephen King....It's my party, and I'll write 'amazing' if I want to."

Based on a recommendation from one of my cigar shop buddies, I read Sheehan's *A Bright Shining Lie* and Boot's *The Road Not Taken*—two downers that made me scream at the French government, Truman, Eisenhower, Kennedy...and especially Johnson, McNamara, and Westmorland for all their deceptions throughout the war. My conclusion? The Vietnamese should have been left alone to figure out their own destiny, which in the end they did anyway to their credit.

Since one of my sons is the ultimate Army boy—full Colonel, head of the West Point history department, and resident of a 6,000 square foot house on the Hudson subsidized by taxpayers (not that I am bragging or anything close to it). How about a shout out to our service men and women, in particular the almost 58,000 soldiers who were uselessly killed in the Vietnam Conflict and the many more physically maimed or mentally damaged. As the absolutely trite phrase goes, thank you for your service.

DeMille, Pelecanos, and Finder are top-flight wordsmiths, but there's only so many ways that DeMille's character, John Corey, can save the day or Pelecanos and Finder can devise convoluted plots.

I just finished *The Magus* by John Fowles, a more erudite work than the thrillers. But his style can be so intellectually-challenging that I spend too much time looking up the meaning of his words and expressions on every page. Fowles makes me feel like such a blockhead, so mentally dull that I have almost concluded, just maybe, I ain't nothin' but an ig'rant man!

After reading *The Magus*, I began feeling guilty about not reading other more "serious" books. I took up Trollope, since interviewees in the *NY Times* Book Review section kept lauding his work. After three chapters into *Barchester Towers,* I found myself sawing Z's, so Mr. Anthony was a non-starter. I'm certain that the Trollopites look down at me with considerable loathing as if my higher education ain't so high after all.

What to read next? Maybe the entire *Pentagon Papers*. Twenty-thousand monotonous pages ought to take me to the end toward my eternal ride to the sky.

The Trump watch continues. The guy is a bat-shit crazy blowhard and certainly as incompetent as they come. A blustering real estate developer, he never had more than twenty employees who worked for him. How that qualified him to serve as our president is beyond me. And not a very successful one at that. He declared bankruptcy six times, compared to a man who became a prosperous businessman without one trip to Chapter 11—Warren Buffet.

And the Trumpmeister stiffed everyone he hired—contractors, lawyers, and such—getting mired in numerous lawsuits with the stifees. Other monumental failures of the self-proclaimed art of the deal—Trump University, steaks, airline…did I leave anything out?

Still on the subject of his business ineptitude, what president would select that bumbling Rick Perry as Secretary of Energy? "I would eliminate three departments from the government—Commerce, Education, and um, what's that third one there?" Um, Rick, that would be the department you now oversee—Energy. Or how about Secretary of Commerce, Wilbur Ross, the guy who sleeps through important meetings and is no more than one stage away from dementia so bad that he'll shortly wind up in an assisted living facility?

Trump lies when the truth would make better sense and has a raging sense of colossal entitlement, which must be why he never wears a hat; even a twelve or thirteen hat size wouldn't fit that outsized ego. As a child, he must have been a whiny little brat, a kid who was born on third base and believed that he had hit a triple. That delicious *bon mot* provided courtesy of Barry Switzer. Thanks so much, Barry!

Other than with my old friend and colleague, Tommy Creegan from Tucson, I never paid too much attention before to what the commentators refer to as the great divide between the right and the left—at least not until the *Access Hollywood* tape came out in the run-up to the election.

I have, or at least had, this one close friend, an attorney and devout Methodist over in Knoxville. Over the years, we never had one conversation about politics, never even entered our minds. I sent him off a quick text after the tape that simply noted the president is a total buffoon. His reply blew me away: "I hate Hillary beyond any hate I have ever felt. She needs to be locked up. I believe in Jesus Christ, and Jesus tells me that Trump will be the answer to our country's ills....No more Mexicans, no more regulations on coal, Supreme Court justices who will overturn Roe, lower taxes, doing away with the Iran deal. If Hillary wins the election, I'm moving to another country."

Wow! Floored! That text hit me like—oh boy, here comes some serious banality—like a ton of bricks. Now, I do get the moving away reference about Hillary; since Trump's election, Canada has looked pretty damn good to me. I no longer have a desire to talk with my friend on the phone, much less visit him. Apparently this phenomenon is commonplace across the country; families and friends have been rended by this election.

Did you know that Booth and Oswald both originally escaped from detection after their murderous acts? Is there a way to actually pull off such a feat and get away scot free?

Really fucked up last night. The condo association held a party at the office last night; I went only because of the flyer about the free wine which definitely caught my attention. Eight glasses into a crappy merlot (I never drink Merlot! LOL) and three sheets to the wind, I began expounding on the virtues of a dead president. Drive up to DC, shoot the fucker, and then get out of town and hightail it back to the Lone Star State. But if somehow the powers-that-be caught and killed me after the sordid deed, I'd at least go down in the history books forever. "As far as I was concerned, a real win-win," I slurred, I'm certain only because I was drinking that crappy Merlot.

Some waddling blob of a man—his stomach puffed out way beyond his t-shirt, showing his pasty-white flabbiness—stood next to me during this drunken exposition. He wore a red hat emblazoned on the front with "Make America Great Again" which he would pull off several times to readjust his ill-fitting toupee. The rest of the night, he eye-fucked me, which was probably nothing, but...

-11-
EXCERPTS FROM NOTES OF JANIS MOORE LCP...
MARCH 3 and MARCH 24, 2017

COMMENT FROM ANNE HOWARD: Ms. Moore was equally as resistant as Conrad to turning over the post-appointment notes of her meetings with my dad, once again due to confidentiality concerns. But I overcame her apprehension by telling her that my dad was gone baby gone and that I really wanted to understand what caused my dad to go off the rails. So what harm would come from turning over the notes? She finally relented. Thank you, Ms. Moore.

Patient Preston S. Howard. Clearly depressed so checked first if any self-destructive tendencies. Patient assured that he had no immediate thoughts of suicide. Urged him to call me immediately if he did. Said he would, but I suspect there's some dissembling there.

Got him to discuss some of the causes of his depression: Too much alcohol, admitting to at least a bottle and a half of wine every night. I believe it's more than that. Patient doesn't seem inclined to stop at this time.

Patient in the middle of a divorce. Patient accepts it but seems despondent. Wondered what he could have done differently. Began crying when he spoke about his children; he obviously cares deeply for them.

Also noted that patient seems to be lost…identity tied to his many years of successful work. Patient commented that there is nothing left for him to do with his life. Mentioned several times that he was in what he referred to as the death zone; I suppose meaning his age.

Patient also observed that he doesn't enjoy many of the things he did before: family, movies, dining out, traveling…

Patient then spent some time railing about the president. Patient had so many negative thoughts about the president— thoughts of murder. Not certain how much of this is fantasy, how much reality. Patient assured me no immediate thought to take action against the president…said he doesn't own a weapon.

Right at the end of session, patient mentioned something about a Banks case. Time ran out before we could explore this further. Will have to bring this up at next session if he comes back. Patient seemed put off by the process. Don't know if he'll return.

Patient seemed belligerent from the outset of our second session. Stated that last session was a waste of time. I tried to impress on him the importance of staying the course...explained cognitive therapy and that it takes time; how in the last session it was clear that he gets little enjoyment out of his life, how he needs to identify those activities that in the past he has enjoyed.

Asked patient about his feelings toward the president today....He just shrugged his shoulders. Didn't seem inclined to discuss the matter further.

Reminded him about the Banks case. Patient seemed reluctant to discuss it, other than to see it bothered him a lot and he can't get it out of his head. He kept mumbling something about those motherfucking killers. I encouraged him to discuss this obvious flashpoint, but patient stood up about 20 minutes into the session. Patient said he didn't want to continue and wouldn't return.

-12-
PH JOURNAL MARCH 25, 2017

Cognitive therapy? What kind of psychobabble is that? Right after my strange conversation with my granddaddy, Buster—about ten years after his death (you can check my memoir about that eerie occurrence)—I read up on cognitive therapy. I'm supposed to do positive things that make me feel better like reading, working out, hanging out with friends, and so forth. Well, I *have* been reading, not that it has elevated my spirits a whole lot; I *do* work out, at least whenever I'm not too hungover; all my friends are *work*-related, and other then Conrad and, of course, Tony, I haven't seen any of the others since my retirement.

Conrad calls me every now and then, and we meet for lunch. Our conversations have been strained, as Conrad would continually check his iPhone—why can't businessmen and women ever park their phone for at least a few minutes? And why do couples sit in a restaurant on their phones the entire time, disconnecting from each other as if their lives had dwindled to endless boredom? I must have been totally looped at the end of my marriage; I can't recall whether Donna and I had reached that stage of ennui or not.

I do recognize that Conrad's life, and the lives of other staff, have moved on. The day I walked out of the office for the last time, the door closed behind me, and life went on at Howard, Diamond, and McGowan like I was a nonentity whose history at the firm was now nothing more than a distant memory. I have become a forgotten man, now in a different place, a universe far away from the thrill of a new case, a fascinating client, or one more victory tabulated on the firm's scoreboard.

When I think about it, I get no enjoyment out of anything—zip, nada—well, except my affection for cigars. It's like my happy button has been turned off or gone on the fritz. I'm so down in the dumps that I don't even enjoy drinking my pinot noir other than for the buzz it provides. Things have become so far in the doldrums that I can see the end hovering right over my head, waiting to lower the boom.

I suppose the psycho-lady, Janis, really wanted to help me, and God knows I need it—a washed-up sot like me should get any help offered. But the girl was around 26, almost young enough to be my granddaughter. How do you take advice from a woman who has never experienced the ups and downs of life? Who hasn't felt enough loss, doubt, fear, or disappointment to offer advice to a client?

Okay, enough self-flagellating. It's as unbecoming as an opera diva singing Sonny Williamson tunes. Wait, I amend this last remark: Some years back, Montserrat Caballe did a nifty duo with Freddie Mercury called "Barcelona" that rocked the house.

The Trump watch continues. Hope that someone in the media is keeping track of all the lies that come out of this creep's mouth. People should be shocked when the fabrications are totaled up. Sadly, there seems to be a large group of citizens who are oblivious to the president's constant barrage of fabrications, as if his mendacity is somehow a part of his appeal.

Hillary called these people deplorables; the media refers to them as his base. How have our politics sunk so low that his kind of behavior is not only tolerated but even celebrated?

I notice how Trump always refers to the greatest whatever in history—the greatest election, greatest crowd, speech, scandal, and so on. I'm waiting for him to blurt out "in the history of history." The greatest what? President? Leader? Demagogue? Flimflammer? And what about his "we'll just have to wait and see" line and his "next few days [weeks, etc] you can look forward to [fill in the blank]?" He's so predictable at this point.

I'm getting a bead on this guy. He's as shallow as a kiddie pool and insincere as an empty promise; yet he won't apologize even when he's fucked up to the max. That's gotta be the Roy Cohn influence on him. Got to give the guy his due though; he's running the greatest Big Top since Barnum and Bailey. Send in the clowns!

I wonder whenever his term, hopefully not terms, ends, how he will be regarded in history. Whenever this loathsome president leaves office, hopefully sooner than later, James Buchanan's descendants can cheer that their bumbling relative will no longer sit in last place on the Hit Parade as the worst president ever.

For the first time in my life, I spend hours glued to my television set, surfing for news between the one-note gasbags at MSNBC and FOX, who preach only to their respective left and right choirs, as if their converted audience needs any further indoctrination to support their rigid views? If I want the government propaganda channel, I of course turn to FOX, where you get not only a daily dose but hourly barrage of accolades for the president and hateful fusillades against Obama and Hillary. I thought Barack and Hillary were now a part of the past...old news, but they do make superb piñatas to keep the FOX faithful wound up against politicians they see as vile.

But if you are of a liberal bent—that would be me—then MSNBC is home base. I feel most comfortable in my own echo chamber—okay, I admit to my own intolerant perspectives—and *my* windbags like Joe and Mika, the two Chrises, Rachel, and Laurence, who speak closer to my beliefs. But by the time Laurence comes on, my wine-infused brain can't keep up with the dialogue.

After going back and forth between the news channels, I easily see the chasm between the Right and the Left. And I saw it up close and personal after I completed my memoirs; colleagues urged me to jump on Facebook to pimp the book. I had deleted the FB train some years ago because of all the endless rants about politics and religion. Now it seems even more virulent, as the righties bluster on about anyone with a liberal thought; then on the same FB stream, the lefties jump in with malevolence against the other side. Back and forth they continue, talking over each other, never considering the uselessness of all this vituperation. Really, what is the fucking point!

So last week, I vowed to take a break from Facebook, remembering one of Groucho Marx's many terrific aphorisms: "I find television very educating. Every time somebody turns on the set, I go into the other room and read a book." Since I had already read more than most semi-literate men, I decided to blot out the news and just exclusively watch ESPN for a while—a little bit for the noise—and to catch up on the latest irrelevant games and scores.

What a mistake! I never realized the mountain of sports clichés that spout out more than Niagara Falls: "There's no I in team"..."I gave 110% tonight"..."We've just gotta take 'em one game at a time"..."God was on our side and led us to a win"..."They do what they do, and we do what we do"..."We had a point to prove tonight." Then there's the comments that show up later on YouTube as memorials to absurdity: "Playoffs? Playoffs?"..."Practice? We're talkin' about practice." And so it goes.

But I do have one more thing to say about ESPN. Who is this flannel-mouthed, black idjit (as they say in Texas) named Steven A. Smith? Not that I've got anything against people of color...why, some of my best friends are black. But this guy spews one opinion after another as though he is the final arbiter of all things related to sports.

Steven A. Smith kind of reminds me of Laura Ingraham from FOX. Not their ethnicity or gender but instead, their need to engage in raging harangues—bull throwers who blame this person or that with no understanding of the facts or appreciation of nuance. Speaking of Laura, so long as you keep up your Newspeak vitriol, why can't LeBron do more than dribble a basketball?

Speaking of FOX and ESPN, why is it that the foxy women commentators on FOX sound like a bunch of bubble-headed bleached blondes while the ESPN ladies not only look like eye-candy but have the additional quality of knowing what the hell they're talking about.

My plan lasted for just three days, so today I relented and watched a segment on FOX with Trump walking along a rope-line, surrounded by a bevy of Secret Service agents. As he walked along the cordoned-off line, he swaggered with his customary self-importance, talking to his admirers with feigned sincerity as he soaked up all his admirers' applause and hurrahs.

A thought came into my head while watching the rope-line circus. If I could find out where and when he shows up at one of these events, maybe I could squeeze up one shot close enough to blow the fucker away. How awesome would that be? The only trouble would be that one of those Secret Service agents would terminate my life in a light speed, mini-second. Have to think that one over.

I know that hate is a wasteful emotion. It gnaws at your brain like an oozing cancer that will eventually pollute your entire mind and then move down the rest of your body. Why can't I have happy thoughts like Al Franken's SNL role as Stuart Smiley: "You're good enough, you're smart enough, and doggone it, people like you."

-13-
PH JOURNAL APRIL 5, 2017

Good day, bad day. Started out on the upswing, but first a little back story. When I was living high on the hog out in Rob Roy, I joined an upscale gym at Lamar and Sixth Street just off of downtown called Mecca. The place was billed as a luxury environment, and the prices certainly reflected this hotsy-totsy description. I had to fork out five-hundred bucks to join and another one-fifty per month for the privilege of working out.

It was still a gym though, and the same kind of patrons showed up as they did at Gold's or Anytime Fitness. This one quartet of workout partners was especially memorable—four dudes on the back side of forty, all with their heads intentionally shaved to baldness and wearing wife-beater shirts to show off their bulging biceps and triceps. I would refer to them as the Mr. Clean Quartet or the Coneheads, but only to myself. If I had mentioned either of these slights out loud, one or more of those fellows might have cleaned my clock.

Another kind of workout fellow was especially annoying, one I referred to as a grandstander. This guy would strut around in his muscle shirt, carrying a gallon jug of what likely was some kind of protein enhancer and constantly staring into one of the many mirrors placed all around the gym so he could admire his perfectly sculpted body. As he worked out his muscles with barbells whose weights I could only dream about pumping, he would forcefully moan like one of those professional tennis players who grunted as they hit every shot. When finished, the grandstander would throw the barbell down violently as if some part if his back had been displaced.

When I moved to the condo, the location, cost, and annoyance of the Mr. Clean/Coneheads and grandstanders at Mecca made the cozy (and free!) condo gym more sensible. But before I go into this particular morning, a little background about my workout routine, or what Donna would often refer to as one of my many ruts that made me too predictable.

I carry my iPhone and ear buds so I can listen to my playlist of awesome classic rock tunes. There must be an evil gnome who fucks with my ear buds every night because they are always twisted to the point that it takes me a good five minutes to untangle them. Sometimes I will ask one of my kids about this mysterious contortion; each of them responds in a similar way. "Don't you have better things to do with your time than worry about your ear buds?"

My song routine (rut…whatever) begins with two adrenalizing tunes, "Thunderstruck" by ACDC and "Bad Reputation" by Joan Jett and the Blackhearts. Once you're on the treadmill and turn these songs on, if the heart hasn't quickly spiked up to a minimum of one-hundred-forty beats per minute, then you've already put one leg in the grave, so you might as well crawl all the way in the casket and close it tight. These foot stompin' songs are followed by Van Halen's "Best of Both Worlds," "Do Ya" by ELO, and the two "city" melodies—"Suffragette City" by David Bowie and "Paradise City" by Gun and Roses.

Last but definitely not least, a word about Toni Basil. She produced an album called *The Very Best of Toni Basil*. The photograph on the cover shows her wearing pigtails and a cheerleader's outfit, apparently the one she actually wore in high school. She looks quite fuckable, ready to jump right into the star quarterback's car for a tumble in the back seat. Her song, "Time After Time," concludes the playlist.

Toni has been a multi-talented artist: She and Karen Black portrayed LSD-hazed prostitutes to a T in the movie *Easy Rider*. She also became acclaimed as a professional dancer, frontlining a dance troupe called The Lockers. I saw The Lockers' electrifying production once when watching Don Cornelius's *Soul Train* on WGN; although, I honestly was glued to the show only for the hotty black women wearing minis up to their twats who danced toward the camera like strippers sauntering around the stage with a jump-me expression on their faces. Okay, Toni, enough about your coolness.

So this morning, as I slogged along on the treadmill, sweating out last night's wine-fest, a lady walked into the condo gym wearing a denim, medium-blue mini-skirt and an untucked gray tee. It was difficult to gauge the size of her cantaloupes because of the draped tee, but they did appear quite substantial.

Her cropped black hair gave her a kind of a dykey, guyish look; she could have been the doppelganger for the gifted British actress, Olivia Colman. This woman wasn't a street-stopper like say, Jessica Biel, but she wasn't a two-bagger either but, instead, more like a tweener...like Olivia.

Looking back afterward on the exchange in the gym, I concluded that the similarity between Olivia and the woman went beyond just the overall appearance; it was more their countenances, how their faces could move with bullet-train speed from glee to condemnation to puzzlement to disgust.

She interrupted me in the middle of "Do Ya" by ELO saying "Hi there, good lookin" as she stepped up on the treadmill next to mine. Now, I'm not Robert Redford by any stretch of imagination, but I've been told by more than a few gals over the years that I am a somewhat fetchin' kinda guy, whatever the hell that means. Still, after her remark, what I saw was a bright, multi-colored neon flashing on and off, saying "come on down!" So I was figuring, maybe this retired seventy-plus has-been still had a little gas left in the tank!

"I really need to get a few pounds off my butt," she continued, doing a booty sway back and forth a few times in a showy-off way. I took a gander down below and replied, "That butt looks quite fine and pinchable if you're open to that kind of thing."

She didn't bite, at least not on this one; her stinging temperament, though, would appear a few minutes later. Instead, she began a long-winded conversation about how she had just moved in, how lonely she was (*Neon light really flashing now!*), and she wanted to learn how to work the machines.

Fortunately, I had recently completed a transaction to buy my condo and recalled some of the principles I learned back in my law school days about offer and acceptance. So, being the gentleman that I am (not), I offered…and she accepted. The next hour, I taught her how to work the lat machine, bi's, tri's, back, and so on; all the while, she kept rubbing her gazongas up against my arms and back.

The Johnson down between my thighs has been dormant for a long time, kind of like the Poas Volcano in Costa Rica. But like Poas, there could always be an eruption on the horizon.

My dating skills had definitely rusted at this point of my life. Donna was my last date over forty years ago, and I never included my many dalliances as even remotely counting as dates. So after introducing myself, I stumbled through our initial conversation: What's your name? What kind of work do you do? Where did you live before? I almost went with "what's your sign?" as a joke, but since we're now living in the twenty-first century, this line seemed beyond lame. So on and on I nattered, yadda, yadda, yadda…embarrassing and faltering chit-chat.

As I was going through this litany of complete balderdash, I suddenly noticed the woman's eyes, the hue of pure turquoise. I had never seen such dazzling, even mesmerizing eyes that, depending on how the light hit her face, would alternate between a hue of blue and green. In fact, thinking back, I can hardly recall any women with eyes that color.

"My name is George" the lady got around to answering. "I retired from a software outfit in Silicon Valley and moved to Austin where property values are lower. I don't have to worry about earthquakes, fires, and mudslides all the time, and one of my daughters has lived down in New Braunfels for several years."

"What a minute, you said your name is *George*?

"You got wax in your ears? Yes…George. Short for Georgeanna."

"Thought I heard it right. Are you a lesbo? With your hair and that sort of manly walk, you sure look like one. By the way, do you know what a lezzie brings with her on her second date? You probably don't…a U-Haul full of her belongings."

George gave me a look that could be taken as somewhere between contempt and amusement, the kind that Olivia might have used in *Broadchurch*, and then said, "That was a very personal and cheeky question, Preston Howard. You should be ashamed of yourself."

"I suppose I should be," I answered, "but I'm really not. It's just how I roll. Just so you know, though, some of my best friends are mackerel eaters."

"You get a black mark on your report card for being a smartass, so try not to get any more, or you're going to detention after class. To answer your sassy question, I definitely don't go down on women …hetero all the way."

I have always been astute at deducing a woman's age, but she had one of those indeterminate appearances where she could have been anywhere between forty and sixty. "Good to know," I remarked. "How old are you, *George*?" I couldn't help but make funny with her name again.

"Enough with the jokin' around fella. I'm sixty-seven."

"No way, George." You look like you're around forty, maybe forty-five."

"I take good care of myself—eat right, work out four or five days a week, think positive thoughts. By the way, your tutelage on the machines sucks. Don't ever give up your day job to become a fitness trainer. You get an F, as in failure."

"So you knew how to work the machines? Why did you ask for my help then?"

"How else was I gonna get you to pay attention to me? I saw you at the condo party, where you made a drunken but hilarious fool of yourself, but since you're an anti-Trumpite, we do have a little, and I mean little so far, basis for friendship. By the way, how old are you, Preston?"

"I'm eighty-five," I lied.

"Wow, you look great for eighty-five! Wait a minute, I'm calling bullshit on that one. How old are you, *really*?"

"Okay, I'm really seventy-three," I fessed up.

"You don't look so good for seventy-three, Preston." George laughed heartily, hopefully because she was kidding and then reached a hand out toward me and tweaked one of my nipples.

Definitely had a live wire on my hands!

Then George announced right out of the blue that a dinner at Ruth Chris Steakhouse would work just find for her. The woman was moving right along and had extravagant taste, but whatever...I could afford it, and it would be a diversion from the dreariness of my present circumstances.

George continued, "I've noticed you walking around the condo like a lost puppy. You weave all over the parking lot like a drunken sailor, and I would imagine that your breath stinks like wine all the time like it does right now. I expect you to stay sober when you take me out."

Now why did she have to go ruin what otherwise had promised to be a memorable night, where the little blue pill would make its way down into my system, and in no more than an hour urge my cock to wake up and take care of business? I told my new and odd acquaintance that I'd have to rethink our plans. George ignored my remark. She said she'd expect me to pick her up on Friday at seven p.m. and make sure to make a reservation. Jesus, how can I stay sober around Ms. Wild and Crazy Dog and get laid? A real conundrum.

Now for the bummer part of the day.

***

Walking back to my condo, two sourpuss-looking men stood in front of my unit; they both wore ill-fitting gray suits that looked like they had been bought off the rack at Kmart. Frick and Frack identified themselves as secret service agents who needed to speak with me immediately about some comments I made last February. I knew right off the bat where this meeting would be headed.

Mr. Frick told me that a resident who had met with them expressed a concern that I had made threats against the president; Mr. Frack, pointing toward the obvious gray government-issued vehicle nearby, ordered me to accompany them to their office. I told the Frick/Frack brothers that it has always been my policy to stay away from law enforcement offices unless I was under arrest.

And thus what started out as a tense impasse almost turned into an out-and-out brawl— screaming back and forth and then quite a bit of pushing and shoving. When I began bellowing that I was being kidnapped against my will by aliens, and residents came outside to watch the drama unfolding, Messrs. Frick and Frack calmed down a bit. I offered a compromise. If they wanted to enter my condo, we could the sit down and have a rational conversation—probably their first encounter with an unhinged citizen who asserted his rights.

Once inside, I offered them a beer, wine, or something stronger. They declined the offer, saying they were on duty. I told them that my policy has always been to never drink until the sky is over the yardarm, but it's got to be five o'clock somewhere so come on guys. Live a little. They didn't find my banter in any way as humorous I did.

These two guys were unalike in so many ways. Frick looked like Fatty Arbuckle—so obese that his pants were unbuttoned and his belt on the very last hole, his full head of disheveled, bleached-blond hair looked like it hadn't been washed in a month. Surely the Secret Service had regulations against this kind of appearance; I bet he never worked the presidential detail. Frack totally contrasted his partner—rail thin and close-cropped hair like a Marine with a nervous tic in his left eye and a twitchy right leg that looked like it had a mind of its own.

They both acted way too tight-ass, probably the kind of guys who saw the glass as half empty. They bought into the maxim that life is a bitch and then you die and only used the missionary position when

121

fucking their wives. Not that Frick could ever find his dick located somewhere below all that corpulence. They both sat totally erect in the living room chair—quite an achievement for Fat Body—and had scrunched up mouths and faces as if they detested that I had faced them down outside.

So then we got down to business. Mr. Frick first advised that they were with the protective division of the secret service, whatever the hell that was. He went through my Trump rant at the condo association party. Mr. Frack advised me that I had violated federal Code 18 Section 871, which constituted a felony when I threatened the president. Then one of them (can't remember which) asked me what my intent was then, and still is at this time, to kill the president.

My turn to speak. I told them that in fact I hated the president and wished that someone would rid this pestilence from the earth. But then, I assured them that first off, I was drunk out of my mind last February and had no idea what I was saying. Not exactly true. Somewhere in the recesses of my brain, I recalled that lying to a secret service agent constituted a crime. Then I advised them that further, I don't even have a gun and had no intention of buying one (which, until that very moment was true—more on that in a minute).

Mr. Frick (or was it Mr. Frack?) advised me that my threat was taken seriously and would be classified as a level-1 enhancement. I should have been elated at this news since it turned out this classification was the lowest one on the totem pole, but I was so pissed at the entire episode that my hair was, metaphorically speaking, on fire. One of the dudes notified me that I would receive a letter shortly, outlining their decision, and they would be alert for any further malfeasance on my part. Big Brother working hard on behalf of our citizenry!

When the Frick/Frack partners departed, my first reaction was to pull out my baseball bat, walk over to the "Make America Great" slob boy's condo, and bash his head in so hard that whatever tiny amount of his brain existed would spill out all over the ground. Now that wasn't exactly a Stuart Smiley pleasant thought, was it?

Then I realized that this course of action was not an especially nifty move…more involvement by the authorities, an arrest, conviction for aggravated assault, and likely civil suit. Dumb idea. At least I've learned enough from this experience to keep my mouth shut out in polite society about this sorry ass excuse of a president.

Now here's a great question: Why don't I own a gun?

-14-

PH'S JOURNAL APRIL 8, 2017

Dipped my foot into the water so to speak last night...first real date I've ever had since wooing Donna so many years ago. I don't count bar pick-ups as dates...too many to even remember. I have no guilt about these fleeting liaisons. Most of my illicit jumps in the hay took place back in the seventies (well, maybe some later than the seventies). Women were welcome with their favors before the fear of AIDS caused the ladies to become more cautious about spreading their legs.

As instructed, I picked up Ms. George—by the way, last name Robards—promptly at seven p.m., a reservation set for a half-hour later. As for her admonition about alcohol, I must have forgotten about that one because I downed three vodka and tonics before the appointed hour, hoping that her booze detector would not ding.

For a woman who initially appeared—oh, what's the word? Lesbo?—she came to the door stylishly well-decked-out in black leather mini skirt, six-inch heels, a sheer lavender blouse, and a matching lavender push-up bra that showed off some serious cleavage that had been sadly camouflaged at the gym by her gray tee. She had clearly taken the time to apply just the right amount of makeup, so she didn't appear like a tart; her spiked, black hair had obviously been meticulously attended to at a salon.

It's so easy to stereotype people. Based on our first encounter, I had her pegged as a space cadet, one of those women who would park her car at the mall and later couldn't find the car if her life depended on it, so she would have to ask a security guard to drive her around for a half-hour in the vast parking lot looking for it. Then she'd holler out, "Oh my goodness, I can't believe it was so close to the mall entrance!"

We started out with some of the normal getting-to-know-you superficial crap. She had been a hard-charging executive in Silicon Valley, absorbed totally in her work. When she came to Austin to be closer to her daughter, her condo was a lease/purchase agreement in case the move didn't work out as planned. I glossed over my renowned legal career, making it seem like I had been employed at a piece-work factory, and when I mentioned my so-far mediocre occupation as a novelist, I left out the rather significant fact that my royalties would barely pay for more than a Uber ride on my next trip out to Bergstrom.

The dinner was going as I expected, a downer. But then my perception changed during the course of our meal as we discovered a common link. We had both spent time during the sixties in Chicago, and when George could name the starting infield for the Cubbies in 1966—Ernie Banks, Glenn Beckert, Donnie Kessinger, and Ron Santo—I immediately began rethinking her space-cadet pigeon-hole.

Then we bemoaned the infamous trade when the Cubs gave up on Lou Brock in 1964, trading him to the Cardinals. Lou Brock was one of only four players to hit a home run over the cavernous center field wall of the old Polo Grounds in New York and was later inducted into the Hall of Fame. For Brock, the Cubs got the arm-hobbled pitcher, Ernie Broglio, the even-on-a-good-day middling Doug Clemens, and the thirty-nine year-old, over-the-hill, sly curve-ballin' lefty Bobby Shantz. Come on, pull out the guillotine and execute the dumbbells who engineered that trade. Off with their heads!

"While we're talking about that trade," George told me, "there is this group of muckety-muck Cubs fans in Washington, D.C., called the Emil Verban Society, who from time-to-time give out a "Brock-for-Broglio Judgment Award" for stupidity. In 1990, the society gave the award to Saddam Hussein for invading Kuwait."

I never heard of the outfit, but from the moment George began expounding on the whatever-it-was-called society, I became so enamored with her that I was ready to propose marriage…or at least ready to get laid. Then I realized that the vial of blue pills was sitting in my bathroom vanity…crap.

What really floated my boat were those turquoises which George would flit up and down in a coquettish way, surely knowing that it captivated me. I almost wanted to jump in and float around inside those eyes.

I have barely even one shred of recollection about my first date with Donna, other than it took place in 1966, and I am certain we didn't have any conversation about sex. Donna wasn't by any stretch of the imagination a prude, but she did have a strong sense of respectability. We never even kissed until the third date. And sex? Beyond getting beyond second base, maybe even third base, until we married…fuhgeddaboudit. After all, it was the sixties.

I decided to get the real scoop on the now-captivating George Robards. "What the hell was the nipple tweak all about the other day?" I asked her. And off to the races she went. She married at twenty-five to a man who smooth-talked his way into her heart; he turned out to be a lazy, boring dipshit, but at least she bore a daughter, Alexandra, who she described as her only accomplishment from the union. So three years later, George began checking off the box for "divorced" on her employment forms.

Later, she visited a longtime friend and college roommate at Stanford. She noticed that her friend's husband appeared overly compliant to his wife's every demand. When George inquired about this interplay, her friend said that they had a special relationship, what is termed a Domme/submissive dynamic. The wife rules the roost at all times, controls when, where, and how sex takes place (for her only; he is normally chaste at all times), and enforces her will through various mechanisms such as whippings, nipple clamps, humiliation, and sexual frustration. George told me that as she listened to her friend's strange tale, she became so turned on that her nether region became inflamed and wet.

Somewhere in George's bizarre story, she used the term "uxorious" when describing the husband. I had to immediately call a time out and google the word, contrary to my standard restaurant protocol of a parked cellphone. Three cheers for the iPhone!

As George starting going into further detail about how Dommes control their submissives, talking about other cringe-worthy subjects I had never before heard about, I had to interrupt her, telling her that enough was enough. While the account of her sexual longings wouldn't scare me out of the restaurant, my little fella down below was a zero on the peter-meter, as flaccid as a strand of cooked linguine.

No way was I gonna have my ass beat, my nipples aching, indulge in any other creepy shit, and most of all, get a case of the blue balls, not that prostate-less men would ever catch the painful testicle malady. When I'm horny these days, I have no hesitation about spanking the monkey and no way was this pressure reliever ever going to become verboten.

Then George put a hand over mine, squeezed it slightly, and said, "My needs have changed over the years. I figured out that number one, most of the so-called submissive men were just living in a fantasy world, and didn't really want the D/s relationship; they just sought the icing without the cake; submission to a woman as a way of life never really appealed to any of them. Second, it was just too much damn work for me."

"So where are you now?" I asked, wary that maybe she would move on to some even weirder shit, maybe like her fucking and sucking a donkey or something else you might encounter in Juarez, ("You want to see my seester?"). Fortunately not…

"All I want at this point is an honest, positive, and intelligent man with a great sense of humor," she replied, "and who doesn't have any addictions." She pointed at my glass of pinot noir I had ordered previously over her reproving glare. "That gets in the way of being with a complete man. Of *you* being a complete man."

Sometimes it's just better to shut the fuck up rather than say anything about my constant, raging drunkenness…no defense to this frailty anyhow.

"So here's where I am right now," she said, finally getting to the point, whatever the hell that was. "I've had my eye on you from the moment I first saw you—immediate attraction on my part—even when you were totally sloshed that night at the condo party, railing on about Donald the Freak. And then I found out you're not only a famous lawyer, but a writer to boot. Wow, so much promise! Sooo, if and when you get off the booze—and from where I sit, that's a pretty big if and when—then we can discuss a serious relationship and sex. Plus, I never have sex on the first date; I don't want to be thought of as a slut."

Shit, I knew I wasn't getting laid tonight. This date turned out way sucky. "So if we have sex on the second date, then you're not a slut?" I asked her. "Good to know."

George didn't bite on that one, and she clearly hadn't finished getting to the meat and potatoes. Why can't women be a lot more pithy and simply move on to the point?

"So once you get yourself straightened up, we'll talk about sex," she continued as I had an irresistible desire to feign an overelaborate yawn but thought better of it. "Are you a considerate lover?" George asked.

"I've always been a kind of wham bam, thank you ma'am kind of guy," I answered, a little bit in jest…or not.

"No funnin' around about sex," George replied earnestly. "If you're a flop in the sack, well…forget it."

"Can we talk more about the Cubs?" I asked her.

George got the hint, so we went on to her travels after retirement throughout Europe and the Far and Middle East. She actually knew who the vice-president was (the so-called "man in the street" has no clue other than isn't that the dude with the white hair?) and most of the current senators. She failed on the names of many of the US representatives, even from Texas, but I couldn't fault her since I don't pay much attention to them either. We had many of the same other interests in addition to travel—bridge, hiking, and reading. She had actually read Churchill's six volumes about WWII, something I had accomplished some years ago. Quite a slog, but fascinating.

Later, as I escorted George to her door, she lowered the boom on me. "You don't listen, do you, dipshit? I had told you no drinking, and you show up with alcohol on your breath. I can detect vodka, asshole. I've already told you, I'm not going to bed with you tonight," she said, "but remember our first date." She took a step into my body and gave me the most delectable, wet, French kiss that had ever been placed on my lips, right up there with Rick and Elsa's kiss in *Casablanca*, including George's left arm wrapped around my shoulder.

Definitely and fortunately, though, not the one in *Brokeback Mountain*. I mean, come on, watching two guys goin' after it is just a bit too much for me.

But understand, I'm not homophobic….Some of my best friends are gay.

My head became dizzy from the intimacy, and Poas felt a rumble down below. While I was still reeling from the lip-lock, George said, "Whenever you get your drinking under control, ask me out again, but not until then. You're a really interesting fella, but you need to get your life in order. And remember this kiss."

As I relive the night, it is clear that there had never been even one moment of awkwardness—the best time I could recall with a woman…ever, including Donna. I feel melancholy tonight. Due to my one notable frailty, there probably is no future for sex or anything else with Ms. George Robards.

-15-
AUSTIN AMERICAN STATESMAN STATE AND LOCAL SECTION, MAY 10, 2017

Donna D. Howard, 69, filed a petition for divorce yesterday with the Travis County District Clerk against her husband, Preston S. Howard, 73. The basis cited for the divorce was insupportability, specifically that there were disagreements and differences that could not be resolved. In Texas, this filing is considered a no-fault divorce.

Ms. Howard's attorney, Howard Cashman, stated that his client and Mr. Howard had mutually agreed to the divorce. Mr. Cashman further advised that his client and Mr. Howard have already worked through a financial settlement which will be implemented once the divorce is finalized.

Mr. Howard is a reputed Austin attorney who has handled numerous cases both in Travis County and throughout the country. One of his most publicized and notorious cases involved his representation of Austin detectives Willard Banks, James Buhl, and Theodore Williams, who were charged with murdering Leroy Wallace, Shanice Wallace, and their three children in East Austin in 2007. The dismissal of charges against the three officers in 2008 created a furor throughout the Austin community.

When contacted, Mr. Howard's attorney, Stan Petchel had no comment.

-16-

NOTE FROM ANNE HOWARD

While my mom and dad were, on the one hand, sad about their divorce, as was I, they were also both relieved to get through this difficult moment in their marriage without too many complications. I was especially pleased that my dad did the right thing, making sure that Mom was well taken care of so she would be financially secure for the rest of her life. In his memoir, Dad commented about his inadequate IRA. What bullshit! The fact was, he made a boatload of money through his practice, training programs, speeches, and settlement with his firm for his partnership share to the point he could have retired comfortably in his fifties, but his passion for the work impelled him to stay at the grindstone way past seventy.

Mom is definitely in a better place and feeling good about her future. But my dad...that's another story. He seems lost in a swamp or maybe a dense forest with no way out. In both his words and actions, he seems to have given up and has no reason to keep on living. I really worry about him right now.

I began thinking the other day about the fond memories of Dad during my college experience. We drove off from Austin, hooked up with I-20, and motored all the way to Atlanta in 1997 where I matriculated to Oglethorpe, a small liberal arts school that must have cost Dad an arm and a leg. He drove us all the way out in my clunker of a car with no air conditioning...in August...in the South. But never mind, as he drove along, smoking one Fidel

133

Castro-sized cigar after another, he would tell many of his wild yarns about his work. A special time!

The day after I moved into the dorm, we met for breakfast at a diner next to the Marta, where Dad could jump on the train and ride down to Hartsfield for the flight home. As we sat discussing my excitement about the next four years, suddenly Dad started bawling and had to leave the table. I was at first flummoxed by this behavior and didn't figure out until after he left that I was his last child to leave the nest, and the moment hit him hard.

On graduation day, Senator Max Cleland gave the commencement address—the Max Cleland who earned both a Silver and Bronze Star for valorous service in combat during Vietnam. The same Max Cleland who lost two legs and an arm during the 'Nam debacle. And the Max Cleland who lost his senate seat to that slime-ball Saxby Chambliss who charged Cleland with being unpatriotic for some votes he took in the Senate. My dad gets apoplectic even today whenever he talks about Saxby Chambliss, not only for his underhanded political tactics but for having been his classmate in law school. Dad says that it's difficult to claim he went to the Harvard Law School of the South, while in the same breath admitting that Chambliss went there too.

After the graduation, Dad slipped me a tidy sum of money, told me how proud he was of me, and then floored me when he said, "Sweetheart, with this terrific liberal arts degree, you are now qualified to say, 'Sir, will that be with or without fries?'" I was beyond pissed at my dad for that remark until a year later, as I listened to one wretched client after another at the Texas Unemployment Board pour out their miseries at having no job and no money. It's amazing how much smarter my parents became as I got older.

-17-
PH JOURNAL MAY 19, 2017

An indoor gun range sits in an unassuming part of South Austin. I had passed it numerous times in my travels around the city but never paid a bit of attention to the place until now.

Decided to check it out today. Pickup trucks with gun racks sat throughout the parking lot, so I figured that many of those owners voted for The Donald. As I walked up to the entrance, a sign covered part of the front door which pretty much confirmed this observation.

"NOTICE
This place is politically incorrect.
WE SAY
Merry Christmas
One Nation Under God
We Salute Our Flag
We Give Thanks to our Troops
If This Offends You
LEAVE"

This greeting made me realize before I even walked in that I would need to be on my p's and q's. I knew for a fact that the patrons inside would have rather unyielding views about America, home of the free and the brave. My disgust for the man currently occupying the White House would have to be kept under wraps.

Walking inside, it felt like a frenzied, out-of-business sale, as if the enemies of the Second Amendment would be sweeping down at any moment to clamp down on gun owners' unalienable right to buy their AR-15s and shoot up shit. Mostly men of all ages, the good ol' boys wore baseball hats or cowboy hats, and many of them spat tobacco juice into Styrofoam cups… the embodiment of macho Texas fellas.

The right-wing slant didn't just stop at the front door. Inside, a t-shirt was draped over a stand-up, cardboard figure of Hillary. The t-shirt read: "DEPLORABLE LIVES MATTER." Another sign stated "Due to a price increase on ammo, do not expect a warning shot. Thank you for understanding." And yet one more, an outline of a body target full of bullet holes in the head and middle of the chest that read "Free body piercing by Glock."

As I walked around the range, weapons were stacked galore around the enormous room—big guns, little guns, automatics, semi-automatics, double action revolvers. Whatever you wanted, they had it, and if they didn't have it, they'd order it for you.

I met the owner, Joanne, a fortyish lady with heavy makeup, who wore a too tight-fitting, black blouse and equally snug, black short-shorts, both of which did little to hide her creeping pooch-belly. Joanne probably had to worry incessantly that as middle-age took over and ravaged her body, she would turn to flab. Several earlier photographs of her were displayed around the room maybe ten or fifteen years earlier when she wore the same type of black, figure-hugging, come-thither outfits and carried an AR-15.

We made some mindless chit-chat for a few minutes while she set up my membership at the range. Then, in an accusatory way, she said, "You're not a Muslim, are you? We're not big on rug-heads hanging out here."

I just about blew my top over this remark but held my tongue. I had a notion that every other gun range would be staffed by NRA nutbags, and since buying a gun was the objective, I simply told her that as far as I knew, my Presbyterian membership card still remained valid, omitting that I was expelled from church back in my younger days due to my wise-ass, Jesus-mocking comments to the minister.

She pointed toward my t-shirt and said, "What does that mean," referring to the inscription on the shirt: "Mustache rides—twenty-five cents." Not wanting to get sideways with her just yet, I replied, "Ask around. Someone here will probably know."

Joanne introduced me to a salesman by the name of Wally, who would show me the ropes, help me buy a gun, and take me to the shooting range. I was hoping for a lady. There actually was a woman selling her wares at the range; wait, that didn't quite come out right.

Wally turned out to be knowledgeable and accommodating. Being a newbie and a fussy customer, I probably drove Wally nuts with my questions—the differences between a semi-automatic handgun and double action revolver, how the weapons are loaded, and so forth.

Wally was a middle-aged fellow with a stomach paunch—way bigger than Joanne's—a head with only a few wisps of hair, and some kind of red splotches all over his head that appeared infected, like he needed a dermatologist appointment STAT. He was the kind of unremarkable man who, when he walked down the street (other than the head malady) would have been disregarded by anyone passing him by. But fortunately for me, Wally had the patience of Job and answered every question as if I really wasn't a nimrod who had been so oblivious to weaponry for more than seventy years.

My initial preference was the .38 Special, only because the semi-automatics seemed too intimidating with all their moving parts that seemed complicated. My lifelong lack of mechanical proficiency screamed for me to go with the .38. But after I told him that the gun would be used for self-defense—now that was quite the major fabrication—Wally urged me to go with the Ruger Security 9. He assured me that anyone who tried to get in my condo would be in for quite a surprise. Since he seemed to know his stuff and promised to help me with my first experience at the range, I went with the Ruger.

Off we walked to the range, and right away I had buyer's remorse. Couldn't even load the goddamn Ruger, so Wally gave me a speed loader to insert the rounds…still a pain in the ass. He demonstrated how to place the clip into the Ruger, press the safety off, and position my hands when firing. Then he showed me how to clip up a target and move it down the range. Even with mufflers on, every time someone else on the range fired a shot, my whole body shuddered, disconcerted by every report close by.

Wally set the target for ten yards away, saying that when you qualify for a concealed weapons permit, you fire from that distance. Concealed weapons permit? Now, that little wrinkle made my endeavor even more attractive.

Pretty pathetic first time. With the Ruger violently recoiling, I hit only three out the ten rounds into the target, the three only along the edge of the target. In a real-life setting, even those bullets would have hit nothing other than air. After fumbling with the speed loader again and firing the same pitiable result a second time, I threw up my hands in frustration, and called it a day.

Wally guaranteed that with more practice I'd get proficient. My thought was that the Blusterer-in-Chief didn't have anything to fear from me, at least not yet. I told Wally that like Arnold, "I'll be back."

As I walked toward the exit, holding my newly purchased deadly firearm, Joanne gestured toward me, so I walked up to the front counter. Grinning like a mule eating briers, she pushed a quarter toward me and with a leer, said, "See ya 'round, Preston." I concluded that even NRA off-kilter women got off on their pussies being licked as much as any other gals.

I finally got up the nerve to phone George and see if she had softened up; it had been over a month since our first date, and I wanted to check up on her temperature. She asked about my drinking. I told her I was working on it. She hung up on me with not even a polite goodbye. Befuddlement! So much for dating in the twenty-first century—concession or rejection. I must still be living in the seventies—gold chained, fun lovin', disco-dancin' lounge lizard.

-18-

LETTER FROM STAN PETCHEL JULY 14, 2017

Dear Preston,

Enclosed is the final order of your divorce from Donna, including the financial settlement. While I do not anticipate any complications arising from your divorce, I always encourage my clients to put this document in a safe location in the event that some issue arises after the divorce. Please email me or call if you have any questions or concerns.

I realize that this letter represents a fundamental change in your life. Some of my clients never get over the scars left over from the end of a marriage. I would encourage you to see the positives of this moment and put aside any negative feelings that lingered from the divorce. I have counseled all my clients to seek out psychological help so they can get on with their lives.

Sincerely,

Stan

-19-
PH'S JOURNAL JULY 15, 2017

Psychological help? Been there, done that, Stan. Definitely wasn't my cup of tea, as the expression goes. I wonder if Stan uses the same fucking boilerplate language when he writes the final letter to his clients. Sure sounds like it.

Who would practice…what is it called now…"domestic relations" law? Among all the specialties, it's got to be the most mind-numbing of all, except maybe for estate planning. Snooze. Husbands and wives at the end of their tether, one or both of them seeking a way out of their misery. Every now and then, Stan does get a case with a little excitement. He told me about one divorce several years ago where an unhinged wife—the other party—attacked his client, Stan, and the judge in the courtroom!

So when Stan's wife asks what happened at work today, he could relate this or some other fascinating anecdote to her; she would sit at the table, trying to feign interest in another of his interminable stories just like Donna did with me. I wonder whether Stan's wife ever fantasizes about how much better life could be without him….Donna for sure did.

I've spent the better part of tonight rethinking my marriage to Donna. We did have some memorable times; we both delighted in traveling around the world. We hiked the Kalalau Trail along the Napali Coast in Kauai, the Path of the Gods on the Amalfi Coast in Italy, the Drakensbergs in South Africa, the Rainmaker on the west coast of Costa Rica, and right here in the good ol' US of A, Rainier, Mount Hood, and the John Muir Trail in the Sierra Nevada Range.

Costa Rica tugged at our hearts the three times we flew there—warm, educated people, stable government, varying topographies, delicious coffees, and the list goes on. I still work out with my now somewhat tattered Costa Rican t-shirt that proudly broadcasts "No Army Since 1948." The Ticans were an authentic people who seemed to lead contented lives. *Pura Vida!*

The first time Donna and I traveled to Costa Rica, we decided to drive our rental car from Arenal, where we had watched lava spewing down the mountain at night in dribbles of orange light, to Monteverde along what appeared by map to be the quickest route—only twenty-five miles...piece of cake. More than six hours later, along a boulder-laden, slippery-mud backroad, we finally arrived at the cloud forest town.

Just before Monteverde, while still in the middle of no-man's land, we stopped so I could drain my main vein. A wizened man sat by the bathrooms, pushing hotels in Monteverde. By his voice—clearly an Anglo—I asked him where he was from and why was he out here in nowhere land. "Uh..." he answered reluctantly "...from Idaho, and I just like it here." He was as much from Idaho as I was from Qatar. When he told me "You can't pahk the cah there," I figured right away a Bostonian, maybe one of Whitey Bulger's pals on the lam.

From Monteverde, we drove down the Pacific Ocean to Quepos. The first night we sat in a quaint bar, watching a brilliant sunset moving downward toward the western horizon, red rays illuminating the sky above the Pacific. A small apartment house sat across from the bar where in one of the cramped units, a man sat on his bed, also viewing the same sunset. He seemed so at peace, like he had found the perfect place to live with no complications or annoyances. At that moment, I wondered what it would be like to live in Costa Rica, like that man in the apartment, getting away from the constant hubbub of my life in Austin. But I knew immediately it was just an ephemeral fantasy that would never materialize.

Surely that one common enjoyment should have been enough to sustain any marriage. But there's more to matrimony than gallivanting around the world. I confess, but only to myself, that I have always had serious intimacy issues, a built-up wall that has kept me at full length away from anyone—Donna, my co-workers, even to some extent my kids.

There's no point in ever going back to the psychobabble lady to figure out what makes me tick. Time has passed me by, and it seems pointless to figure out at this point what makes me tick. I just "yam what I yam."

So I sit here in my noiseless condo, holding a letter from Stan Petchel that speaks to my complete failure as a husband. Maybe I need to turn on some George Jones sappy tunes like "He Stopped Loving Her," "Still Doin' Time," and "If Drinkin' Don't Kill Me" to fit the melancholy that presses down on my heart.

-20-
PH'S JOURNAL MAY 23, 2017

How fortuitous! I've been thinking of late about the three boys in blue, the guys I often refer to as the Three Amigos, and who do I meet up with today at the cigar shop but Willie Banks?

I ignore Dr. Ghazini's condemnation and don't even give a damn if cancer invades my mouth, tongue, or esophagus from tobacco. In spite of Dr. Ghazini's annual scolding about my cigar usage, there's no way I'll ever give them up. Doesn't make any difference if it takes ten years off my life; the way I look at it, every day at this point is gravy anyway.

Puffing away on a cigar is an agreeable pastime, and it still gives me at least a modicum of pleasure. I've always wanted to use the word *modicum*. Lo and behold, there it is—the very moment to fit it into the narrative. But, as usual, I wander away from the point; what was the point anyway?

Oh yeah. My refuge has always been an upscale shop in Northwest Austin called Heroes and Legacies which sits in the swank Arboretum; I worry, though, about how much longer the shop will stay in business. The owner has told me that his rent has been increased up to sixteen grand a month, which is probably not out of line for the Arboretum, but damn, how many cigars does the owner have to sell to make his nut every month?

Like so many other changes in Austin, the city is no longer the sleepy little town when I first moved there in the mid-seventies. Construction drives the city in all directions—condos and new businesses—like the universe expanding. More tech nerds flock in to fill the many software startups emerging throughout the city. There's even discussion about a MLS team opening here.

Heroes has always been a top-of-the-line cigar shop where you can sit in a luxurious nut-brown leather Barcalounger, puff on a few overpriced cigars, and engage in some normally light banter with the many Neanderthal Republicans who patronize the place. These guys are of the same ilk as the good ol' boys at the gun range; the only difference is that they spend their money on expensive cigars rather than killer weapons and don't spit 'baccar into Styrofoam cups.

Most of the guys here believe that anyone who isn't a dyed-in-the-wool Republican is either a Commie, atheist, deviant, or some combination thereof. Unfortunately, with the advent of the loony tunes pretender residing in the Oval Office, the conversation has entered a more edgy stage. More on that in a bit.

Since retiring, I have spent considerably more time at the shop and gotten familiar with the many neo-Fascists who hang out there. There's Colonel Mike, maybe 70-plus years old, originally from Philly, who of course now struts around proudly like a peacock wearing his red "Make America Great" hat every time he walks in. Colonel Mike is afflicted with any number of illnesses—Parkinson's, diabetes, and a heart condition that the doctors can't seem to pinpoint. He enjoys talking about the Commies he mowed down in Vietnam; he was the fellow who recommended the Boot and Sheehan books.

Then there's Milt, a gray-bearded fellow well into his eighties whose face is chock full of wrinkles and who is the only patron who smokes a pipe. I tried a pipe once, a pricey meerschaum. It was quite tasty, but there was too much fiddling around—light, tamp, light, tamp—a repetitive exercise like playing with a paddle ball.

Milt wrote lyrics for several rock bands; I think he used to toke a whole lot along with his musician buddies because his mind is a few fries short of a Happy Meal. Billy Bob—now there's a real Texas name for you—used to work the rodeo circuit. I believe that Billy Bob got thrown by bulls way too many times or else he has early onset Alzheimer's because Billy Bob and, for that matter, Milt, both have difficulty keeping up with the flow of conversation.

And then there's Howie, Larry, Klaus, Charley, Todd, and so on. They are all part of the entourage that make my visits to the cigar shop entertaining, at least when the TV is muted so I don't have to listen to FOX. Why does every cigar shop around the country tune in to the government propaganda machine? I suppose because the normal cigar clientele is way to the right, Republican, and Trump-adoring.

If you haven't figured it out yet, there's not a whole lot of cigar-loving women in Austin. A mid-thirties lady did walk in about a month ago, wearing a black miniskirt and fuck-me high heels with serious cleavage pooched out from her peach blouse. She selected a thin, four incher and sat there smoking for about an hour, completely disregarding all of the lecherous old men, of course, excluding the virtuous Preston. She would move the cigar around her mouth like a phallus. I believe the other guys enjoyed the show; I know I did. Then she stood up and walked out without ever saying one word. We're still discussing what her story was all about; I'm hopeful that she'll return for an encore.

Last week the FOX commentator railed about the disgrace of our immigration policies, with brown-colored men, women,, and children invading our country from the southern border. Larry turned to me and asked, "You agree with FOX on this one, don't you, Preston?" I told Larry that if he researched his lineage on Ancestor.com, he would discover, as I would, that we were both immigrants ourselves. "Myles Standish didn't ask permission from the Wampanoag Indians before the Pilgrims stepped off the Mayflower and came onto land at Plymouth Harbor," I concluded. Larry waved both his hands downward toward me in total disgust as if I had committed a heinous thought crime and violating every tenet of the FOX propaganda machine.

As I walked into the lounge today, the boys were arguing over minutiae about basketball. Who was the greatest shooter? Rebounder? Dribbler? Greatest of all time—Michael or LeBron? Now I am as much of a sports trivia guy as the next; I can even tell you the starting line-up for the 1956-57 Boston Celtics—Cousy, Sharman, Russell, Heinsohn, and Jungle Jim Loscutoff with the ultimate sixth man, Frank Ramsey, coming off the bench. But my favorite name on that team is Togo Palazzi, who was Cousy's roommate not only with the Celtics but at Holy Cross too. I met Togo once as a kid at a Cousy basketball camp and was certain that he didn't major in physics 'cause he was dumb as a box of rocks. Even today, I still recall Cousy sarcastically congratulating Togo for the uplifting words he offered to all us youngins.

Anyway, this back-and-forth in the cigar lounge went on for at least 45 minutes, and it sounded like the fellows had been at it a long time before I arrived. Finally, I couldn't take the sports minutiae anymore, so I interjected: "Can we please change the subject? Let's talk about Texas highway construction bonds and where they could best be used in the state." Now that should have been a show-stopper if there ever was one, but after getting booed by the whole crowd, the dialogue moved onto greatest baseball hitters, home run kings, and so on. I struck out…so to speak. *Groan.*

I let this strand of the conversation endure for a while longer. If I had really wanted to wow the boys, I could tell them the starting lineup for the '54 Cleveland Indians in the World Series and name their four all-star pitchers as well—Wynn, Garcia, Lemon, and Feller. But who really gives a shit, right?

So I decided to really get their collective goats: "Wada you think about Mueller getting appointed as Special Counsel? It's a red-letter day if you ask me. The Prez should be peein' in his pants about now; he's in the deepest of crapola and well deserved if you ask me." Well, that for sure got the conversation off of baseball! I got yelled and sworn at to the point that I thought some fisticuffs might be in the offing.

Not certain how long it will take for several of the cigar aficionados to get over their heartburn toward me over those remarks.

Fortunately just at the peak of their pique—how's that for an outstanding homophone—Willy Banks walked in the shop. He gave me one of those ear-to-ear grins that I still remembered, but as usual, the smile couldn't hide his deadened eyes, so unemotional, almost sinister. We moved off to a different area of the lounge, taking me out of the direct line of fire.

Willie is a mulatto, a term like Negro that my daughter, Anne, despises. She accuses me of being a closet racist; she has never figured out that once I guessed those and other terms—Chinaman, for example—bother her a whole bit, I just start messing with her in the worse way. One of Dad's guilty pleasures. Plus, the term "mulatto" is a permissible description of a light-skinned people with a mix of black and white ancestry. I looked it up in the Internet—what Senator Ted Stevens once referred to as a series of tubes—so it must be true.

Willie has smooth, unmarked skin. He has maintained his weight around 175 and must still work out just about every day; his biceps looked toned up, even a little bulged, under the snappy aqua blue, linen short-sleeved shirt. His beige pants appeared expensive, as did his leather crocodile shoes. He completed the outfit with a beret that matched his shirt. I don't ever recall Willie wearing this kind of lavish get-up; he always showed up at my office in grungy, baggy clothes. His suit during the trial was threadbare, his tie and shirt clashing.

I asked Willie what he had been up to since retiring, careful not to inquire about his wife. I had some recollection that Willie was on wife five or six at the time of the trial.

He filled me in. There was a fourteen-day cruise to the Caribbean he had just returned from, one on Viking to various French cities, a paddleboat out of Portland along the Columbia River, and a drive up California's Route 1, including Catalina Island and wineries all along the western ridge of the state. He got the idea of the winery tours from my retirement talk. Not sure of Willie's current matrimonial state, I asked who accompanied him. He said a different babe each time; a man of his means had his pick of the litter. Pick of the litter? Now that's one expression I had never heard before when discussing women.

Then he started in on his Cuba lark...flew into Mexico City and then on to Havana. He drank gallons of Cuba libres and mojitos and also bought four boxes of Cohibas. When he flew back to Mexico, he bribed an immigration official so there'd be no stamp recording his entry from Cuba and returned home with his precious cigars, fortunately for him not searched by Customs. I've done any number of nutty things during my life, but sneaking into Cuba always seemed beyond my reach or maybe the anxiety I would feel over something so risky.

As he handed me a Cohiba—a damn good smoke—Willie gabbed on about his good fortune. When I asked what he meant, Willie said, "When Jimmy, Ted, and I got indicted, I thought my world had come to an end. But you were my salvation,

Preston. You got us off, and when I stop to think about it, I owe my life and my current…I guess you'd call it prosperity, entirely to you, counselor."

I asked Willie how he had become so prosperous; he winked at me and changed the subject. WTF.

-21-
PH'S JOURNAL MAY 24, 2017

Can't get past the conversation with Willie Banks yesterday. Willie intimated, in fact, almost blurted out, that he, along with Jimmy and the Splendid Splinter, pulled off a fast one. The only conclusion I could make from Willie's remarks was that the bastards stole the money from the Wallace's house and are now living in high cotton.

I saw a photograph of Jazmine Wallace at some point before the trial, an angelic face with a playful smile and eyes both sunny and alive. I pulled the picture from the file and kept it...no idea why I did that. I sat looking at Jazmine's picture today, thinking about how extraordinary she must have been, a girl so full of promise and hope. Her death, and that of her brothers DeShawn and Tyrone, were never avenged. What a tragic result.

My mind keeps wandering back to the Banks case. A constant, niggling pinprick in my brain. Something was off, something that stunk like a month-long dead rat stuck inside the wall of a house. Thinking back to Conrad's praise over the Banks case at the retirement party, I feel nothing but disgust and shame, as if I am a fraud who has known in the deepest recess of my brain that I conned the justice system...or at least contributed to it.

I feel guilt now beyond any I have ever felt for my part in this travesty. There is now no doubt that my clients were, and still are, as low as any sleazebags I ever represented. From the outset, I intuitively knew in my heart-of-hearts that they were lying.

They must have had a hand in the skullduggery of Maurice Holloway's disappearance. Why did I give them any bright ideas about how Holloway might turn into a vanishing witness? I did give them a warning to stay away from the man, but they might have taken it as a hint. What did they do? Kill him? Pay him off? And it wouldn't have been inconceivable that one or more of them had a hand in Janard Coleman's death right after the trial.

Speaking of Coleman, Tony Nelson pulled my fat out of the fire when he recommended that I include Janard on the witness list. Who knew that Sam Evans would turn out to be as much of a crook as the Three Amigos and would get all crazed over my questions about Coleman?

The Austin paper nailed it in their editorial condemning me for my dubious remark that justice had been served. By the end of the trial, I knew for a fact that Messrs. Banks, Buhl, and Williams were guilty as hell, and I played more than a small part in this mockery of justice. *Shame on me*!

-22-

PH'S JOURNAL AUGUST 3, 2017

TV has turned into 24/7 political entertainment, something like the old soap *As the World Turns*. You can't make this shit up or write a TV/movie script that captures the insanity at the White House. Or as Ozzie Osborne once sang, "Crazy Train. "

Trump appoints Anthony Scaramucci as Communication Director on July 21st. Then the Mooch calls Priebus a fucking, paranoid schizophrenic; about Steve Bannon, he says "I'm not trying to suck my cock." Pretty graphic—hilarious in a pathetic kind of way. A few days later, the Mooch is given the old heave-ho.

At the same time, Priebus is out and General Kelly is in as Chief of Staff. Kelly seems like a standup enough guy, but if I were him, I'd be thinkin' along the lines of Satchel Paige: "Don't look back. Somethin' might be gainin' on you." The merry-go-round goes around and around. Where it stops nobody but the Confuser (or is it the Confused?)-in-Chief knows.

For some reason, his so-called base stays with him through every lie, every obfuscation, every diversion that he pulls out of his ass. Who are these people anyway? What is wrong with them? Can't they see that the king has no clothes? My take on these folks? A bunch of people are fearful that their way of life is threatened in the new America—too much brown, not enough white bread, and all those Muslim heathens, plus jobs leaving for minimum wages in China, Vietnam, India, and so on.

I was watching one of those morning shows yesterday, the one with Kelly Ripa, who has got to be the most self-absorbed twit on television. Who cares a flip what she did this past weekend or what big-named celebrity she just hung out with. There's some guy with her on the show—Ryan something or other. He looks kinda light in the loafers if you ask me, but he is apparently straight as an arrow. My point? The Trump worshipers must all tune in to watch the Kelly show every day, glued to her every word of insipid banter the same way they dote on Trump's every smoke-screening falsehood.

I've become a real buddy with Wally from the gun range—not the kind of buddy I'd want to have a beer with. He's about as exciting as a college professor lecturing on entomology. But Wally definitely knows his stuff, and he's worked to improve my shooting skills. I now know how to load the Ruger, or better yet, load up three or four clips; my scores have improved to the point that I consistently hit at least eight out of ten right in the middle of the target…still working toward perfection.

Then if I ever get the chance, the Prez goes down, in his case like a lump of pudginess. Only trouble is, I don't really look forward to getting plugged by Frick and Frack's colleagues-in-arms.

I had an epiphany last night, or at least as much of one that seven glasses of pinot noir could muster. How much more can I obsess about Trump? How much about the Three Amigos? I spend too much time consumed with horrible thoughts cluttering around in my head. So last night, while in a wine-induced haze, it came to me: Forget about all these losers and do something positive with my life. Maybe I need a hobby, something other than sitting around in this silent house, something that will get me out and about, making some kind of contribution, however small, to this helter-skelter world.

I'll give it the old country try. If any idea I conjure up doesn't pan out though, I guess it'll be back to my fixation with the loser president and the three shady cops.

-23-

EMAILS BETWEEN PH AND CLIMATE REALITY PROJECT AUGUST 7 THROUGH SEPTEMBER 11, 2017

TO: Climate Reality Project
FROM: Preston Howard
SUBJECT: Enrollment in your organization
Dear Sir/Madame:

I recently retired from practicing law in Austin, Texas. I have had concerns about environmental issues for many years. Since the new administration's intention to withdraw from the Paris agreement and the actions of Secretary Scott Pruitt to ease or eliminate safeguards against corporate attacks on our environment, my concerns have escalated to alarm.

After reviewing your website and the options available, my desire would be to join your Leadership Corps so that I can make a difference either at the local level or across Texas or the country. It is exciting to think that my work on behalf of your organization would help in any way, big or small, to save our country, and even our planet, from destruction.

I have always been such an admirer of Al Gore; it would be an honor to work in an organization led by him. He was an effective senator and vice-president (although I do have some reservations about whether he invented the Internet). Also, his Nobel Prize was richly deserved.

Please advise at your earliest convenience how I can join the Climate Reality Project as a part of your

Leadership Corps and when your next training session will be conducted.
Sincerely,

Preston Howard

TO: Climate Reality Project
FROM: Preston Howard
SUBJECT: Enrollment in your organization
Dear Sir/Madame:
I wrote to you one week ago about joining the Climate Reality Project and your Leadership Corps. No one has gotten back with me to date. Please contact me as soon as possible since I am very excited about being a part of your organization and want to get moving on this important work.
Sincerely,
Preston Howard

TO: Climate Reality Project
FROM: Preston Howard
SUBJECT: Enrollment in your organization
Dear Sir/Madame:
Two weeks have gone and still no word from anyone at the Climate Reality Project. Is the website monitor taking a long coffee break? Or on an extended vacation? Whatever the reason, the dipshit running the website needs to be replaced!!!!! Or maybe you guys and gals are just grubbing for financial contributions, but I'm not checking that box on the website just yet when there seems to be some incompetency rampant at the CRP.
Sincerely,

Preston Getting-Really-Annoyed Howard

TO: Climate Reality Project
FROM: Preston Howard
SUBJECT: Enrollment in your organization
Dear Sir/Madame Idiots:
Now into the third week without any reply. What would happen if my law firm ran its business this way, where the website manager ignored potential clients' requests for representation? Pretty obvious—my firm would go under in less than a minute. Get a clue and answer my fucking email...make that EMAILS, plural, several, NOW FOUR, REPEAT FOUR (!!!) without any answer.

Totally-pissed-off Preston Howard

TO: Climate Reality Project
FROM: Preston Howard
SUBJECT: Enrollment in your organization
Dear Incompetent Asleep at the Wheel Shitheads,
Let me try one more and different approach. Please tell Mr. Gore that on my graduation day from law school, his dad, Gore Senior, spoke to the assembled students about the importance of our country recognizing China. While I did have to insert toothpicks in my eyes to keep from falling asleep from the excessive boredom, it really was a worthwhile speech; a few years later, Tricky Dick did in fact, recognize the Chinamen.
Preston   Waiting-on-Pins-and-Needles-for-an-Answer Howard

TO: Climate Reality Project
FROM: Preston Howard
SUBJECT: Enrollment in your organization

Okay, no point in sugarcoating the conclusions about this pathetic, bungling, and slothful non-profit. Please tell Mister I-Would- Be-President-But-For-537-Votes:

1. I was cum laude too from Harvard, that would be of the South.

2. You should have left your tongue in your mouth with the Tipper kiss onstage at the 2000 Democratic convention, or better yet, you should have gotten a room.

3. From now on I'm not recycling anything— not a scrap of newspaper, plastic, bottles, or cans. It's as insignificant as a piece of sand shifting a half inch in the Mojave Desert.

4. In fact, I'm gonna start carrying my recyclables down to the Colorado River—only a three minute walk from my house—and toss them into the water.

Take that Mister Environmental Man.

PS: Pay more attention to your organization and less to your press clippings.

-24-
PH'S JOURNAL SEPTEMBER 13, 2017

What conclusions to draw from my trial balloon in rejoining the human race? First and most obvious, Al is a major disappointment; I wonder how many other people have been led down this same primrose path, so excited at first to be on the front lines of the environmental war only then to be turned away like rejected paramours. And second, while I am reluctant to call the Environmental Man a rip-off artist—after all, we are fellow Tennesseans—how many other cons are out there, sucking gullible folks into a variety of schemes?

One scam that seems to attract seniors—the people whose arteries are drying up and brains are in decline—is the IRS swindle. I know this one for a fact because it's been perpetrated on me twice. A few months ago, I answered my cell phone and a guy comes on the line saying, "You need to call the following number immediately; otherwise, your home and retirement fund will be seized by the IRS." So I wrote down the number and did as the gentleman directed.

The fellow on the line sounded faraway, and the inflection in his voice resembled an African. I asked, "Is this the IRS?" I gave my name.

He answered, "Yes, and you're in serious trouble."

"Oh goodness me! I don't want to be in trouble with the government. Who are you, sir?"

"This is Officer Johnson," the dude replied imperiously.

"I didn't realize the IRS hires officers," I observed.

"Of course, we're all officers here at the IRS."

And now my punch line: "Well, Officer Johnson, blow me, you cock-sucking motherfucker."

The guy went off on me, matching my obscenities with more of the same and then hung up. I don't get how a guy who was trying to rip me off could feel offended that I had caught him at it.

The second time, the police were on their way to arrest me unless I coughed up $10K plus interest currently owed; by the way, we will take a credit card as payment. Having been through this train wreck once before, I had a prearranged come back: "I'd be more than happy to pay whatever I owe. Please give me your address so I can come down to your office and beat the living shit out of you and your buddies." Click. Damn, I couldn't even get the satisfaction of a second round of tasteless retorts.

Since having been the prospective victim of a scam, I looked into other swindles—remote PC repairs, fraudulent check for cash exchange, pets for sale, collection agencies, timeshare resale, work from home, and of course, the infamous rich Nigerian prince scam. The list is endless, and many people, being both gullible and greedy, are more than willing to part with their money without a second thought.

My experiences, while limited in amount, have gotten me to thinking, something that always seems to wind me up in trouble. LOL. Do I have the balls to pull off my own version of the swindle game? However, my idea of a scam goes beyond the bounds of polite society and instead into the realm of homicide, of committing a murder in the name of the better good. Worth considering anyway.

I think Tony N. called me about the time Laurence came on MSNBC. My recollection is that he just wanted to check up on me and have lunch tomorrow, but I was pretty tanked and not sure. I'll call him back in the morning after the cobwebs clear out.

-25-

E-MAIL FROM TONY NELSON TO ANNE HOWARD SEPTEMBER 14, 2017

TO: Anne Howard
FROM: Tony Nelson
RE: Your dad

Hello, Anne. I am sorry for the length of this email, but I feel compelled to let you know about a meeting I had with your dad earlier today. It distressed me terribly, and while I don't want to interfere in the Howards' private affairs, your dad is such a close friend of mine, and I am concerned for his welfare.

I phoned your dad last night, but he was so in-the-bag that his speech was completely incoherent. He then phoned me this morning, and we agreed to meet for lunch. I know he enjoys the grilled chicken salad at Bartlett's, so we agreed to get together at one p.m.

As usual, he was sitting at one of the booths by the bar when I walked in. It looked like he was on at least his third pinot noir because his words were slurring a bit. Very jarring to see my friend in his cups so early in the day.

We spent some time catching up. I told him about a few of my cases going on at the firm. Told him that it was never the same since he left, how his cases were always the most fascinating at the firm, and how much I missed working with him.

When I mentioned the sad state of affairs in America, he went off, cussing a blue streak so loud and for so long that the hostesses had to come to the table and ask us—meaning your dad—to bring it down a notch. Screaming at the top of his lungs about Trump and his buddies who were part of the DC swamp, your dad's face got red as a beet, and he became mad as a hatter....He wouldn't shut his trap. At this point, people not only at the bar but in other parts of the restaurant, began looking our way.

I told your dad to take a deep breath, and that if he didn't pipe down, this lunch would be a short one. My observation? The alcohol had lowered his inhibitions to the point that he had not even one care what anyone in the restaurant thought.

Fortunately, he finally settled down, like a top that had stopped spinning and fell down inert. I had never before seen my friend in such a frenzy. When I looked at him, he appeared so different from the man I once knew. He appeared dissipated and exhausted, like he hadn't slept for days, even weeks. He had a week-long, scraggly beard, his remaining hair was disheveled like it hadn't been combed in days, and his clothes appeared slovenly—a tattered Tennessee T-shirt with faded, orange-colored UT and seedy-looking sweatpants that had seen better days...and looked slept in for days. I suddenly felt great concern for my good friend; he was clearly in serious need of help.

I simply put it out there: What the fuck is wrong with you? Your dad hesitated for more than a minute, apparently deciding whether he wanted to broach the heavy burden that was clearly weighing him down. Finally, he said, "Does anything bother you about that case?" I didn't have to ask him which one. He had to be referring to Banks, Buhl, and Williams.

When you work for a law firm, you're not supposed to have any kind of conjecture about your clients....They're innocent until proven guilty, blah-blah-blah. But I had retired out of the APD after twenty-plus years before taking the gig with his firm, and in my day, you pretty much accepted that most everyone you took off the street at the APD was guilty.

But at the firm, it was a completely different mindset. Your dad's job, and by extension mine, was to zealously defend our clients to the best of our abilities. That all sounds so warm and fuzzy, but unlike Preston (sorry, your dad) with his legal ethics and all that other lawyerly crap, I was, and still am, a cop at heart.

Every time I got around those three guys—the Banks trio—my skin crawled like I had some kind of contaminated cooties on me. When he first took the case, your dad handled it like every other one—all business and professional-like. Then I still vividly remember right after the grand jury indictments and another meeting with his clients, Preston and I met for a drink—in his case, multiple drinks—at the Doubletree on 15th. We talked over the case and some additional work he needed done involving Janard Coleman. Then, like a bolt out of the blue, your dad said how things just weren't adding up, and I can still remember his exact words. "Tony, do you think we're representing three rotten, lying crooks?"

I had to tread lightly on this one at first because I had never seen him exhibit any kind of indecision about his work. He always operated like a Whirling Dervish, pushing and prodding the staff, especially me, to pull out every stop in defense of a client. So here he was, Obi Won, as everyone on the staff called him, the ultimate Jedi legal warrior in the country, coming across like a wishy-washy kind of guy…not the Preston that I had come to know and admire.

But I finally did agree with him as much as it pained me to believe that there was any kind of hanky panky in my beloved APD. Your dad added, "Tony, we've been dealt the cards, so we're just going to play them. If we're in for a penny, then we're in for a pound." I made a mental note that those were some pretty cheesy clichés, so I piled on with a few others. "We'll just have to hold our nose, or as Chief Dan George said in *The Outlaw Josey Wales*, 'we'll endeavor to persevere'."

Back to the here and now. "I can't get the fucking case out of my head," he said at lunch, his head burrowed into his hands so the words came out muffled like a mumbling Mexican with a dick in his mouth. Sorry, Anne, sometimes these little inappropriatisms (is that a word?) just slip out, but you're not a little girl any more. LOL.

"Ya know, Tony," he remarked, "I interviewed several of the jurors after the DA's office withdrew the prosecution. They all made the same point. There was a lot of smoke, but the prosecution couldn't ever light a fire to the case." Then your dad asked me, "What do you think happened to Wallace Holloway? And what about Janard Coleman? Do you think one of the Amigos, or several of them, smoked one or both of them?"

I told your dad that I had the same questions. It all just seemed too convenient that Holloway would have taken off without a word to anyone. And Janard? The world was, for sure, a better place without lowlifes like Janard around. But still, murder is murder, no matter how you slice it.

Then we sat there in silence, both of us nibbling without any enthusiasm on our grilled chicken salads. At this point, your dad had swigged down at least his fifth pinot, to the point that he seemed almost incomprehensible. I told him I'd call a cab because he wasn't driving home.

Later, as I guided him into the cab, he looked up at me forlornly and said, "I'm not sure which thing obsesses me more—The Donald or the Three Amigos." I leaned into the cab, placed my hands on his shoulders, and told him, "Get this shit out of your head, Preston. Otherwise, it's gonna be the end of you." Not sure my words registered with him; I'm sure he went to the house and called it an early day.

So Anne, that's the gist of my meeting with your dad. Like I said before, I am terribly concerned for him…as you must be. If you want to call or write me, we can commiserate or maybe discuss some plan for getting him help. It will at least be worth a try; although, in the end, Preston will be the only one who can figure out that he has a serious problem and deal with it.

As always, your friend,
Tony

-26-
NOTE FROM ANNE HOWARD SEPTEMBER 14, 2017

When Tony Nelson emailed me today about his bizarre conversation with my dad, I was beyond upset to say the least. Tony called Dad later to check if he was okay; afterward, he phoned me, saying Dad was, as now appears his normal state, totally buzzed.

Tony became apologetic for fumbling the ball; he had kept close tabs on Dad since his retirement and realized there was a major problem, but late hours at work and a new woman in his life had sidetracked him from contacting me until today. I told him I understood. Our lives always have such an inconvenient way of intruding.

Tony asked if I knew anything about interventions for alcoholics. I told him no; although, the thought had crossed my mind several times. He thinks my dad's situation is so dire that it's in need of an intervention, as in right now. Tony had read up on it, saying that it's a must-do if Dad is going to have any kind of life going forward. He gave me the names of several outfits in Austin that provide services to deal with people in Dad's situation.

I took down the names. I also asked Tony if he would participate. He said PDQ. I had trouble picturing my dad agreeing to an intervention. He's such walled-up man when it comes to feelings. I can just hear him now: "What kind of bullshit is this anyway!!" But for certain, Dad has hit rock bottom, and if I do nothing, he will die sooner rather than later....I will feel guilty for not at least giving it a shot.

Fortuitously, dad had called yesterday, relishing the emails he sent to the Al Gore organization and the telephone calls he had with the bogus IRS agents....How he so enjoys a good joke.

The ones he played on Mom were over-the-top funny. Mom played the accordion in her childhood and looked forward on Saturday nights to watching *The Lawrence Welk Show* and getting all bubbly over Myron Floren and his beer-barrel polka songs. Wait a minute. Bubbly? Lawrence Welk? Unlike Dad, I am a little slow on the uptake (a belated groan!)

Dad and my Uncle Bobby, Mom's brother, mercilessly ragged Mom over that instrument. Bobby would pull out old photos of Mom, back in her chubby, younger days, sitting on a chair, holding the accordion on her lap, wearing nerd-like glasses and a plain maxi-dress with a floral print and penny loafers—the ultimate little girl geek. Bobby and Dad would roar with laughter, much to Mom's chagrin.

Back in the eighties, a friend of my dad's took a driving tour of the Creole country and stopped at an accordion factory. At my dad's urging, the friend wrote a postcard from the factory, written to my mom at home, which read:

Dear Donna,

I am at the Savoy Music Center in Eunice, Louisiana, where the owner, Marc, is working on a custom-made accordion to my specifications. I told Marc that you are a good friend and an enthusiastic accordionist. Marc suggested that you come by soon and he will give you a real deal on a trade-in for your beat-up old instrument and fix you up with a whiz-bang squeezebox.

> *Your buddy,*
> *Myron Floren*

I can still vividly remember my mom coming in from the mailbox on an early Saturday afternoon, walking up to Dad, and holding the postcard from Myron Floren up toward him. "I know you put someone up to this shenanigan, and frankly I am not as amused as you and your mischievous buddy," Mom said, with not even a glimmer of a smile on her face. She had become more and more annoyed over the years. She then went ballistic when her brother, Bobby, sent her a postcard two weeks later with a photograph of an accordion orchestra. Bobby wrote,
> *Sis,*

> *I couldn't pass up buying this postcard and sending it. Thought immediately about you!*

> *Bob*

Dad vowed on a stack of Bibles that his brother-in-law and he were not in cahoots on this practical joke (not that we had any Bibles lying around in our house). Mom still gets mildly apoplectic anytime someone talks about the Myron Floren/accordion and orchestra pranks.

But Dad outdid himself with this last accordion joke on Mom. The San Antonio office had just hired a new secretary named Maria who had emigrated from Honduras. Short and slim with short, black hair and brown eyes, Maria had an effervescent spirit and an inquisitive way, so when Dad took her out for the customary new employee lunch, Maria peppered him with many questions about the office and then about his life.

When Maria asked about my mom, Donna, Dad decided to lay a total poppycock story on her; what the hell, the two women were never likely to meet anyway. "My wife was an internationally famous accordion player, playing at venues all over the world," he started out. "Vienna, Prague, Berlin, Madrid, London."

When Dad repeated the story to me, he told how Maria said, "Reeely?" with a heavy, loud Hispanic inflection.

"Yes, really," Dad answered. "I was sight-seeing in Paris back in the sixties at the same time Donna was playing a concert there. I just happened to go to the concert and was so enamored with the way she played that I went backstage afterward, introduced myself, and asked her out for dinner."

"Reeely, Meester Howard?"

"Call me Preston, and yes, really. After being together for only two days, we realized that we were totally in love, so Donna gave up her career as a famous accordion player for me, we got married a few months later, and the rest, as they say, is history."

"Reeely, Preston?"

"Really."

Unfortunately for my dad, the firm held a Christmas party for the staff that same year, and

Maria showed up. As Mom circulated around the room, Maria caught a glimpse of her and in a voice heard by everyone, shouted, "Doña, Doña, I want to hear all about your career as an internationally famous accordion player."

Dad overheard Maria's comment and broke out in fits of laughter; my mom glared at Dad and stomped out of the room, clearly not enjoying the gag as much as he did.

-27-
EMAILS BETWEEN GEORGE ROBARDS
AND ANNE HOWARD OCTOBER 18, 2017

TO: Anne Howard
FROM: Georgeanna Robards
SUBJECT: Your dad

Anne,

I am not in the habit of getting involved in the affairs of other families. However, your dad gave me your email address last night when he showed up at my doorway three sheets to the wind... make that ten sheets.

I have become quite fond of your dad. We met here at the condo and had a wonderful date at Sullivan's some time ago. He mentioned you during the dinner; he clearly feels very close to you. He is a brilliant and fascinating man, and I would so enjoy having a relationship with him; however, he has a serious drinking problem. I have made it clear to him that until he gets off the bottle, there is no way we can be together.

When he showed up here, he started babbling about an incident tonight. I've already figured out that he is quite the embellisher. So I am not convinced of the veracity of the events, but...he claims he went to some dodgy country and western club and began dancing with a platinum blonde floozy. He kept saying fat-bottom girl repeatedly. I should have realized that your dad is a fan of Freddie Mercury. He told me that the woman had trailer park written all over her.

He claimed to the lady that because of his Vietnam experiences and PTSD, he was totally impotent. The woman, and he pointed out that this term was expressed with considerable looseness, said she would cure him of his flaccid cock, grabbing him by the hand and directing him out to the parking lot where they got in his car. She went down on him and shortly thereafter he had a considerable explosion in her mouth. Then he hollered, "My God, it's a miracle." She was apparently pleased with her ability to cure your dad's infirmity, left the car, and returned to the club, maybe to save some other poor man with a similar disability.

The strange thing is, he had tobacco juice all over his right shoulder where the woman would have placed her shoulder while they were dancing. First off, I hope he didn't kiss her…*gross*. Second, I have my fingers crossed that she wasn't a him. *Double gross*.

After telling this sketchy tale, he mumbled for some time about killing someone, at first about the president, and then about some cops he represented. His thoughts were frightening, even delusional. After that, your dad began crying for some time, before falling asleep on the floor of my living room. I am just going to let him sleep it off and deal with getting him back to his condo tomorrow morning.

Your dad is really in pain. I am willing to help in any way possible….I care for your dad a great deal and want him to get well. BTW, everyone calls me George, so you don't have to refer to me by my given name.

George

TO: Georgeanna Robards
FROM: Anne Howard
RE: Your dad
George,

Thank you so much for contacting me and expressing your concern for my dad. It's timely that you have written because I have similar anxiety that my dad's drinking has reached gargantuan proportions.

As we speak, I am exploring a possible intervention and checking out organizations that offer this service, all the while realizing that Dad will be resistant to any such endeavor. But hopefully, an intervention will allow him to see the dimensions of his addiction and the effect it is having on people close to him. Hopefully, a lightning bolt will strike and instill some self-perception and humility in him. God knows, he can use some.

Since we have never met, would it be possible for us to meet for lunch or dinner, preferably sooner than later? Dad hasn't mentioned you, which is neither here nor there....He has become pretty closed off from discussing his comings and goings. Please let me know a convenient time and place for us to talk. I live north of town as you are, so it should be easy to figure out a suitable restaurant.

BTW, you nailed it on the head about my dad's tendency for exaggeration. He never went to Vietnam! As a matter of fact, he went down to the Army induction center in 1969 and applied to be an officer. He wrote down on the application that he had a terrible speech problem (which he actually had some years before), and during the physical, he couldn't get a word out of his mouth....He told me that the Force had somehow overtaken him, and he simply couldn't get even one word out of his mouth without stammering like Mel Tillis.

When he reached the end of the line, a doctor told Dad that the Army couldn't have an officer with a speech problem. He told the doctor, "Well, d-d-d-damnit. And I s-s-s-so w-w-w-wanted to go to N-N-N-Nam and sh-sh-shoot some f-f-f-fucking C-C-Cong." He walked out of the induction center a free man, saved from the hell of death or maiming in Vietnam. He told me later that he never had even one feeling of remorse for that dodge; too many of his friends had already died over there for such a hopeless cause.

At least Dad had a somewhat plausible excuse, as opposed to Trump, who had corns on his feet and thus avoided the draft. I suppose he couldn't fire a rifle with foot corns because his sighting would get unaligned or maybe he would slip and fall from so much pain from the corns while tromping around the jungles of Vietnam. How lame! LOL

Please get back with me ASAP.

Anne

-28-

EMAILS BETWEEN GERI CREEGAN AND PRESTON HOWARD SEPTEMBER 15 – OCTOBER 19, 2017

TO: Preston Howard
FROM: Geri Creegan
SUBJECT: Call today

Thanks as always, Preston, for your call today. You have been like a rock over the past five-plus years, taking the time even while you were working to fly out to Tucson and spend time with Tommy. As you know by now, Tommy's Alzheimer's has taken a serious turn for the worse. He is now totally confined to his bed; he doesn't even understand how to stand up or sit down and needs constant assistance.

His decline has happened so quickly. I can remember it was only about eight months ago that you took him out for lunch; while you waited for Tommy to come back from the bathroom, you saw him walking down the street, oblivious to his surroundings. You had to run him down and remind him of where he was. In a sad kind of way, it was funny, especially when Tommy begged you not to tell me what happened! Looking back, that was one of his last moments of lucid thought.

Tommy has stopped eating; his weight has got to be down under 100. Every time I look at him now, I start bawling. I've been crying for so long now, I can't even remember a time when I felt any joy.

Your good friend,
Geri

TO: Geri Creegan
FROM: Preston Howard
SUBJECT: Visit

As always, Geri, it was a pleasure to call and speak with you. Tommy and I have so much history together, working together to organize cops all over Arizona, driving all over the state, and telling outrageous tales about our many exploits. LOL. He is one of my true and good friends. I know his time is short on this earth. Please know that I will assist you in any way as you get through this tough ordeal.

Preston

TO: Preston Howard
FROM: Geri Creegan
SUBJECT: The time is short

Preston, Tommy is on his last leg. He probably won't last beyond the end of today, maybe tomorrow.

Tommy always admired you so much and used to talk about you constantly. You both have had a friendship that few people ever enjoy.

I have a very touchy subject to broach with you: my family and I would really appreciate if you would give the eulogy at Tommy's funeral. It would mean so much to all of us. I realize that it might be too emotional for you; I know my nerves are raw to the point that I would be unable to stand up there and talk about Tommy.

I will understand if it is too overwhelming for you. But think it over.

Geri

-29-
PH'S JOURNAL OCTOBER 20, 2017

I don't shed tears often; although, I have a vague recollection of crying at George's condo the other day. Did I do that, or was it a dream?

But today is an exception; I bawled for over an hour over Tommy's death. He has finally gone on to his greater glory, or so he thinks...or thought—off to the Promised Land where the streets are paved with gold. On the one hand, I feel a deep loss for as good a friend as I will ever have. But I also know for certain that Tommy's pain has ended, his suffering brought to its inevitable conclusion.

I have many thoughts today about death, knowing that there is an expiration date on my own life, at this point sooner rather than later. I have aged into the Zone of Death, and there's no reversing my status as a senior citizen on borrowed time.

Tommy and I would argue every now and then about religion, never with any acrimony but instead with a bunch of jesting back and forth. I subscribe to the tenets of Ronnie Reagan the Younger, who is an atheist and says he's not afraid of burning in hell. I'm not afraid of dying...just want some idea of what happens when I pass on. If Ronnie the Younger is right and there's nothing at the end, then what does it mean to be dead? No consciousness remains? An eternal sleep?

I really shouldn't worry a whole lot about the end of my time anyway. The earth won't be around in another billion or two years; either the sun will flame out or the Milky Way will collide with the Magellan Cloud, causing our minute acre somewhere in the cosmos to pulverize. When I stop to think about it, I'm even more insignificant than a gnat in the universe. More like a no-see-um. The God of Random Chance looks at me with the same indifference as a leopard cares about its impala prey, except that it's a delectable meal.

Maybe I should rethink my view, prostate myself before God, accept Jesus into my heart, and then meet up with Saint Peter at the Gate of Heaven. I'll shuck and jive Peter into believing I'm worthy of entrance; although, if Peter reviews my tumultuous life, he'll probably give me the heave-ho. And where would that leave me?

Why am I thinking so much about where I stand with God? Maybe because of a close friend and author here in Austin, a committed Christian who I suspect prays for my soul every now and then. She told me about her dad who had been an atheist his whole life, believing that followers of the Good Book were weak people. My friend's step-mom said, though, that her dad had been slowly opening his heart to God as time went on. When the Twin Towers fell on 9/11, my friend felt the time had come to have a tête-à-tête with her dad, so she flew out to Seattle. They sat down in her dad's back patio; she spoke for hours about the need for him to open his heart to God and asked him to kneel down and accept Jesus into his heart. He listened and suddenly knelt on the floor of the patio and decided the time had come for him to become a devout Christian.

What to make of that moment? My friend was gratified that her father came around to Jesus. And I'm certain he feels relieved that he made this decision. I'm just still not, as yet, convinced that it works for me.

Then I had a client a few years ago who had a NDE after he was admitted to the hospital when an ulcer bled out and sent him into a death spiral. He recalled hovering above the OR, watching the hospital staff desperately trying to save him. Suddenly he was in a tiny room where he could hear his grandmother talking to other people in the next room. As he began opening the door to the next room, his grandmother called out, "No! You can't come in because it's not your time yet." Next thing he recalled was waking up in the hospital recovery room. He re-thought his cynicism about religion and now frequents a Baptist church every Sunday. Once again, it's a mystery with no answer, at least for me.

I have no reason to disbelieve my friend or my client or to mock them. They are both sincere people and firm in their conviction that the Bible is the answer to life's questions. It would be a comfort to think that my family and friends who have embraced God go onto a higher plane, a place of love and serenity, like in "Welcome" by the Blind Boys of Alabama

Can't decide whether to speak at Tommy's funeral. I know that Geri wants me to talk, but goddamn, I start bawling like a panty-waste at any service. The thought of embarrassing myself in front of so many people who know me feels appalling.

Plus, in my current state, with my boozing at an all-time high, I'll be pretty shaky at best.

I'll prepare a eulogy just in case my nerves feel soothed to the point that I can speak without breaking down. Geri admonished me to keep my tribute to fifteen minutes. That's rubbish! I could speak for several hours about our adventures across Arizona and our affection for each other. I actually dedicated my memoir to Tommy and spoke at length about him—his even temperament, compassion, humble manner, and wicked humor. If I can get through the service—at best a questionable outcome—my closing line will be "I shall miss Tommy terribly and hold him in my heart for whatever time I have left on this earth."

I phoned George. She didn't pick up; she just sent a text saying that after showing up at her place drunker than skunk, it would be better if I quit calling right now; then she wrote, "Get your shit together if only for your sake!"

-30-
PH'S JOURNAL OCTOBER 24, 2017

There were lots of weepers at the Tommy's funeral yesterday. Fortunately, my tears were spent through and through the day before at the viewing. Now that's a morbid custom. Who wants to see a rouged-up, waxen corpse and listen to people murmur, "Oh, he looks so good," like folks did at Buster's viewing. Who the fuck looks good when they're dead?

Surely not Tommy, whose body had emaciated to the point that his Tucson police uniform bagged everywhere on his body. At least he was going out with a bang as a Tucson cop, with the department's Honor Guard alternately standing motionless by his casket.

I lost it at the viewing, passing by his casket, and then standing in front of a TV screen showing slides of the alive Tommy. So vital, positive, smiling all the time—not those BS saccharine grins that so many pose with but instead the genuine thing. Mental scraps of our times together kept running through my head while at the same time, one slide after another zipped by, telling a photographic story of his life as a father, husband, and cop.

After less than an hour, I couldn't take the sorrow any longer, so I said my goodbyes to Geri and her three articulate, well-bred kids; although, they weren't kids anymore….How the time flies by. I left the mortuary sniffling, wiping away tears, and blowing my nose into a Kleenex, all the way to my rental car.

Tommy's funeral was a testament to his standing in the community; there had to be at least seven-hundred people there. I've seen bigger funerals. Like when a cop gets killed in the line of duty and officers from all over the state and even the country show up....Sometimes more than two-thousand people attend.

When my moment in the sun came, I sucked it up and stood up in my wedding/funeral suit, a somber, grey, light woolen, and nary a tear fell down my cheeks as I spoke about my magnificent friend and colleague (for only twelve minutes, so there, Geri!). I felt relieved that first off, I pulled off the eulogy without embarrassing myself which, given my pain-numbing hangover from the night before, was a miracle and second, that somewhere out there in the ether, Tommy knew that his buddy had spoken some words that brought some little comfort to his family if even for a few short moments.

Tommy and Geri were lifelong Baptists, the kind of folks that not only went to Sunday service but also to couples Bible study on Monday, Wednesday night devotion, and men's early Friday morning religious discussions. If you ask me, that seems like an awful lot more spirituality than a parishioner needs to get into the gates of heaven, but if it floats their boat, who am I to criticize?

It turned out that the resident minister had taken sick and the associate preacher had been on vacation, so Geri scurried around at the last minute to find a pinch-hitter. The gentleman was one of those Whiskopalian fire and brimstone types who spoke about God's wrath, unfaithfulness, and repentance. I figured that the minister—actually Episcopalian clergy are called priests—didn't know Tommy very well, or even at all, since Tommy was as devout a Christian as I had ever met, in no way unfaithful, and definitely not in any way deserving of God's wrath or repentance.

Being a Whiskopalian minister priest, Mr. Fire 'n' Brimstone didn't disappoint, emphasizing the one theme that many ministers fall back on during a funeral. "We should not despair about Tommy's death," the pious man said, "because it is all a part of God's plans."

I screamed wordlessly!!!! Did Tommy feel better that God's plan was for him to die from losing his mind? Does Geri feel all warm and fuzzy that God's plan was for her husband to die before his time and leave her a grieving widow? Does any parent buy into God's plan when their child dies when running out in front of a car? Or in a car wreck? Or from an overdose? Or does a wife feel just peachy about God's plan when her husband gets pulverized in a horrific train or plane wreck? Get the point? Or am I beating the proverbial dead horse?

But maybe Governor Greg Abbott accepted God's plan after he became paralyzed from the waist down at twenty-six when a tree limb ran over him while jogging in Houston. He figured that although he'd never again waltz across Texas, he could still lead a productive life.

After the service, I asked the priest about how he wound up ministering to his flock. The man said that he had originally served as a Catholic priest and had gone to what he thought was a Catholic retreat; it turned out, though, to be an Episcopalian one. He decided right then and there that he felt more comfortable in the Anglican denomination, so he converted. Just as he was telling me this odd story, a woman walked up—quite the looker—who he introduced as his wife. Let's see…Catholic priest…no women…no marriage. Gee, ya think he just had a thunderbolt strike him at the retreat, and suddenly he became a Whiskopalian? Not. Sorry, my cynicism was dripping down all over the floor.

Following the service, Geri arranged a tasteful Mexican luncheon in the courtyard of the church; but God dammit, she stuck to her teetotaling ways even when three-quarters of the folks were either cops or their spouses who would for sure have looked forward to a libation or two. Now me, we're talking four or five, for starters.

I had planned to mingle for just a few minutes and then boogey to the closest watering hole. But I ran into many cops, both on the job or retired, many of whom were former clients. So I got a lot of "So how's retirement, Preston?" My pat answer, along with a false, crooked-looking grin was: A little of this, a little bit of that. You know, just trying to stay busy while knowing full well that my life sucks a big one.

-31-
PH'S JOURNAL OCTOBER 25, 2017

I flew home on Southwest through Denver and on to Austin Bergstrom. As I was walking through the terminal, I felt a hand on my shoulder from the rear. When I turned around, the Splendid Splinter stood there, arms out, waiting to embrace me. I hardly recognized Teddy at first; he had always been a little bit on the pudgy side going toward flab, but now he had blown up like the Fat Lady Doris Bleu from the circus. He had gotten so obese that he walked with a cane; when he spoke, Teddy wheezed and coughed as if every labored word might be his last.

"Whaddaya say we grab us a real drink and wolf down some mid-afternoon lunch, I'm starvin'," said the Splendid Splinter. Why was I not surprised that he would want to gobble down some food? "And I'm buyin' every round," he said. Not being one to pass up free booze, I accepted the invitation straightaway, so we agreed to meet up at the Texas Chili Parlor on Lavaca.

I hadn't been for some time, but as always, time stood still there. The same sign stood above the bar: "Tipping is not a place in China." The bathroom had its usual black, blue, red, and green felt pen scrawlings of political vituperation: "Trump sucks a big one....Lock her up!...Cruz is a sorry excuse for a senator." And so on. The lunch crowd had dispersed, so we could sit toward the back of the restaurant and talk without the usual clamoring patrons around.

Teddy ordered two bowls of Triple X chili with extra onions and cheese; we each ordered Shiner

Bocks, and Teddy told the waiter to keep the beers flowing. As usual, the chili came out from the kitchen post-haste.

It turned out that Teddy was one of those guys who couldn't multi-task; he got so fixated at devouring the all-meat chili—in Texas, beans in chili are as taboo as an observant Jew eating pork—that he couldn't speak at the same time, kinda like a Gerald Ford moment. Teddy's butt splayed out so far over his seat that each cheek jiggled up and down every time he moved his body.

After each bite of the Triple X, Teddy's face reddened more, and sweat began pouring off of his brow onto the food and the tabletop. Although his every bite of chili, every drip of sweat, and every movement of his flabby ass grossed me out, I was okay with the silence; I could concentrate on one after another ice-cold Shiners soothing my throat.

Finally, the Splendid Splinter finished up, wiping off the tiny bits of chili speckling around his mouth. "Whaddaya been up to since retiring?" he asked me as he kept wiping the sweat pouring down his face with a napkin. The waiter could see that Teddy was in need of a steady supply of napkins, so he brought out a ream and laid them on the table. I gave the same rote comeback that now seemed so frequent: "A little of this, a little bit of that, yadda, yadda. How 'bout you, Teddy?"

After Teddy stopped hogging down food, he turned out to be as voluble as a macaw. Told me that since he enjoys food so much, he decided to become an epicure, traveling not only around the country but the entire world, dining at the finest restaurants he could find. He checked off a list of his biggest hits—Eleven Madison Park in New York; Osteria Franscescana in Modena, Italy; El Celler De Can Roca in Grona, Spain; Mirazur in Menton, France; Central in Lima, Peru; and Asador Fixebarra in Axpe, Spain. What the fuck is an epicure, anyway?

"I have a few questions, Teddy" I asked him. "First, why did you select these particular restaurants?" Teddy told me about the wondrous world of the Internet; he had googled the greatest ones in the world and those locations had come up. So he checked 'em out and they were as good as advertised.

"My second question isn't really a question," I commented, "but, instead, an observation. Not to put too fine a point on it, Teddy (isn't that called an aphorism? Even with my alcohol-deadening brain, I still can pull out these brilliant words!) but just looking at your present condition, you seem to have moved from an epicure to a glutton. I don't mean to be ugly, but it looks like you're eating yourself to death."

The Splendid Splinter took my remark surprisingly well, conceding that he had overindulged since his retirement. "My doctor has told me I've got full blown Type 2 diabetes, and if I don't get it under control I'm gonna have a major heart attack or stroke out at any time. Frankly, I don't give a shit....I'd rather enjoy the hell out of my life and eat fine foods rather than worry about the consequences."

I had another question. "How have you paid for all these extravagant meals and travels around the world?" Teddy simply shrugged, grinned, and answered. "Counselor, you of all people should know the answer to that one." I was flummoxed for a moment but then the light bulb brightened up in my head. The Splendid Splinter is as big a piece of dog shit as Willie Banks!

-32-
PH'S JOURNAL OCTOBER 31, 2017

Sitting in my living room, I am listening to my Nathanial Ratliff and the Night Sweats playlist— "S.O.B.," "I Need Never Get Old," "Look it Here"— his gospel and rock-infused music blends into a unique sound that captivates me. His shows are always sold out, so I've never had the chance to see him live.

Next up on my queue was Slobberbone, an alt-country band…make that way alt, almost rock group. The first two songs up were: "Tilt-a-Wheel" and "Whiskey Glass Eye." I learned about the group when reading the book, "Black House" by those renowned wordsmiths, Stephen King and Peter Straub. Since I insulted the King of Horror previously, I thought that as a fellow author, I should make a backhanded apology to Stephen and mention the book (as if I am really a fellow author and Stephen needs any trumpeting of his body of work).

By and by, Stevie-boy, would you consider donating your brain to me when you pass? I could always use a helping hand to improve my sometimes lacking skills in scripting words and phrases.

Whenever I listened to Nathanial Ratliff, Slobberbone, or any of my other favorites, I turn the hi-fi up to blast-off, along with the sub-woofer. Another fellow lives in the condo below me, and he has never complained once about the music. I have concluded that the man either enjoys the tunes or is deaf or dead. If he is deceased, I am sure the stench will at some point reach up to my floor, the death smell of a dead raccoon, only worse.

As I sit here listening to the Night Sweats and becoming increasingly lit up—what else is new?—I review the scribbled, at times blitzed handwritten notes over the past month's long assault on our democracy by the so-called leader of the free world. Not included in this array of fuckups are the constant barrage of tweets assaulting the media and anyone who disagrees with him, and his deceitful claim of "NO COLLUSION." Why does he use capital letters so often? Did he take English grammar in school?

10/2 Finally gets around to visiting Puerto Rico. *Two months* after the worst hurricane disaster in the state's history. PS, Donald, it is a state for your information, and the head of the state is a governor, not a president. So what does the Chief Ignoramus do but toss paper towel packages to the assembled folks like shooting a basketball. Nothing but net. The man has as much class as John Belushi in *Animal House.*

10/12 Administration pulls out of UNESCO, citing anti-Israel bias. I had to Google this one because I've never paid a whit of attention to this United Nations agency. So let's check this one out: We're now against an organization that promotes sex education, literacy, clean water, and equality of women. Another admirable contribution by our country to opposition against such worthless goals. Three cheers for the US of A!

10/13 I'm going highbrow here: Triskaidekaphobia is the Greek for "thirteen" and "fear." How's that for a bit of showin' off about Friday the 13th! The Trumpster (rhymes with the

Dumpster) says he won't certify the Iranian nuclear deal. Another blow to stability in the world.

10/15 Trump pays $1.1M out of his campaign fund for legal fees related to the Mueller investigation, a great deal of it for the li'l young'n, Donald Junior. The old man continues to rely on OPM, just like he always did to make his shady real estate deals.

10/18 Another legal blow to Trump's Muslim ban, which he instigated as another sop to his base, also known as white people fearful of anyone who doesn't look like them and who have a delusion about returning to the good ol' fifties when Ike was president and blacks had to use their own toilets and drinking fountains and ride in the back of the bus, at least until Rosa got fed up with the whole second-class treatment deal.

10/30 Finally, a spate of positive news. Trump's military ban on transgender soldiers is banned by a federal judge. My son/daughter—my nomenclature on this family issue has never been clear in my mind—has decided to stop pulling the Republican lever in elections; it's now all D's all the time. Mueller finally gets around to the first round of what I expect will be a bevy of federal indictments arising out of the Russian probe. First, George "Coffee Boy" Papadopoulos gets charged….Shit, I'm so wasted now. I'm not sure about the spelling—and Manafort too. If only all days could be this magnificent!

The Donald spectacle is kinda like the Jerry Springer show, where God's gift to humankind gets his so-called base ginned up and in a lather: "THERE'S NO THERE THERE, NO COLLUSION,

THE DEEP STATE, FAKE NEWS, WITCH HUNT." Whenever Donald, AKA Jerry Springer, holds one of those look-at-how-wonderful-I-am rallies, check out the audience sitting behind the deified Donald—a bunch of white men and women with a sprinkling of one or two token Uncle Toms to show his bogus compassion for them, all of them wearing the obligatory red shirts and hats saying "Make America Great Again."

Check out photographs of the Trumpster's followers, their red faces grotesque in apoplectic rage over...what? Muslims, brown people, blacks, liberals, and worst of all, those insidious Socialists. Except, when it comes to my Medicare...now, that's different. Don't ever call Medicare socialist, and by God, don't put even one finger on my Medicare.

What about the folks who don't show up at these rallies, the ones who spend their time watching *The Bachelor* and *Big Brother* on TV? The ones so self-absorbed in their own lives that they have no clue what's going on around them? I should be enraged at them, but they're just regular folks, trying to lead quiet and often desperate lives with no thought at what's going on right in front of their eyes. How can they? Between mortgages, car payments, food, insurance, and so on, who has the time or energy to worry about the decline of our republic?

-33

EMAIL FROM ANNE HOWARD TO TONY NELSON OCTOBER 30, 2017

TO: Tony Nelson
FROM: Anne Howard
SUBJECT: Intervention

Hi, Tony. I have been working feverishly to set up an intervention for my dad. The date, time, and location for the intervention is November 1st at 4:30 p.m. at Conrad's office. Sorry for the late notification, but it's near five-minutes-to-midnight for my dad's welfare, and there's no more time to waste.

I had trouble coming up with a location, but Conrad says that he will make certain the staff vacates the office before that time. Conrad has given my dad an excuse about some lingering issues regarding a case that needs his attention. Will you be able to attend?

An intervention specialist from one of the addiction recovery clinics will serve as the mediator. She was leery about the location, saying it wouldn't really be a neutral site, but I had to balance Conrad's office versus searching around for a better place when time is, in my opinion, of paramount importance.

The specialist suggests that everyone attending write out their concerns about my dad's behavior and read them during the intervention. This approach will insure that the meeting doesn't get out of hand; there will be plenty of emotions flying around as it is. She suggests a meeting that doesn't go past an hour and a half, preferably just an hour. Please put together your thoughts in advance.

The other people who will attend other than you will include me, my two brothers from New York, my sister from Arlington (formerly my brother), Conrad, and a new friend of my dad's by the name of Georgeanna Robards. I was at first apprehensive about inviting her, but after meeting her for lunch, I am convinced that she will be a good choice for the intervention. She is a truly engaging woman and clearly has affection for my dad. After much gnashing of teeth, I decided against inviting my mom; there's still so much lingering rancor between them, so there's no sense throwing gasoline on that fire.

Please confirm that you are able to attend.

Anne

-34-
EMAIL BETWEEN ANNE HOWARD AND GEORGEANNA ROBARDS OCTOBER 30, 2017

TO: Georgeanna Robards
FROM: Anne Howard
RE: Intervention
George,

I so enjoyed having lunch with you. We hit it off really well, and independent of my dad, I believe that we could be good friends. I can see why you are attracted to my dad and vice-versa. You both have common interests in books, movies, and, of course, those Cubbies! Dad has told me innumerable times that there's two things he thought would never happen in his life, and he's still scratching his head that the Cubs would win a World Series and we'd have a black president.

I was watching television with dad during the Cubs' seventh game victory in Cleveland and that night in Grant Park when Obama and his family triumphantly walked out on the stage in '08 to the roar of Barrack fans. Both special nights still sear in my brain as do my dad's joyful tears. The best of nights!

I am probably going out on a limb here by including you in the intervention that we discussed at lunch, but my instinct tells me you will be a good addition to the meeting. So if you're up for it, please consider this email an invitation.

The intervention will be on November 1st at 4:30 p.m. at Conrad Diamond's office on 13th Street. I've been there so many times but have never paid attention to the address, so just Google it. There is parking in the back of the building.

Besides you and me, the other participants will include Conrad (former partner with my dad), Tony Nelson (Dad's close friend and former investigator), my two brothers, and the brother, now sister, that I mentioned who has transitioned. The addiction recovery specialist suggests that we all read letters rather than just blurt out whatever comes to mind. That way, you can deliver a message to Dad that has been thought out. So please work on your presentation in advance.

Thank you so much for helping out, George. If this doesn't move my dad to some kind of action, I have no idea what we'll do next.

Anne

PS: I have looked into Al Anon, a support group for people who have loved ones facing alcohol abuse. I am going to start attending local meetings. If you have an interest in coming along, I would look forward to you accompanying me; I will need the support! I will let you know when and where.

-35-
PH'S JOURNAL NOVEMBER 2, 2017

Fuck a duck. My family and friends blindsided me yesterday like an NFL receiver who catches a pass across the middle of the field unaware that a safety will clobber him almost senseless in a microsecond. After that bout of emotion thrown my way at Conrad's office yesterday, listening to their anguish over my...all right, undeniable alcoholism, I feel like I've gone through a hand-crank clothes wringer.

My feelings of shock and confusion are bearing down on me as if a boulder has pushed down on my body to the point I am paralyzed. What should I feel about this assault by my family and friends? Rage? Shame at my addiction? Motivation to change? All of the above? I can't even begin to ask the right questions, much less figure out any answers.

As I listened to my children, Conrad, Tony, and...Jesus, how did George get sucked into this operation?...all of them reading from notes, quietly crying, in some cases out-and-out bawling (shut the fuck up for Christ sakes, George!) venting their frustrations over my wretched behavior, all I could do was bow my face into cupped hands and feel shame that I had so terribly disappointed all of them.

I was so wrung out after the intervention that I almost passed out in Conrad's parking lot, so George drove me to the condo. Someone fortunately worked out how to get my car home. George sat with me afterward in my living room, thankfully keeping her trap shut, while I tried to process what had just taken place. After about an hour, she stood up, kissed me on the forehead, placed a kiss on her right hand fingers and caressed those fingers lovingly across my cheek, and then left without a word. It's clear that this woman really cares for me; I'd better start paying attention.

Today has been one of serious reflection, like a Buddhist monk, sans robe, who seeks isolation and quiet time. I have a criminal attorney friend who became a Buddhist and jumped right into a six-day retreat of complete silence. Now, thus guy had always been a yapper who couldn't keep in mouth shut even if his life depended on it; how he lasted six days has always mystified me.

I turned off my phone, television, and for a time, even my laptop. I am on the verge of crossing the Rubicon after which I will become a lost soul with no family, friends, or point of living. I am, for sure, at the end of my rope.

Eventually, I jumped on the Internet and began Googling facilities that dealt with alcohol abuse. The outfit that caught my attention was the Betty Ford clinic; I always admired the First Lady who had the fortitude to admit her addiction to alcohol and opioids. If she had the balls, so to speak, to fess up and confront her demons, why couldn't I?

Then there's the case of Joe Walsh, one of the A-list guitarists and singers with groups like the James Gang, the Eagles, and a few others. Alcohol hit Joe so hard that he hit the bottom of the barrel, right where I am sitting at the moment. Don Henley and Glenn Frey did their own intervention, saved his ass from total destruction, and got Joe on the path of sobriety for now some twenty-five years. RIP, Glenn....I miss you.

I've had one previous experience with Betty Ford. Conrad and I had an under-performing lawyer in our office back in the nineties who we suspected of having either an alcohol or drug addiction. We confronted him, he confessed to a cocaine problem, and we convinced him to go to Betty's facility in San Diego. A month later, he returned a new man, clutching his gold AA coin at every opportunity. He stayed off the coke, but as it turned out, he was still a pitiful excuse for lawyer when sober, so we fired him. I sometimes wonder whether he went back to snorting up his nose.

The website talked about a 12-step holistic treatment program, which makes me nervous— sounds like a disguised AA. How do I accept God into my heart when I'm a nonbeliever? And the holistic treatment sounds a little too close to the approach of Janis Moore, the twenty-six-year-old psychologist. Will Betty's system really get me out of this hell hole?

I telephoned the 800 number and spoke to a lady who sounded timid, almost like a wallflower, telling her that I am getting on a plane to their Tampa facility on Sunday the 5th to undergo treatment for my condition. Ms. Wallflower threw up a lot of folderol about insurance approvals, pre-testing, whatever. I advised her that insurance wasn't a problem (actually, Conrad is paying the tab, decent of him) but she kept throwing up obstacles, so I pulled the old let-me-speak-to-a-supervisor maneuver.

Conrad always had a sign on the door going into his office that read, "It's all about me." That attitude must have rubbed off a bit on me; I tend to insist on getting my way. Maybe the lack of acceptance is one of the traits of an alkie. I'll have to ponder this burning question whenever I arrive at Betty's house.

Let me make an observation about telephone operators and supervisors, not the ones here in the US, but those faraway Indians in Bangalore. The first contact goes something along these lines. "Hello, this is Fred. How can I help you today?" Not really Fred, but Sanjay, Rohan, Muhil. Always overly polite and normally incomprehensible. Speaka de English for Christ's sake! So I ask for a supervisor. Fifteen minutes later, a gal or guy gets on the line, once again well-mannered but syrupy and still unfathomable. "Please connect me to a US agent," I ask. "Oh, I'm so sorry, sir. We are unable to connect from here." Ah, the frustrations of an interconnected world.

Back to Betty Ford. A fellow picks up the line and tries a soothing, understanding routine, but I have no patience with bullshit and began brow-beating him like a drum. After going around a bit, I finally said, *I am in serious trouble and need help now!* I will be flying to Tampa on Sunday; will someone be at the airport to pick me up? After a little more wrangling back and forth, he asked me to call back with the time my flight would arrive in Tampa. The power of persuasion—no, make that exasperating importunity!

Now for a few preparations before my trek into the unknown. I phoned Anne and the other kids, Conrad, and Tony, and after first informing them of their back-stabbing intervention, I did at least grudgingly thank them, and told them I'd be off on my Betty Ford excursion this Sunday. Since all of my technological support—laptop, iPad, and iPhone—would be verboten at the clinic (what Grinch in the Ford bureaucracy passed this fiat?), my communication will be limited to short emails at their facility or a letter.

Who writes letters anymore? Definitely a long-lost practice, like reading an actual newspaper or book that you can hold, smell, and leaf through the pages.

My last call was to George. After laying out the plan, I asked her for a big favor. Would you please drive down to Tampa and pick me up. "George, I'm concerned about walking out of the clinic and running to the first bar for a drink." She signed off without hesitation, which I had anticipated; after all, the woman loves me. Boy, do I have way too much hutzpah, or what?

I actually had two deceitful motives in mind for her help. First off, I still have the hornies for George; maybe with some miles between Tampa and Austin, we could pull off for a little rest, relaxation, and most important, playtime.

The more sinister intention was I asked George to bring a pre-prepared bag of extra clothes, plus my communication devices. What I wasn't about to divulge was that my Ruger would be packed along with everything else; I will keep my fingers crossed she won't scrounge around in the bag, or if she does, the gun would be secreted in a place that she hopefully wouldn't locate.

The Trumpster has been making the rounds around the country, boasting at his rallies about how in all of US history, he has the best economy, stock market, foreign policy, and so on. I'm waiting for him at some point to use the line, "In all the history of recorded history…" *Yuck!* Anyway, I might get lucky and cross paths with one of his rallies on the way to Austin. Then it'll be bam, bam, bam *"Ashes to ashes, dust to dust. Too bad, Donald. You're no longer with us on this earth."*

One more errand tomorrow, and then Sunday it's off on Southwest—always remember, folks, two bags are free—into the world of sad sack addiction patients. Since alcohol will be a serious no-no at Betty's place, should I load up on Bloody Marys during the flight? Or maybe I can sweet talk the flight attendant into letting me use an IV bag to mainline a bunch of Jim Beams? Just keep 'em comin'.

Is this humor sick, or what? Do you think Anne or George might think this demonstrates a lack of commitment? What have I got myself into here?

-36-
PH'S JOURNAL NOVEMBER 3, 2017

I made one more trip to the gun range this morning, getting in one more practice so my kill-shot skills are at a level close to an Olympian in the twenty-five meter rapid fire pistol competition. The minute I walked in, the owner Joanne lit my fuse—in fact, exploded it.

She was wailing like a banshee at a man who had just complained about the life-sized blowup of Hillary wearing the "Deplorable Lives Matter" t-shirt. Then the man jumped all over—actually screamed at—Joanne for having no compassion for the murdered children at Sandy Hook and their distraught parents.

"If the teachers had guns, Sandy Hook would never have happened," she testily answered. "Plus, guns don't kill people; people kill people." The NRA would be proud of Joanne as she mimed those predictable sayings. At this point, Joanne became apoplectic. "Get the fuck out of my gun range, you Commie-lovin' bastard," she shrieked.

"You're a sorry-ass excuse for a gun range owner; you and your ilk are a bunch of right-wing crackpots," the man responded accusatorily as he stood toe-to-toe with Joanne, jabbing his finger toward her face. Several of the good ol' boys hanging around the shop, fellas wearing cowboy boots and name belts and chewing wads of tobacco bulging in their cheeks, began sidling up around the man with threatening glares. The man's face blanched like someone who had just been circled by a bunch of ravenous wolves. Realizing that he was a minute away from a serious ass-whippin,' the man began skedaddling out of there without further ado.

To add further insult to injury, Joanne hurled one last stinging remark as the abashed gentleman hurriedly reached the front door. "You are hereby forever banished from this gun range!" she pontificated like a female Caligula.

I suddenly felt more out of place in that gun range than a homo at a DAR meeting, so I decided to tempt fate and find out how much Joanne really wanted a moustache ride. I left my gun case outside the range—*violation.* Carried the box of bullets right up to the firing line and loaded them into the Ruger—*violation.* Rapid-fired the ten rounds, one of them into the target of the shooter next to me—*oh my, violation, violation.* Left the gun facing away from the range toward the door as I step backward to drink some water—*violation,*

"Mr. Howard, you are abusing the range policies," she screamed into a mike over the intercom, clearly still in a snit over the previous altercation. "You must immediately cease and desist, or you will be in serious trouble with *me!*"

Cease and desist? I thought I had retired from the Howard *et al* law firm almost two years ago. "You are not the fucking queen of the world, Joanne. That privilege belongs to your pathetic-ass hero, the self-proclaimed King Donald. Therefore, I am self-banishing myself from this second-rate excuse for a gun range." I gathered all my gear post-haste and hightailed it out of the shop before the ass-whippers had an opportunity to take out their rage on another

Socialist, never to return or be seen again at Joanne's gun range.

I packed some clothes and toiletries for the trip on Sunday; another bag was prepared to be left with George. Tomorrow, I'm having lunch with Anne and George together at The Roaring Fork. When did these two women become such good buddies? I can already picture them conspiring to keep me on the straight and narrow path after the Tampa journey. God damn, I want a drink so bad…maybe just a sip or two, or even more, of my much-adored pinot. Do drinks of wine make a noise in the forest? They'll never know.

-37-
PH'S JOURNAL DECEMBER 1, 2017

Left the clinic today after thirty days of incarceration, I felt like Ray Liotta in *Goodfellas* as he walked out of prison and sees Lorraine Bracco leaning against her car in a suggestive pose...the same way George did this morning. Her pose gave me a huge woody...oh baby, oh baby. She must have a sensitive antenna or picked up on my prurient leer as right off the bat, she said, "Forget about it, junior. You're still in my woodshed, so no handsies just yet." Crap, the cold shoulder once again. When will the deep freeze thaw out?

George has been kind enough to pull off I-75 and check into a motel, so I can spend time reflecting on the past thirty days and writing into my journal. On the one hand, the last month has been like my teenage years, slow as you go, never gonna end.

But I did learn about my addiction, the triggers, coping mechanisms, meditation, attending AA meetings, using sponsor and other support groups, and nutrition, There actually are grapes on vines suggested by the clinic other than the ones in a pinot bottle, like grape juice. Although my only experience with grape juice has included several splashes of Tito's, a superb vodka produced right there in Austin.

Here would be a great story: When I walked out of Betty Ford, the sky opened wide up and I felt the finger of God placed on me. Actually, nothing even close happened, not even one aha moment hit me like a thunderbolt. Instead, what I felt was fear—the dread of relapse, letting my family and friends down, getting back into the habit of throwin' 'em back, and worst of all, giving up on my life, the place where I sat at the moment of the intervention over a month ago. I don't want to go backward, but the need for a drink sits over my head, waiting to thrust down on me like the sword of Damocles.

When I showed up at Betty's house, one of my good friends, Dan Ruggiero, walked in the lobby a minute or two after me. I represented him on a case from my early days in Austin. And no, in spite of the surname, he had never been mobbed up. Dan must have spent considerable time barking at the moon or powdering his nose; he had obviously become a frequent Betty customer. He addressed every attendant by name the moment he walked in, like he had been bosom buddies for years with each of them.

Dan's appearance—medium height, unremarkable features—would never draw a great deal of attention in a crowd, but he had a mischievous smile and eyes that twinkled like the Cheshire puddy cat that had just gobbled up the canary. That smile and eyes matched up to the swindle he ran back in the day—a police solicitation business.

"Good afternoon, Mr. Smith. I work for the Austin Police Association, and we are seeking funds on behalf of the poor police widows and orphans who need our help." There were all kinds of monkeyshines surrounding this pitch.

A solicitor like Dan would reap ninety percent of the profit, after expenses, while the police union got a puny ten percent. Any police widows, at least the ones whose husbands were killed in the line-of-duty, received at least a lump sum half-million bucks in federal and state payments, plus their spouses's pension, plus tuition payments to a state school for their children. No wonder that at the biennial Texas Police Memorial ceremony, all those salivating policemen lurked around the wailing but sex-starved half-millionaires. And here's the crowning point: When was the last time anyone had ever heard about or been to an orphanage? "Goodnight, you princes of Maine, you kings of New England." Thank you Dr. Larch and John Irving for such a masterful phrase!

I helped Dan with the legalities of setting up his operation and hooked him up with the Austin union leaders who would enjoy the ten percent largesse of Dan's work. He lived large, taking Donna and me, union leaders, and his sweet, deaf girlfriend, Renee, out to elegant dinners at Austin's finer restaurants, ordering bottle after bottle of Pouilly-Fuissé whites and Châteauneuf-du-Pape reds.

Dan had a great scam goin' on until one of his solicitors got caught by a businessman/victim who taped the solicitor saying he was an Austin police officer....Whoops. Both the long arm of the Austin law and an *American Statesman* investigating reporter—that same shithole, Terry Palmer, who often bedeviled me—came down on Dan like a ton of bricks, and his operation was finis.

He disappeared from Austin faster than the speed of a million light years, and until this moment at Betty's *hacienda,* I had never heard from him. He still had that same look on his face, as though his next flimflam waited right around the corner.

He was wearing a clearly expensive three-piece suit with three huge Macanudos stuffed into his coat pocket. An attendant held out his hand and harshly told Dan to turn over the cigars. "No tobacco products here, Dan. You know that already." Dan winked at me as he turned over his contraband to the attendant.

"Looks like you're back in the high life, Dan," I told him.

"Higher than high," he replied. "Let's get checked in and go through the usual bullshit orientation. We'll catch up. Later. Do I have some stories for ya!"

And how. Later, he told me a tale that sounded outrageously implausible, except given Dan's previous behavior, nothing could be too far-fetched. Since he was down on his luck and Renee offered no monetary contribution to the relationship, he discarded her faster than a bullet train speeding down the rails. Cold as an iceberg, but I figured, if you're a scammer, compassion wasn't a part of your repertoire.

He met a hippopotamus–sized woman named Lydia who had recently finalized her divorce and walked away with a settlement that would take care of her for a lifetime plus. Dan glommed onto Lydia's money. "She took care of me—any trips, jewelry, cash, anything I wanted," he explained. "She gave me her moola, and I gave her my compassion, obviously for her flabbiness. It was a mutually beneficial deal." Worse than frigid, I thought. This guy made Machiavelli look like an honorable man.

"She was so fat," Dan continued, "that I would never let her fuck me from on top. I woulda been squashed to smithereens. So it was the missionary position all the way if I could find the hole down there between her legs and not get repulsed from the obese flaps enveloping me on each side."

"Lydia did have one positive quality," he said. "She had a tattoo with a tail that started on her back, moved down to her ass, came back up on her front starting by her navel, and then travelling up to her boobs where the snake tailed into a cock. Hovering above the cock right where the cleavage began, a red-lipsticked mouth awaited. LMAO!

"But there's more!" Dan went on. "When we went out in public, Lydia would wear a backless dress that exposed the tail moving down toward her ass; then the front side of the dress was exposed down the middle so the other side of the tail moved up to the ending cock as it got ready for insertion into the mouth. Needless to say, I enjoyed people-watching as men and women stared in horror at the spectacle."

Now I laughed so hard I worried about pissing in my pants; my prostrate-less bladder can take a little bit of jangling, but this story was pushing the old bladder to its limit. This conversation reminded me of the movie, *Patti Rocks*, where two guys spent almost one-half of the movie driving in a car, discussing every repulsive experience about women that guys talk about in private...not that I've ever done anything so revolting. That's my story, and I'm stickin' to it.

"But I'm not finished," Dan went on. I told him I might stroke out if he continued. "Now comes the best part of the story," he answered. I simply nodded; Dan was so wound up telling this story that a herd of water buffaloes galloping toward him wouldn't stop him from telling the rest of the yarn.

"As much as I enjoyed Lydia's money, her porkiness had begun to gross me out to the point I could hardly look at her; she was so obese that Mama Cass looked like Twiggy. At the same time, I'm starting to snort down gargantuan quantities of coke, so my perception of reality became way, way skewed. So I stole a bunch of her money, diamonds, and other jewelry, and took every piece of my gold jewelry that she had bought me, and took off.

"In my haste to leave, I forgot that Lydia had some shady friends with names that ended in i's a's and o's; it got back to me from some mutual friends that she called a few of these mean-acting fellows and took a contract out on my life. Come on, really? After all the compassion I had shown her, she wants to rub me out? I suppose Congreve was right," he finished. "Hell hath no fury like a woman scorned" as the saying goes."

Tell me you're finished, I said; I can't take any more! "Not quite," he said. "Since I now had Costra Nostra-like gentlemen on my trail, I had to do some fast thinking. So I changed my name, turned all the jewelry into liquid assets, moved up to Maine, and opened up a gourmet restaurant in Portland. It's been a pretty successful venture, even written up in the *New York Times*. Trouble is, I can't keep off the coke, and while the restaurant is a living, it's not generating the kind of cash I'm used to. Plus, I have to work my ass off every day but Sunday. So, when I get out of here this time, I'm thinking of calling Lydia up and seeing if she'll take me back."

"You're kidding me, right?" I asked Dan. He just gave me his devilish grin and a sparkling puddy-cat-ate-the-bird wink.

***

While I've been frolicking away in Tampa, Roy Moore has become engaged in a battle royale for the Senate election in Alabama against Democrat Doug Jones. Roy is definitely my kind of Republican. He was tossed out twice as Chief Justice of the Alabama Supreme Court—the first time for refusing to get rid of a monument of the Ten Commandments in the rotunda that he had erected in the Alabama Judicial Building and the second time for defying a US Supreme Court decision affirming same-sex marriages.

Now, it turned out that in the past, he had been hitting up on teenaged girls. If he wins, Roy will feel right at home with some of his right-wing hypocrites in Congress. It's too bad Denny Hastert isn't still hanging around D.C. Roy and Denny could discuss their experiences diddling young girls and boys.

What a providential development! The Master of the Universe, Donald the Boob, the tin-pot, banana republic dictator of all time—the man who outshines Robert Mugabe as the worst humanoid on earth—will be showing up in Pensacola on the 8th (only a week away) for a Roy More rally. He will, of course, boast at the rally how in the history of American politics, he is like Muhammed Ali—The Greatest.

Now the tricky part. How do I convince George to hang around Florida for another seven days rather than speed back to Austin? The old North Carolina four corners slow-down offense might do the trick. Hey, George, how does this sound? I've never been to the Redneck Riviera, so let's hang out on the pure white sands of Pensacola for a few days. Surely she'll buy it. And don't call me Shirley.

-38-

DECEMBER 4 THROUGH 7, 2017 EMAILS BETWEEN GEORGE ROBARDS AND ANNE HOWARD

TO: Anne Howard
FROM: Georgeanna Robards
RE: Your dad

Since we talked by phone on the day your dad got out of what he refers to as the Bastille, we have been wending our way, and when I say wending, I mean really moving like a turtle across I-10. I wanted to drive back to Austin ASAP, but he seems content to dawdle his way across Florida. We are currently at a lovely hotel right by a gorgeous beach that is as white as I've ever seen.

There is some good news and bad, so I'll begin with the good. Your dad looks as good as I've ever seen him—eyes clear, face no longer pasty like before from his drinking, smiling, pleasant to be with, content. He seems averse to alcohol, and hopefully that will continue. He is committed to attending AA meetings, a positive; although, he jokes about what higher power will be his savior.

Now for the bad news, and I really need your advice on an ethical dilemma. Before I left Austin, I checked his bag which he had asked me to bring with his electronics; I wanted to make certain he had something warm in case it got cold on the drive back. Lo and behold, I found a gun and three clips alongside filled with bullets. Chilling.

I didn't think much of it at first, but now that we're in Pensacola, four days away from Trump flying here to deliver a speech, I have become completely unnerved. Your dad has made noises about shooting the president before, and in putting two and two together, it's clear to me about his intention.

So what do I do? If I confront him, he will conclude that I have invaded his personal space, and he won't ever trust me. Contacting the Secret Service is clearly not an appetizing choice, actually not even an option. Yeah, I'm the gal that turns in your dad. Not even going there.

Any advice, Anne? Help!!!

Your friend,

George

TO: Georgeanna Robards

FROM: Anne Howard

RE: My dad

Holy shit...double shit. The Secret Service is out....I can just see the headlines: "Austin Lawyer Attempts Murder of the President." I also understand your need to maintain my dad's confidence.

But, you have to do something to stop him. *Anything* to keep him from pulling the trigger. If he decides to go to the rally, stay glued to him every second. Being a bigtime sports fan, conjure up an obscure football linebacker and tackle him if necessary. You absolutely must not allow this assassination to take place!

Please keep in touch over the next few days.

Your new found buddy,

Anne

TO: Anne Howard
FROM: Georgeanna Robards
RE: Your dad

The Trump rally takes place tomorrow, and I am beside myself. I know that he has murder-lust on his mind, but he is totally mum about the rally. He spends his time walking along the gorgeous beach, keeping his thoughts about the next day to himself, and singing gospel songs like "Battle Cry" by the Kingsmen and "God Put a Rainbow in the Cloud" by the Blind Boys of Alabama. How can a man who believes Jesus and God are frauds (kind of like Marx's opium of the people line) still enjoy this kind of music? Quite the dichotomy, but I have figured out that your dad is a walking contradiction of values and actions.

At least we have gotten in a whole lot of hand-holding along the beach—quite romantic—and have spent much time talking about our lives and aspirations (even as seniors, I suppose we still have hopes!).

When your Dad is sober, he is, in two words, *da bomb.*

I'll keep my fingers crossed tomorrow for a positive outcome. I don't want for you to read in *The New York Times* tomorrow that your dad has been arrested or killed in an assassination attempt.

A distressed George

PS: If it becomes necessary to tackle your dad, I will conjure up the Philadelphia Eagles linebacker/center Chuck Bednarik and violently toss your dad to the ground (only in my dreams). Concrete Charlie, as he was called, wasn't so obscure though. Inducted into the Hall of Fame, he was the last player to go both ways—defense and offense. He called all the players who only played one-way "pussyfoots." Too much information!

-39-

PH'S JOURNAL DECEMBER 9, 2017

Fuck, fuck, motherfuck. So close and yet so far. George insisted on coming with me in spite of my resistance to the idea, so I should have picked up right away that she was on to me.

We got into town for a mid-afternoon lunch. The weather was bitingly cold, so rather than wander around, we found a cozy restaurant to hang out and chat. "I sure would enjoy a cold brew," I told George. She rolled her eyes, and said, "No way, Jose." Coffee and tea the rest of my life? Grape juice? Yuck and suck.

Then she floored me, suggesting, not insisting, that I live with her.

"Why would I do that," I asked.

"So I can keep tabs on you, numb-nuts."

"So, at some point in this co-habitation," I continued, "will I finally get into your pants?"

"I have decided that you will get, as you so crassly say it, into my pants before we get back to Austin…if you behave."

"Oh boy!" I yelled, gathering some attention from nearby patrons. "But to be truthful…" I continued…

"I hate that expression 'to be truthful,'" she interrupted, "because when I am talking to you, it is implied that when you speak, you will be truthful. Please continue with your 'truth.'" She air-quoted the last words with the index and middle finger of both hands.

Jesus, I have a firecracker on my hands, I thought. "What I was going to say, before you so rudely

222

interrupted me..." I winked at her so she clearly understood this remark was a joke—lord have mercy, she can be so touchy—"...was that since my prostate operation twelve years ago, I haven't been inside a woman. Even though I do carry around the magic blue pill, I'm not even sure the plumbing works down there anymore."

"Oh, you poor little boy," she replied sarcastically. "I feel so sorry for you. Let me aks you this," she went on, using the oft-spoken black usage. "Your tongue still works, doesn't it, sweetheart?"

I felt my face redden, which she seemed to enjoy thoroughly. All I could do was nod in the affirmative.

"Just so you know, Preston," George went on, "I am multi-orgasmic, so you will be working between my legs for quite a long time...so get used to it."

Boy, oh boy. What to make of this woman who has somehow stealthily taken over my life.

Anyway, back to the Trump fiasco. The rally was to begin at seven p.m., so we began making our way over at around five. Since it appeared there would be no rope lines, my only opportunity would be to get in line at the Pensacola Bay Center and hope the body scanners that would surely be in place wouldn't go off when I walked through.

I enjoyed the anti-Trump protesters standing around as we made our way to the Center, shouting every negative comment about the idiot-scum president. One sign read "Trump Supports Pedophiles," which I particularly enjoyed.

A huge line snaked its way around the building, so I played the old-man-I'm-freezing-card and found some amiable—as if that word even fit the pro-

Trumpers—people who allowed George and me in line. As the line started to move and we got closer into the entrance, I felt my armpits start beading up (Arrid XX—48 hours protection…not). Sweat begin forming on my forehead. I wondered if John Wilkes Booth perspired the moment right before he pulled the trigger and assassinated Lincoln. Other than that, Mrs. Lincoln, how was the play?

George stood to my right where the Ruger lay hidden beneath my coat; she took my arm, squeezed it lightly, and whispered in my ear, "Sweetie, come to your senses. Between the scanners inside and the Secret Service everywhere around us…one of them standing a few yards away"—she pointed toward the somber Marine-crew-cut-looking kinda guy with an ear piece and some sort of metal insignia on his lapel—"you're doomed. Let's go back to the hotel." She reached up and lightly kissed my cheek.

And that was that. As anticlimactic as it gets, like when I went to Yankee Stadium on September 30, 1961, to watch Roger Maris break Babe Ruth's homerun record and he whiffed. He waited until the next day to hit number sixty-one. One of the heartbreaks of my life.

So now I'm back in the hotel and not certain what to feel. Upset? At What? Not killing the president? Mad at George for unearthing my scheme? Relieved? Maybe a little of everything. In the end, I'm not going to beat George up over her likely invasion of privacy; she saved my life from certain extinction, for sure.

Well, it's time to end this part of my saga because George is standing right in front of me with a broad grin, wearing a sheer black teddy and black thigh-high fishnet stockings, along with some fuck-me, black, spiked heels…and holding a Viagra pill out in front of me along with a glass of water. Fortunately, no flogger in either hand! It's gonna be a long night.

-40-

PH'S JOURNAL DECEMBER 10, 2017

I convinced George to break-up the trip even more, mostly because I'm in no hurry to get back to Austin. With Anne, Tony, Conrad, and who knows who else wanting to hang out and talk about my new-found sobriety, it will be a pain-in-the-ass gabfest.

But there's a more impotent (ha, ha, *not,* as it turns out) reason. About halfway between Pensacola and Austin sits Lafayette and a super-duper Cajun restaurant—Randol's—which serves the best gumbo in Louisiana. George seems to be the adventurous type, so she will enjoy something she's never experienced before. We're driving from the hotel to the restaurant in a few minutes, so I want to spend some time beforehand replaying the last day.

I had told George on our first date about my nonchalant view of sex with women, but with her, there was no wham-bam-thank-you-ma'am. It was a night of touching, exploring, embracing, and kissing that ranged between tentative brushing of the lips to mouth-wide open, full-throated tongue exchanges. As an old Jewish high school buddy used to say, "Oh voy, oh voy!"

But there's more. The magic little blue pill worked its magic. My prostateless cock worked as intended, once, twice, but the third time was not the charm! The old fella down below just couldn't operate the machinery that last time. Dammit, I ate three oysters and only two of them worked.

George never gave me a respite. Between the intervals of our serious thrusting back and forth, I was pushed down between her legs (no resistance on my part LOL), and yes, as advertised, this woman was beyond orgasmic. She exhausted me like a marathon runner felt at the end of a race. Down the road, she might wind up giving me the Big One, a cardiac arrest so mammoth that the ball game will be cancelled due to something a lot worse than rain. But at least I'll go out with a smile on my face.

I am replaying our trip across I-10 today, a snapshot of George that keeps whirling around in my brain like an LP stuck on a phonograph. She sits across from me on the passenger side of the car, her legs tucked underneath her body and right arm draped across the side of the door. Her peach-colored, silk blouse is completely unbuttoned and pulled back, tauntingly showing her breasts, which, even though she is sixty-seven, still have serious uplift. She grins lustfully, like a woman sitting at a bar working on a pick-up with a man sitting next to her and talks as if it's no big deal to sit there exposing herself. What a slutty, prick-teasing, wonderful woman.

We replayed the epic sex-a-thon, me telling George in that way I used to with my one-night stands, "You're the best I ever had." George asked me if I wanted to get slapped so early in the day, so I rescinded my comment and told her that truly, I would never forgot last night. She seemed to accept my revised version, and after saying I definitely was not a flop in the sack (whew, that had me worried), she then untucked her legs, hiked her skirt up high, spread her legs slightly, about to expose her totally-shaved nether area, sans panties. I told her that I'd never concluded whether the pink-bearded clam down there was ugly as sin or a beautiful sight, so it would be advisable to maintain her shirt at its current level until I could make some determination on this momentous issue.

"I never realized how much of a little hussy you are," I remonstrated. "You're gonna give me a hard-on, and I'm tryin' to rest the little fella."

"It's not as little as you think," George answered, "and you'll have ample opportunity to find out again tonight. And just so you know, Preston, I'm gonna be the biggest and baddest hussy you've ever been with." What on earth did I get myself into!

When we pulled off to a rest area—being seniors, our bladders ain't what they used to be—George tucked herself back in. As we moved back onto I-10, I was relieved that she stayed fully dressed and got off the sex train for a bit. I told George that I held no rancor toward her for finding my Ruger, which seemed to alleviate her concern. Then I told George that since I still have the pistol, it would be such a shame to waste not using it. I spent the rest of this leg of the trip telling her about the Banks case. She became engrossed with my story but not so much with my new and improved—just like Tide—plan for the Ruger.

***

Just returned from Randol's. George thoroughly enjoyed the shrimp gumbo with the dark roux and the crayfish etouffee. As an additional reward, an A-plus group played there on Sunday—Dwayne Dopsie and the Zydeco Hellraisers. Dwayne and his group played three hours of rockin' Cajun music to George's excitement.

I taught her how to dance the two-step which fit Cajun music perfectly. I told her she'd have to learn it anyway when we get back to Texas. I didn't have my Preston name belt, cowboy hat, and boots, but never having done the two-step, she didn't know the diff.

I did the standard dance move with my hand wrapped around her neck, kinda like Harvey Weinstein must do when he has an actress victim on his studio couch, his hand pushing her down toward his exposed cock. BTW, if I ever tried that stunt with George, she'd give me what for. She did have trouble at first shuffling her shoes across the floor rather than feet moving up and down off the dancehall, but she finally got the hang of it. Two-steppers everywhere would have been proud of our display.

Sometimes, the Hellraisers would play a faster 2/4 beat rather than the 4/4 more conducive to a two-step. So when the band played a 2/4 tune, George and I agreed to do the lindy hop. She had this one phenomenal move where I would swirl her totally around, and at the end of the turn, she would kick up her right leg perpendicular to her waist. She must have taken dancing lessons at a more exclusive class than mine, and it showed.

We went to and fro, twirling around the room; George definitely got turned on, as did I. As George Bernard Shaw once said, "Dancing is a perpendicular expression of a horizontal desire."

Fortunately, she didn't dance like a white woman; she could sway and grind with the best of the *Soul Train* gals. Halfway through our two-steps, I began getting a woody, and from time-to-time she would gingerly and surreptitiously rub the noticeable bulge in my pants with her left hand as she looked up at me with a naughty grin.

-41-

MAILS BETWEEN GEORGE, ANNE, AND TONY DECEMBER 11-14, 2017

NOTE FROM ANNE HOWARD...DEAR READERS: Due to security concerns, parts of the following stream of emails have been redacted from the materials sent to family and friends, but you, dear readers, get a peek behind the curtain. So, pay attention to the redactions which will be prefaced by [brackets].

TO: Anne Howard
FROM: Georgeanna Robards
RE: Your dad

Well, we're finally back home at last. Your dad is currently over at his condo, gathering his belongings. Due to our successful trip, he is now content to move into my place, which is good not only for the sobriety issue but also for our personal enjoyment.

It's probably gauche to discuss a father's sex life with his daughter, but I am comfortable enough talking to you that on our trip, he popped my cherry, or is it I popped his cherry? Either way, I have found a man compatible with me in so many ways, and just not the sex thing. He took me to a Cajun restaurant in Lafayette that was out of sight. Never tried gumbo before. Such a unique but scrumptious taste. And the crawfish etouffee was to die for. And holy, moly, your dad can for sure dance the light fantastic

We're now making plans for a trip to Vancouver, to take a hike or two and maybe pay for an Alaskan cruise. Your dad says the cruise will remove two

231

items from his bucket list—seeing Alaska and taking a cruise—but he seems dubious about the latter. He's thinking too many humans around in one place and worried there might not be accommodations on the cruise for an AA meeting. After Googling several cruise lines, he asked me whether we could put a hold on his temperance—just temporarily, you understand—purchase the liquor package, and drink to our hearts content. I told him this idea was like a NASA rocket that fizzed out on the launch pad, not going anywhere except in the scrapyard.

Now if we can only keep your dad off the sauce. He has the will right now but will likely become weak at some point, so it's important for both of us to be vigilant. He is committed to AA, so hopefully he will stay straight as an arrow.

When I phoned you after the Trump rally near-disaster, we both had a sigh of relief. I figured we were out of the woods entirely. But with your dad, the hits just keep on acomin'.

As we drove along I-10 toward Lafayette, passing the many live oaks and cypress trees with the hanging-moss that drooped from many limbs down toward the ground, he began talking about the Banks case. Your dad must have been one helluva lawyer; he got those three corrupt cops off from a murder rap. I told him he should be proud that he did such a remarkable job, but he wasn't having any of it.

He said he has felt guiltier as the years went by, consuming him even more than his Trump obsession. He apparently has run into two of the retired officers recently—Willie (??) Banks and the Splendid Splinter. I, of course, being a baseball aficionado, knew who Ted Williams was. Your dad has always been impressed with how often I can hit a home run (groaning as I write!!) when talking about baseball ("bazeball been berry, berry gud to me"). I worry, though, that he'll get so esoteric with me one of these days that he'll mention some player so obscure that I've never heard of him, even more so than Jose Valdivielso from the old Washington Senators (pulled that one out of my butt though!). Since I won't knew who the hell he's talking about, your dad will discard me like an over-the-hill dishrag ready for the trash.

Sorry, I am digressing....So he's telling me about the two cops he met, and in both conversations, he gathered, very clearly, that they stole money as a part of their conspiracy not only to kill the Wallace family but maybe two other men. He then related the whole story about the case from beginning to end and started talking about Jazmine Wallace, one of the young kids killed in the shootout. He got so upset about the girl's death that he had to pull off the road and sat in the car trying to compose himself. Your dad is such a compassionate man, another quality that so endears him to me.

[Here's the bottom line: Your dad has traded his murderous intent toward our inglorious president and is now directing it toward the three cops. I don't remember the third guy. Buwl? Beel? Anyway, as I am sure you know, I am once again in a fit of upset and despair.

Help, help, help! Any advice?]
Your buddy,
George

TO: Georgeanna Robards
FROM: Anne Howard
RE: Your dad

George, I wouldn't get distressed about Dad throwing you overboard. You're the only woman he's ever met who is into baseball as much as him. But just to be on the safe side, I somehow wound up with every baseball card Dad ever saved. I'll turn them over to you, and when he's not looking, you can slyly peek at them and memorize every one of the cards. That way, you will so impress him that he'll think you're the best thing that ever happened to him...which he apparently already believes anyway.

Now to the point at hand. The other cop is named Jimmy Buhl, a guy with thinning hair and a narrow face that gives him the appearance of a ferret. He has the look of a sneak, someone who might reach down into the bucket of a panhandling, blind man and pull out as much money as he can. Buhl has this disconcerting habit that my dad first related to me, and then later I observed during the trial. He would play with his tool, trying to be as furtive as a mouse darting across a kitchen top. Sadly, he didn't hide this deviance very well.

Dad has discussed the Banks case so much with me that I have had to turn him off; after all, it's been almost ten years since the case was resolved. But as I said, I did spend considerable time during the trial, sneaking off from work and sitting in, watching what many commentators in Austin have referred to as The Trial of the Century. And during my time in the courtroom, the ebb and flow of the case was riveting.

Dad told me in the middle of the trial that his chance of an acquittal was zero; the three cops were headed, at best, to prison the rest of their lives. At worst they would lay down on the express bed to infinity up in Huntsville.

Fortunately, I happened to be in the courtroom the day that Sam Evans testified; and wow, did he for sure upset the applecart with his testimony, or I should say, lack of on cross-examination! The courtroom became a hubbub of chaos, people stunned that a cop would take the Fifth on the witness stand. And then later, the district attorney's office withdrew the charges against the officers. What a turn of events, both for my dad and his three clients.

I thought Dad would be pleased with the outcome, but over a period of time, he soured over the case and the fluky developments that led to his clients' freedom. He would make comments now and then about how the case bothered him. The murder of at least five people troubled him—maybe not so much the drug-dealing Leroy and Shanice Wallace but for sure the three innocent kids who the Fates had placed in the crosshairs of the three cops. He would especially agonize over Jazmine, the oldest child, who had such a bright future ahead.

Dad speculated whether $5M had been stashed in the Wallace's house; and if so, did the three cops steal it. He wondered whether one or more of the cops killed Janard Coleman. And last but not least, whatever happened to Maurice Holloway, the key prosecution witness? Was he murdered too along with Coleman? Or maybe he vanished into thin air and is now sipping Mai Tai's in Tahiti?

[Dad would obsess over these questions, over and over again, and at a certain point, I had to figuratively plug up my ears....He wore me out over the Banks case. But, I am going to say something that you might not like. I'm going to get it off my chest about those three cops—Banks, Williams, and Buhl—they were guilty, guilty, guilty and deserve the worse kind of death, maybe by throwing them down into a vat of boiling oil, forced to watch a photo of Jazmine Wallace as they scream in agony and the skin peels gradually off their bodies. I know this thought is horrid, but it's been floating around in my head for going on ten years.]

Sorry about the rant, hope you can still be my friend. Good luck with Dad....You are the best therapy ever for him.

Anne

TO: Tony Nelson
FROM: Anne Howard
CC: Georgeanna Robards
RE: My dad

I am forwarding both George's email to me and mine back to her. As you can gather from the back-and-forth between us, Dad is back at it again, but at least he has gotten off the broken record about your president. LOL. Unfortunately, his newest obsession is for the Banks case, not that I blame him. Those three guys have so much grunge coming off of them that their ooze would slip off and build a pathway behind them; anyone behind them would slip and break their neck....You get the *pitcher*, as they say here in the Lone Star State.

[I hate to keep coming back to and using you like a crutch, but you have always been such a true friend to both my dad and me. Just for the record, I have zero opposition to having Banks, Williams, and Buhl rubbed out (isn't that the Cosa Nostra expression?). An even more frightening thought, after watching my dad agonize for some years over this case, is I am almost open to urging Dad to go through with it, the only drawback being that the cops apprehend him for the deed, make him do the perp walk, and then watch him go through an even more profile trial than the one where he represented the scumbags. But if he could pull it off without the mortification of an arrest and conviction, I say go for it!

Any thoughts, Tony?]

TO: Anne Howard
FROM: Georgeanna Robards
CC: Tony Nelson
RE: Your dad
[Anne, I have been a law-abiding citizen my whole life; although, some of my BDSM beatings of bad little boys might almost qualify as crimes. Don't know if your dad ever filled you in on that wild 'n' crazy phase of my life; if not, I'll tell you about it some other time.

Anything that will calm Preston down and get him off this ongoing preoccupation works for me. So, you go gal! I'm giving this idea considerable thought.

Your possibly-now-budding-and-abetting criminal,

[George

TO: Anne Howard, Georgeanna Robards
FROM: Tony Nelson
RE: Your dad

All right, you frisky little gals. You two have been inhaling way too much ganja this week! Take a deep breath and think about what you're proposing—aiding and abetting Preston in the murder of three human beings. Despicable as they might be, once you go down this road and start planning something this heinous, you're getting into murky, dangerous waters.

Every time I think about Banks, Williams, and Buhl, I get vomitus to the point that the feeling can only subside after I think happy thoughts, like maybe Anne's president being impeached...back at ya, Anne! I have no doubt that Preston has homicide on his mind; he has worn me out over that case, even though it's been over almost ten years.

I'm not saying one way or the other whether I'm in on this deal, but I know almost 100% that Preston will likely carry out this ill-advised plan. He hasn't been able to get his mind off the case from the get-go. And if you think about going down this path as well, there are a number of considerations, the first of which is all future emails *must* be encrypted. You will need a program called 256 bit AES encryption.

When (and not if) the law breathes down your neck, you also can't have this current stream of emails discovered. You will need to totally erase them, which is a little trickier. I would suggest that the three of us meet for lunch sometime *very soon*; I will show you how to install the encryption program and also how to totally delete this series of emails.

Only the beginning of any plan. Preston will have to figure out a way to get the Three Amigos together in a way that doesn't appear suspicious. As follows, there are other concerns: Preston has to get the hell out of the country right afterward, somehow bamboozle the world into believing he is dead, acquire a fake passport, move his money out of the country under an alias and into an offshore bank (e.g. the Caymans), unload his condo, and locate a suitable country to live in, preferably with no extradition treaty with this country

A bunch of countries in the Middle East and Africa, China, Russia are included. They definitely suck, but one country worth looking at is Samoa— good weather, exclusive of tsunamis, out of the way, and they're big into tattoos. Just think of Preston with enormous, colored shoulder tats! Plus it's the home of the Throwin' Samoan, Jack Thompson....Goggle that one, ladies.

Although from what I just read from George, she won't even have to Google the Throwin' Samoan. If she can pull Jose Valdivielso out of the hat, she sure as hell knows about Jack T. Anne, on the other hand, the woman who thought baseball was too dreary and missed the Kenny Rogers perfect game...well, you might have to check it out. LOL

These ideas are just the tip of the iceberg. I will think about other obstacles that might come up.

The crazy-to-get-involved-in-any-way Tony.]

-42-
PH'S JOURNAL DECEMBER 17, 2017

Going to my first AA meeting today. "Hello, my name is Preston, and I'm a fucked-up mother fucker." How's that for an introduction to a bunch of lushes?

Actually, I'm nervous as a Christian Scientist with a severed artery going to this convention of dipsomaniacs. How will they treat me? Do they give shit about me? How do I find my sponsor? Will he be some beak-nosed, curly-haired Jewish guy who talks like he just got off the plane from Brooklyn? And his mother is so proud because he's a lawyer or a doctor?

Don't get me wrong. Why, like my old high school buddy, some of my best friends are Jewish. I was hanging out in South Beach a couple of years ago and wrote to my old Semite buddy, telling him that the only people I saw walking around were either gay or Jewish. He wrote back: "Are the gays Jewish, or are the Jews gay?" Didn't quite know how to respond to that query.

I'm getting way too comfortable fitting into George's place. Her entire condo has been decked out in Oriental furnishings. There are porcelain vases, a teakwood dining room table, a floral room divider between the dining and living room, an ecru Buddha statute sitting beside the Olevia TV (*not* made by the Chinamen!), and an antique Oriental cabinet. I keep walking around the house saying "Ah, so" much to George's sham annoyance, and then I'd go into my "Me so horny....Me love you long time" routine. One time she reparteed, "You keep that bullshit one more time, the pro sashaying down the Saigon street, her likely bare ass almost on total display underneath the super-duper mini skirt, you'll be exiled from the bedroom for a week. The deck boards are pretty hard to sleep on." Wasn't sure if she meant it, so why push my luck?

We walk around her house, touching, smooching, pinching each other's butts, and so on. It's almost too comfortable, almost frightening how we have settled into such an easygoing routine. I haven't felt this kind of contentment in years…in fact, maybe never.

Will this mutual attraction fade out after a bit, like it does with so many partners whether husband and wife, or like us, co-habitors, back to the way it was with Donna—indifference, resentment? Hopefully, this sensation of bliss will continue, and my affection for George will be like Johnny and June once he overcame his drug addiction. Jesus, this sentimentality sounds corny, I know, when re-reading it, but it's what I truly feel.

George has two Quaker parrots, a male named Percy with feathers of various hues of blue, and Zsa Zsa, a female with green plumage. Percy is quite the voluble chap. "Hello." "What's up?" "I'm hungry." George caught me trying to teach Percy "Eat me." She just about sent me to the deck again over that one.

-43-
PH'S JOURNAL DECEMBER 19, 2017

You gotta be shitting me! I showed up at this dilapidated room in a South Austin strip mall for an AA meeting and sat down next to what else than a beak-nosed, brown-eyed, curly-haired guy who introduced himself to me as Siggy…as in Sigmund? Give him a guitar and a cigar and he would be the spitting image of Kinky Friedman. And he spoke like a fellow who spent a lifetime rooting for the Bronx Bombers and just drove in from Crown Heights. I could easily picture him as an Orthodox Jew wearing a Yakama and sporting payos.

Trying to initiate a little gabfest, I asked him if by any chance he was a proctologist. "I've always wanted to find out what it's like to be a doctor who looks up people's asses all day. You ever heard the one about how you know your proctologist is gay? When you feel both of his hands on your shoulders during the exam. Har, Har!"

"Close, but no cigar," he answered. "I'm an orthopedic surgeon."

"Your mother must be so proud," I remarked.

"Speaking of lame Jew jokes, I'm out of procto anecdotes," he said, "but you ever heard the one about the rabbi, the Hindu priest, and the politician?"

As he continued, I wondered why I had opened up this can of worms.

"A rabbi, a Hindu priest, and a politician went hiking. Night fell, and they were exhausted. The hotel on the map was nowhere to be seen. They knocked on the door of a farm and asked if they could spend the night. The farmer said, 'Of course, but I only have a small room with two beds. One of you will have to sleep in the barn.' The Hindu priest said, 'I need no material comforts. I will gladly take the barn.' The rabbi and the politician were settling in when they heard a knock on the door. They opened it to find the Hindu priest standing there. 'So sorry, my friends, but there is a cow in the barn, and I cannot sleep beside such a holy animal.' The rabbi said, 'No problem, my brother. I'll take the barn.' The Hindu priest and the politician were settling in when they heard a knock on the door. They opened it to find the rabbi standing there. 'So sorry, my friends, but there's a pig in the barn, and I can't sleep beside such a filthy animal.' The politician said, 'Okay, let it be remembered that I sacrificed my comfort for the greater good.' The rabbi and the Hindu priest were settling in when they heard a knock on the door. They opened it to find the pig and the cow standing there."

Okay, not bad. I politely chuckled just as the meeting began. I scanned the nineteen people sitting around in a haphazard circle and saw men and women just like me, at least some of them dripping with fear about the possibility of relapse and going down the rabbit hole toward another bout of imbibing and then having to confess their weakness in front of this crowd. How degrading.

As individuals stood up in the circle and said, "Hello, I'm Bob (or Betsy, Wayne, and so on). I'm an alcoholic and have been sober for a year (or two years or months)." Several of them commented that even though sober, it was still a daily struggle, and they had to take it one day at a time.

Siggy leaned in toward me and whispered, "This is your first meeting, Preston, so don't feel like you have to stand up and say anything." What a relief! I felt like a sick patient who had just been told by his doctor that his cancer scare had just been commuted; all he had was a benign cyst in his kidney.

The meeting lasted for about an hour, and the lady who seemed to act as moderator notified us that the meeting two days from now would be open to friends or family and that our own Siggy, who has been sober for more than three years, would speak about the travails of staying free of booze, including what it is like being an alcoholic, the moment of decision to change, and how it feels to stay off alcohol. Who knew that my neighbor was famous for his sobriety? I might bring George along for this presentation by the Jewish ortho sawbones.

As I walked to my car, Siggy walked over and offered to meet me at a nearby Denny's for some coffee. "How 'bout a bar?" I asked mockingly. "A beer sure would be tasty right now." Siggy gave me two thumbs down on that proposal, and off we went to Denny's.

Now, I thought Dan Ruggiero was one wacky son'bitch, but Siggy was not too far behind. As we sat there drinking insipid Denny's coffee—definitely not brewed and served by a Starbucks barista—Siggy related two over-the-top stories from the previous weekend.

He has a pound-bought mongrel that roams around the backyard and takes a particular interest in a duck that waddles around behind a fence in the house abutting Siggy's in the rear. While Siggy climbed a ladder to pull leaves out of the gutter, the dog somehow scrunched under the back fence, retrieved the duck, and pulled the by-now-lifeless quack-quaker back to Siggy's side.

Not certain how to break the news to his backdoor neighbor, he simply put the duck that had bought the farm into a paper sack, laid it by the back fence, and mounted the ladder again to continue his leaf-uncluttering job. A few minutes later, his neighbor, an elderly fellow in his mid-eighties, said in a quavering voice, "Do you know where my duck is?" Siggy looked down from the top of the ladder, pointed toward the sack, and replied, "Yeah, I found the duck. He's in the sack right next to you."

Then Siggy tells me about his visit to the emergency room that same day. "I had a pain in my stomach that I worried might be appendicitis, so when I walked in and spoke to the admitting nurse, I said in a voice like a carnival barker, 'Heaven's sake, this Cialis should have worn off after eight hours, but my ten-inch cock still has a full erection! Someone get over here and help me right away!' Suddenly, five women nurses scurried over toward me, I am certain more to check out my alleged ten-inch erection than to relieve my as-it-turned-out unengorged dick."

"So, what about your stomach?" I asked.

"After waiting around for several hours, just like the other hoi polloi, the attending a-hole resident ordered some x-rays. Turned out that I've got gallstones and have to see a gastroenterologist."

"Don't doctors go to the head of the line at the ER?" I inquired.

"Usually, but this butthole had a corncob up his anus, and he wanted to show off his bleeding heart for the common man. I guess my gallstones were karma for the dead duck. By the way, my last name is Sugarman...Siggy the Sugar Man."

"I definitely won't forget that name. I knew a lady by the name of Sugarman back in the day—quite a delicious woman with a very warm mouth that soothed my cock quite efficiently. But hey, I thought we're supposed to keep our last names anonymous in AA," I pointed out.

"Oh, fuck anonymity. I've never offered to sponsor an AA member, but we've hit it off right away, plus I know who you are."

"How so? I asked.

"Recognized you right off the bat when you walked into the meeting from your pictures in the paper some years ago...the guy with the Jimmy Durante nose who represented those three scumbag cops. Plus, I worked with Dr. Chaudhry on the Jewish-Muslim-Christian Committee to improve religious understanding in Austin. She told me about the smartass who pulled the old stick-it-up-my-ass routine."

"I thought patient-doctor relationships are privileged," I mentioned.

"Some information is just too delightful to keep sacrosanct," he replied. "So, are you married, your wife being the persevering little lady who put up with your shit for only so long?"

"No, my wife, Donna, kicked my ass out the door, and rightfully so. Fortunately, my cohabitating girlfriend, George—she was one of the people at my intervention—has stood by me and made me want to be a better person than I've been. Right now, I'm struggling with the fact that as an atheist, I haven't latched on to a higher power yet," I replied.

"Being a somewhat lapsed Jew, the non-divine Jesus has never played a part in my equation, even when I adhered to the faith," Siggy said. "Higher power to me is the universe. It's a mystical place, full of wonder and powerful forces beyond our understanding. So far, it's worked out well for me.

"Just figure out some *thing* that you can hold onto and believe in, Preston. It can be nature, your love of someone like George—what kind of fucking name is *George* anyhow?—or it can even be an AA group, or like we say, GOD: Group of Drunks! By and by, I would look forward to meeting George; I am sure she is your better half times four."

When I walked into George's condo, she stood by the door wearing a sheer peach negligee which left absolutely nothing to the imagination. "Quite nice," I observed.

"So where have you been, Preston," she commented with no recrimination in her voice. "The AA meeting surely didn't last so long."

"I've been hanging out in a dive bar, throwin' back a bunch of Millers, and talking it up with a couple of trailer park Jezebels," I replied.

"Try again, dunderhead," George said, her doe-eyes looking up tenderly at me, her mouth showing an ever-so-slight smile.

"Darling, it's only my first meeting, and I've already met my sponsor. I had coffee with him after

AA. Great day! Now whatta ya say let's take a rumble in the jungle back in your bedroom."

George stepped toward me, planted a loving kiss on my lips, and said, "I thought you'd never ask. And by the way, Ali versus Foreman, Zaire, 1974, Rumble in the Jungle."

How can a guy luck into such a babe-a-licious woman after all my fuck-ups?

-44-
PH'S JOURNAL DECEMBER 22, 2017

George came along for the next tipplerfest AA meeting. She shed her normal boisterous self, for once keeping her mouth shut and listening to the twenty-plus men and women stand up to proclaim their insobriety, and then my turn came around. "My name is Preston," I stood up and began. "I am an alcoholic and have been sober now for a month and almost three weeks. I thank my higher power that I have been able to get through another day of sobriety and will work on abstinence tomorrow as well. I recognize that every day is a new challenge, and I will face it with all the determination I can muster." It took me some time of intense concentration before the meeting to memorize those few lines.

When I sat down, George placed both of her hands over my right one, squeezed it, and whispered, "I'm so proud of you." Her praise warmed the cockles of my heart (oh God, that's as cheeseball as it gets). I do, though, have to give myself a little pat on the back.

After go-around-the-rosie, Siggy stood up, cleared his throat, and off he went. "Holiday greetings everyone! It's such a pleasure to speak to all of you tonight. I know how painful your addiction can be because I have been there and done that, many times over. For many years, I was what is called a functioning alcoholic. I had a thriving business—a bone cutter—and could get through each day hiding my secret. But my wife, Golda, knew the truth, and being the outspoken person that she was, and is, she kept telling me that the booze would be my downfall if I didn't stop." I felt a nudge in my ribs from George's elbow. I already got the picture, lady; don't rub it in.

"I would get off the sauce for a while," Siggy continued, "but the Adversary—the name for Satan in my faith—would whisper quietly in my ear, and back I'd go to drinking, only more the next time, and even more the next time. This revolving door of alcoholism made every new bout worse, to the point I would hang out in bars until closing time, too drunk to even drive home, so I'd sleep off the bender in my car, outside in the parking lot. It became so bad that for more than a month, I wouldn't even go into the office. How could I operate on someone in this condition? Having been a surgeon, this fall into the depths of insobriety was the knell of doom.

"So after one of these binges, I came home around late morning, and Golda sat in the living room waiting for me. I can still remember what she said like it was yesterday: 'Sigmund'—she always called me by my full name when she really wanted my attention—'the time has come for you to make a choice. I love you dearly, but the alcohol is ruining your life. You either give it up for my sake, the sake of your children, and for yourself, or I am outta here. Our marriage will be poof, your career will be finished, and you will be a pathetic hobo like all those panhandling bums who hang around downtown Austin.' And with that, Golda stood up and walked out of the room, her head high and body erect. And me...I crumbled down to the floor and blubbered, confused, lost, and wanting to leave this earth."

As Siggy stopped for a moment to sip some water from a plastic bottle, I heard a number of people sobbing. George began sniffling and pulled a Kleenex out of her purse to wipe her eyes and blow her nose.

"That was the bottom of the well for me," Siggy said, "a little more than three years ago. So I dug deep into my heart, made the decision to do the right thing, and went off to one of the Betty Ford clinics for two long months. I came home a different man and have stayed off the sauce since then. Sometimes, I ask Golda if I am a different man; she tells me I'm the same man she has always loved, only a sober one rather than a drunk." Siggy stopped for a moment and then finished up. "Just so you know, folks, I fight the temptation to drink every day, just like you. But if I can do it, every one of you can too."

When Siggy sat back in his chair, the room was silent as parishioners silently praying at a Baptist church on Sunday. As people left, many came up and hugged him tightly, obviously moved by his words. As George and I turned to leave, Siggy put his arm around me and said, "I found a Starbucks a few blocks from here...much of an improvement over Denny's. Whatta you say we head over there for some heavy doses of caffeine, so I can get to know your quite nice lookin' lady?"

"Oh, I like you already," George chimed in with a flirty voice.

"I can't take her anywhere," I remarked. "She's a wild thang but has done right by me. George was out looking for stray pathetic puppies one day, latched onto me, and won't let go."

"I'm the best thing that ever happened to you, Preston Howard," George stated. And turning to Siggy, she said, "Starbucks works for me. A helluva lot better than the Denny's you two went to last time." And off we went.

As the three of us sat experiencing one person, one cup, and one neighborhood at a time, I noticed another of George's positive qualities. She can fit into any setting, comfortably making conversation when warranted but also listening to what others say without barging in with absurd remarks. The comfortable talk went back and forth, three ways, but, of course, with George busting my balls every now and then, I suppose to keep me off balance as she so often does. "Siggy, did you know that Preston is a renowned novelist; twenty-two people bought his last book, so we are taking a round-the-world tour on the royalties." I gave her a quick middle finger, almost so quick as to be undetected (I hoped) but silently thanked my stars that she had supported me so I'm not a hoboing panhandler like the people in downtown Austin who Siggy mentioned earlier at the AA meeting.

"How did you two meet? Siggy asked.

"Oh, let me handle this one," I offered. George gave me what I have learned to be The Look when she knows I am about to throw out some serious bull hockey.

I stopped in at the Truman Library in Independence last year," I began. "I was standing right next to the A-bomb display, where many statements excoriated Truman for his decision to drop the bombs on Hiroshima and Nagasaki. I was so engrossed that I didn't notice someone standing next to me, cheek flush against my shoulder, trying to read the display. I looked down at the face below me. George looked up into my eyes, and it was like lightening had struck above Harry's library. Only time in my life I ever experienced love at first sight."

Siggy first looked at me with skepticism and then toward George. "He is so full of shit," George said to Siggy. "The man's almost as much of a Pinocchio as our president, but at least a great more entertaining. I don't even have to pay for this amusement, which I suppose is a plus."

After a few laughs went around the table over this whopper, we got on the topic of climate change, a subject that George and I have been passionate about, and it turned out, so had Siggy. He had the same experience with Al I-was-almost-president Gore; no one got back with Siggy when he expressed interest in joining the Climate Project. Siggy and I agreed that Al gets a loud boo for his and his organization's lackluster approach to potential new members.

Siggy told me about a terrific book by a guy named Jeremy Diamond titled *Collapse*. It's about how civilizations such as the natives of the Easter Islands, the Mayans, Incas, and other Native American tribes collapsed due to environmental degradation. "If you think about the world as one civilization," Siggy remarked, "what do you think is gonna happen when the oceans continued to rise, the sky and lakes became more polluted, food and water becomes scarce, and so on? What's the point of caring out all the issues in our country and the world if we don't have a habitable earth?" He held his hands up in supplication with sorrowed eyes looking back and forth between George and me.

As we got ready to leave, George asked me, "You mentioned your higher power at the AA meeting, Preston. So what is it?"

I looked at Siggy, who winked at me. I just stood up without a word and left.

-45-
NOTE FROM ANNE HOWARD May 6, 2017

Not much news since Christmas. Dad has made a complete turnaround and been a complete teetotaler since his Tampa rehab—what he sometimes refers to as the Bastille and other times as Alcatraz. He is definitely a different man, having gone from a down-and-out drunkard to the vibrant, positive man that I remember as a child.

I told my mom about the far cry from the man she remembers toward the end of their marriage. Her only response was, "Why couldn't he have gotten his life together sooner?" Mom still has a great deal of bitterness toward him, especially knowing that he has gotten sober and found someone else to love; her experiences with the opposite sex have turned out fruitless. Every man she met has turned out to be a liar, humdrum, or a financial leech.

My husband, Barry, and I met George and Dad, along with Siggy and Golda Sugarman at the Roaring Fork for a midafternoon lunch today. I've only mentioned my husband up until now in passing...so sorry, Barry. He has a lot of my dad's qualities—compassion, quite the smartass, and brimming with the most irrelevant factoids known to man. BTW, since I see myself as a liberated woman, I kept my last name. My dad was delighted that I made this choice, but I did it for my own satisfaction, not his. Sorry, Dad.

When we all walked into the restaurant, Dad was toting along George's two Quaker parrots. The maître de acted like one of those puffed-up guys at the Court of the Two Sisters in the French Quarter who once told me as I walked in wearing Levis, "You can't have jeans here." "I didn't come here to eat jeans," I told the haughty man. Never did get service there that night.

Anyway, back to the story. The haughty maître de at the Roaring Fork said, "Animals are not permitted at our restaurant, sir...too unsanitary."

"Whatta you mean?" Dad yelled, getting the attention of just about every patron throughout the restaurant. "These are service parrots. You never heard about them?" George could see this train wreck roaring down the track and walked away, shaking her head. I, on the other hand, had to check out what fantastical tale Dad was about to weave.

"There was a piece on *60 Minutes* last week about the parrots," he continued, "and how they bring equilibrium to people like me who have serious anxiety issues. I developed PTSD during the Boer War, and it's affected me ever since. Horrible thoughts enter my head sometimes about...well, like pulling out a knife when someone contradicts me...and maybe doing unmentionable things to...*him*!"

As we were seated—not by the maître de but with the parrots—George glowered at my dad. "Stoooop it, Preston. You are just the limit!"

"Whatta you gonna do?" Dad answered her. "I'm just a bundle of fun; can't help myself. And you love every minute of it, Georgie-girl."

"Why did you guys bring the parrots?" I asked them.

George advised all of us that their trip to Vancouver and then Alaska had been locked down several weeks ago. When our lunch ended, George and Dad were driving down to New Braunfels where they would turn the parrots over to George's daughter, Alexandra, while they were gone.

When the waiter asked for our drink orders, Dad said, "I want a triple Manhattan, and go heavy on the bitters." George looked up at him with a you–are–so–full-of-crap stare, and Dad recanted the order, saying "Oh wait, I just remembered I'm on the wagon. Give me an Arnold Palmer."

"Such a good boy," George said mockingly.

George has been my dad's salvation. He clearly loves and admires her and seems willing to seek her approval at all times. I haven't picked up any relapse on Dad's part, although George advises that my dad has weakened a few times, but George would take him for a long walk or make him drink down a root beer float to fill his system with sugar. I am hopeful that he will stay on the straight and narrow so he can lead a productive life. Knowing George, she will watch him like a hawk and insure his sobriety.

George and Dad are all agog about their Alaskan cruise; well, at least George is. They are flying out to Vancouver, spending several days touring the city. Dad is excited about the sunset view in the bar of the Sylvia Hotel and the farmers market at Granville Island. Then they're off on a Norwegian Cruise Line eight-day Alaskan cruise.

Dad theatrically bitched about George putting her foot down over the all-you-can-drink liquor package, asking how he could otherwise embalm himself against the mass of humanity on the cavernous ship. He did note, though, that the cruise line offers a daily AA meeting at night, just in case the Three Sirens attempt to lure him with alcohol fumes. When they return to Vancouver, they're renting a car, driving across the Canadian Rockies, and flying back to Austin from Calgary. I'm so happy for them…sounds like the trip of a lifetime.

While George explained their itinerary, Dad would several times crane his neck toward the parrots and whisper, "Percy…eat me. Perrrcy, eat me." George finally interrupted her vacation story and smacked Dad's hand. "Get a grip, Preston!" Dad simply gave her what I refer to as a love smile, where two people care for each other so much and have their own secretive way of interacting.

Siggy and Golda were an outstanding addition to the lunch. Golda reminded me a good deal of George; she watched over Siggy like a Great Pyrenees shepherding a flock of sheep. Siggy talked a great deal about the disease known as Donald Trump. There was no disagreement to his comments from anyone at the table.

After the Trump bashing, Siggy went on a roll of Jewish jokes. "Why do Jewish men like to watch porno movies backward? They like the part where the hooker gives the money back."

"Why do Jewish men have to be circumcised? Because a Jewish woman won't touch anything unless it's twenty percent off."

"What's the difference between a Catholic wife and a Jewish wife? A Catholic wife has real orgasms and fake jewelry."

"All right already. Enough, Siggy," Golda interrupted with a brash New Yowk, New Yowk, accent. "I do recall having one orgasm twenty years ago. Enough about our sex life." Everyone had a guffaw over that comment at Siggy's expense.

As we left the restaurant, there were hugs all around. I had wanted a margarita so bad during the lunch, but hanging around a bunch of Mahatma Gandhis, I forswore the booze throughout the meal.

When I got home, I began thinking about some of my fondest memories of Dad. When I was only seven, he taught me how to spell "zygophyllaceous"—some kind of flowering plants—a point of considerable pride to me. When he asked me, I could spell it on cue, apparently to impress any guests at the house.

I will never forget my first date with a guy whose name is forgettable. When he walked in, Dad ordered him to sit down, asked him what time *exactly* we would return home, and then threateningly said, "You're not planning to drink are you, young man?" The kid had a quavering lip and replied in a shaky voice, "Oh, absolutely not, sir."

"Just so you know, fella," my Dad continued, "if I find out you or my daughter were drinkin', I'm gonna whip your ass." My date couldn't get out of the house fast enough, and I wilted like a dead flower; although, I realize now that Dad was just being protective of me.

Later on, I had a somewhat regular boyfriend who Dad referred to as Charley Manson (not an inexact description of the boy—Mohawk haircut, tattoos on his arms and neck, studs in each earlobe and nose, and Doc Martens). Dad started to notice that every time the kid hung around the house, toilet paper would be missing. I became so paranoid about Dad's complaints over the loss of toilet paper that I began pilfering some from my high school to keep the house supplied with the wiping material. It turns out that the fellow was, in fact, a lot like Charley; he enjoyed physically pushing me around, and he hit me in the schnoz a couple of times. Thus, the end of that relationship. I never told Dad that last part of the story…he would have hunted down Charley to the ends of the earth.

-46-
PH'S JOURNAL MAY 10 THROUGH 14

We checked into a hotel overlooking Stanley Park and made reservations at a highly regarded Italian restaurant called Lupo. Vancouver is truly a world-class city—clean, ethnically diverse, and oh my, those Canadians are just so polite. I remember the hilarious movie *Canadian Bacon*, when the finagling American president and his staff were trying to figure out a reason to declare war on Canada. One not-so-brilliant aide came up with the following half-baked idea: "I don't like the way they say '*aboot*.'"

I sprung for first-class seats on the way out here. George for certain deserved the best treatment for all of the different ways she has helped me come alive again. She was so animated from the moment we took the Uber out to Bergstrom, through the terminal, and throughout the flight. She acted like a little girl taking her first trip to Disney World. Of course, when we stepped out of the Uber at the airport, George had to note gratuitously, "Gee, Preston, the Uber run has totally drained your royalties from the novel." What a smarty pants!

George walked in with a new joystick enhancer—Cialis—and as she shook the bottle of yellow-brown pills, she announced that this drug has a longer effect of eighteen hours, which she advised I will need on this trip.

"You're gonna give me the Big One, George, the greatest congestive heart failure of all time. And then, you won't have your little, lost puppy to order around anymore."

"You could take out a million dollar life insurance policy with me as beneficiary, sweetheart," she replied. "Your family and friends will think I'm a Black Widow like Theresa Russell, but at least I'll be a spider living in the lap of luxury. Whatta ya think?"

"I do think you remind me a bit of Theresa, a kinda trashy but gorgeous look, Georgie girl. Too expensive, but I will buy a cheap-ass burial policy, so you can burn me up and toss my ashes wherever."

"I'll take your back-handed complement about Theresa in a good way…I think. I thought you'd do anything for your true love," George answered with a big grin. "Speaking of ashes, assuming that you fly away from this earth before me, where *do* you want your ashes strewn?"

"I have it written in my will—either across my grandfather Buster's grave in Tazewell or in Cape Town on a path just outside of the Kirstenbosch Gardens overlooking Table Mountain. It's a serene place full of all the flora throughout the country. You, by the way, will receive the bulk of my estate; I just changed my will to reflect this intent."

George appeared thunderstruck by this remark. "You are already spoiling me rotten, Preston, and you know that I am not expecting any special consideration." She stopped for a moment, and then with a smug grin said, "But since you seem to be in such a pampering mood, does your will provide that the South Africa trip will include first class plane accommodations? I will, of course, lament the loss of your companionship, at least for a week or two, but I would so much rather enjoy an interminable flight

Justice Delayed is Justice Denied

where I could sleep comfortably." That George...always the wisenheimer.

The next three days were, as the expression goes, a total blast. We spent the first day exploring the cavernous Stanley Park, a paradise of greenery and well-planned walking trails. We met a young, engaging couple by the name of Larry and Bridgette Conway on the trail; they had been out of Texas School Law for a few years and both worked for the same Austin malpractice firm. They didn't appear to know any of the sordid details about the Banks case or at least didn't let on that they knew.

Larry and Bridgette told us they were hiking the Stawamus Chief the following day. They had rented a car and offered to bring us along. Not exactly one of my more intelligent decisions to agree. The three plus miles up and down turned out to be challenging for us old folks; I could've pulled it off with no sweat maybe ten years ago, but it about did me in. George, being the feisty lady, plowed through it, and we did feel exhilaration at the majestic view on the top. But when we got back to the hotel five hours later, we agreed to order room service and stay in for the night. George decreed no sex that night; I wasn't sure whether she was cushioning me from further exertion or was completely tuckered out herself.

We spent the better part of the last day traipsing around Granville Island. The farmer's market was worth the visit—various ethnic foods, produce, and handcrafted products. When we left the market to find a restaurant, I—of course it would be me—spied an establishment that made its own gin and served any kind of martini you could ask for. "George, my loving and wonderful Princess, let's stop here and see how their dirty martinis stack up to the many others I've tried." George crossed her arms, tapped her right foot, and raised her eyebrows. Message received loud and clear. "Ten-four," I said with an exaggerated sigh.

At the end of the day, we took a taxi out to English Bay right by the Sylvia Hotel. George sweet-talked the maître de into ushering us to the last seat by the window with a photo-worthy view over the Bay. As the sun gradually moved downward toward the western horizon, many shades of red, purple, and orange lit up the Pacific Ocean. I heard several people in the bar wowing the sunset. Now, I'm not the kinda guy who normally gets his socks knocked off by these kinds of moments, but it was gorgeous, a moment where George and I held hands and brushed our lips together several times as we viewed this dazzling scene.

As I have gone to bed since arriving in Vancouver, and in that place between awake and sleep, I have been frequently reliving the past few months, not necessarily the sex, not the constant buzz about George's attention and love, but instead, the question about her as my higher power. I desperately want to please her and keep off the firewater, and she has been both a tower of strength and, I suppose, a crutch. But in the end, I have come to the realization that it is only up to *me*. If I don't gut it out and stay off the booze, then it falls squarely on my shoulders. Scary thought.

Another phenomenon about my slumber. When I reach the REM state of sleep, recurring dreams invade my subconscious where a conflict occurs between Cheap Trick's "Dream Police" and an agent of wickedness, the Beelzebub of Bourbon. This collision between good and evil goes on for some time in the dream and is never resolved much to my awakened despair. I haven't passed this on to George just yet; it would be something else she'd have to worry about.

The Three Amigos continue to trouble me like a tiny prickle in my head that I can't itch. The injustice perpetrated against Jazmine and her siblings weighs down on me as if a tiny voice speaks to me frequently now, saying "Right this terrible wrong! Avenge their deaths!"

Tomorrow's the day. Off on the Alaskan trip—numbing days of too many loud kids, annoying cruisers who think they've gone to embarking heaven, and too many watery miles between ports. Maybe I can get on board, plant myself in our room, and go into a fetal position for eight days.

-47-
PH'S JOURNAL MAY 14-22, 2017

Off we go into the wild, blue yonder though the water is not blue, but rather a kind of unclear, dishwater gray. Wanting to make the trip as memorable as possible for George, I purchased a stateroom, which provided a sizable living room, separate bedroom, and spacious balcony—also mentioned among the ritzy class as a veranda. Nothing is too good for my lady friend. I'm looking forward to smoking the exorbitant Cubans I bought in Vancouver, acting like the King of My Realm Above the Sea.

The steward for our area is from Indonesia, a dark-skinned, small fellow who was a little too loquacious and obsequious. I suppose he was pitching for a premium tip, which he would receive irrespective of this over-the-top behavior. I thought about telling him to take it down a notch.

Just to throw him off his game a bit, I asked, "Do we have to worry about the norovirus on this cruise." "The what?" he asked. He's either a new employee or the cruise line doesn't train the staff on the types of various shipboard infections (influenza, Legionnaires disease, and so on). George gave me the timeout hands sign, so I shut the hell up.

The seven o'clock dinner seating turned out to be the kind of nightmare that I had anticipated on this trip. Our table of eight people was amenable enough. There were couples from Saskatchewan, Chicago, and Little Rock. The food was five-star—well maybe four—but our waiter kept serving unlimited bottles of red wine, and my mouth kept salivating. George leaned over and murmured, "Think happy thoughts about you kneeling between my legs later tonight." "Is your pussy a better thought than that wine?" I whispered. "It better be," George answered with a slight titter.

But the wine deprivation was not the nightmare. A group of eight Indian kids sat right next to our table. They were the kind of Indians from Bangalore, not the Native American kind. Just so you know, some of my best friends are Native American....Wait, I've only known one such person, a guy from South Texas who was a Lipan Apache, and he was a dickwad.

Back to the Bangalorians. Between the ages of around six to twelve, they acted like crazed chimpanzees, screaming, jumping up and down on the table, and creating more chaos than a TNT implosion of an old hotel in Vegas.

I walked over to the children, who were acting like feral dogs, and in a voice one teeny octave lower than a scream, said, "Shut up! You're annoying all the diners around you." They responded with a look of bafflement, as in "who is this loon, and what right does he have to admonish us."

After about two minutes, the bedlam started up again, so rather than take another shot at calming down the kiddies, I went to the maître de and complained. He clearly was not eager to get involved in what he saw as a spat between neighbors, but I insisted. He located the parents at another table close by (from Mumbai?) and asked them to get their children under control.

A few minutes later, an Indian (from New Delhi?) approached our table and indignantly said to our group, "What right do you have to interfere with what our children do?" Since none of the other folks at our table got up to the plate (oh jeez, groan), I stood up, and after appraising that the guy was of slight build—even though I am seventy-four, I'm still in good shape—I walked up to him and calmly said, "Dude, you either shut those children up so they're under control for the rest of the trip, or they be gone." "And if I don't?" he responded with menace." I moved right into his space and answered, "Or you and I are going outside for a serious conversation." I pointed toward the doorway at the other end of the room. He considered whether to take up my dare and decided to have a talk with the little ape-kids; they remained exceedingly quiet for the rest of the meal, and in fact, for the remainder of the cruise.

As the fellow walked back to his table, I said in his direction, "I'll pray for you tonight. I remember a few Hindu Vadas from my time working in the Peace Corp back in the day. The dude turned back and glared at me as if he might reconsider my threat and take me up on it, but he thought better of it. Let's hear it for the manly-man….That would be me!

When I sat back down, everyone at the table except George clapped. 'What a show off," George snarkily remarked. "You're lucky he didn't go outside with you. I would have been totally pissed if you had gone to infirmary and ruined this trip." Gee, and I had so wanted to impress her.

The lady sitting in the chair next to me asked, "Were you really in the Peace Corps?"

"Of course," I rejoined. "Right after I returned from Nam and overcame all my injuries from jumping on a grenade, saving the lives of thirteen grunts, and winning the Gold Star. I worked on building homes for the poor in Nepal, what is now called Habitat for Humanity—Jimmy Carter got the idea from me. I hung out a whole lot with the Dalai Lama—truly righteous dude—but he didn't play bridge worth a shit." I didn't let her in on the only lie in the whole story (as if!); she didn't seem too concerned with the detail that the Lama's prayers are to Buddha, not ones for Hindus.

"Amaaaazing," the lady said. "You have led such a remarkable life...so filled with great deeds. Your wife," she nodded toward George, "must be so proud of you."

George placed her right hand over her forehead, looked down at the table, and covered her left hand over her mouth to suppress the laughter that was about to screw up my prank.

"Oh, you just can't imagine how much my lovely wife has supported me over the years, especially that time I climbed Mount Everest."

George couldn't hold back what would have been an explosion of laughter, so she excused herself from the table. At least she was gettin' into the swing of things

For the next few days, between marathon sex in the stateroom (make that all over the stateroom, I might observe), we wandered around the ship—not a boat, I am reminded by several passengers—losing money in the casino, watching a show, and dancing cheek-to-cheek and pelvis-to-pelvis (is that pelvises or pelvisi?).

Speaking of sex...finally, once again one of my favorite subjects, George told me last night to sit on the edge of the bed with my legs hanging down almost on the floor. She then sat on top of my trunk with her back to me, and thrust back and forth on my Cialis-inflated thingy-dingy. After George came, she began weeping.

"I didn't know my cock was so large it hurt you," I said mockingly to her back.

"Shut up. You got me all emotional," George whispered hoarsely.

"You've definitely been around, George. That's one position I've never been in before."

"Unlike you, dipshit," George was definitely now getting her wind back, "I went for quality rather than quantity."

I was about to say that the point of my sexual encounters back in the day was to put notches on my belt but thought better of it. Time to change the subject to close a reminder of my past, multiple indiscretions. "So, George, I have a question. I know that the rose is not yet off the bloom for us, but what do you ever think happens if it does? Conrad once told me that a guy could get turned on by a woman who used whips and chains, kind of like you did, but he would eventually get as bored with it as...I used finger air quotes when I said "regular sex."

"Conrad has a limited interpretation about sex," George replied. "If and when we get indifferent about our bedroom fun, we'll discuss it. Don't overthink shit, Preston; just enjoy these wonderful moments we're having."

"So if we get bored," I asked, "can we become swingers?"

"You're dreaming! You can be such a nudnik. That's a no-no in my book."

For a gal who used to be the queen of BDSM and has participated in sexual positions that I've never even thought about, she has become quite the square in her senior years. Maybe a good thing though.

***

I've never been easily awe-struck other than the view on the Path of the Gods looking back north along the Amalfi Coast and the sight standing on Camp Muir with Mount Rainier looming atop of me. But on the third day—finally something other than seawater—the Hubbard Glacier moved up close to number one on the hit parade.

As the ship slowed and some anonymous voice announced the glacier coming into view shortly—the broadcaster wasn't even close to the deep, southern Red Barber drawling voice—some calving floated by. George and I moved to the balcony, took a seat in the plush chairs, and I lit up a ridiculously overpriced Cuban. I have never tasted one that outpaced a well-made Dominican or Nicaraguan. It's just the thought of trying forbidden fruit.

Back to the point. The immense glacier slowly moved into view, ultimately turning into a massive, white and blue tinged panorama across our entire sight. It turns out that Hubbard was six miles wide, its massive width blowing George and me away.

But there's more. Every now and then, a colossal block of ice would splinter off, causing an explosion like the sound of dynamite, and fall into what is called Disenchantment Bay with more than a regular splash—maybe like the Stay Puff Marshmallow Man in *Ghostbuster* doing a cannonball into the water. George and I kept oohing and aahing as every block fell off and plunged into the water.

But the story doesn't even end there. The couple in the suite next to us had similar reactions, crying out at the eruptions from the glacier. The woman then exclaimed, "Wow, this is almost like nature!" George suppressed a giggle, but I couldn't let this comment go without a retort that could be heard next door. "I kinda thought this was nature, but maybe I'm wrong." George then laughed heartily. No answer though from our neighbor.

We then sat there in silence, holding hands and continuing to watch the show. George looked over toward me and said, "Preston, I love you so much." Finally the L-word; I knew it would come sooner or later. I feebly replied, "Me too." "That's a pretty pathetic answer, big boy," George rejoined. So I stood up, kneeled on one leg, took her right hand, and said, "I love you with all my heart, George. Is that better?" "Much improved," she answered, pulling up my hand and kissing it.

"You don't have to get nervous about the M-word," she continued. "The retiree health insurance I have from my firm in California is way too lavish, and I'd lose it if we marry. We'll just have to live out our remaining days in sin. Any of our Baptist friends might disapprove—do we have any Baptist friends?—but, who cares. Although a commitment ceremony would definitely work for me. Think about it."

I'm athinkin'.

***

Our next stops were Juneau and Ketchikan. The capital had to be the most dismal one in the country. With around 30,000 plus citizens and no roads leading in or out of the city, it's got to be a drag living or legislating here.

Of course, Sarah Palin oversaw the state here as governor before she ran as vice-president along with her running mate, John McCain. That's the lady who proclaimed her foreign policy experience because she saw Russia from her window. The lady who once said she gained her knowledge from reading everything; who reads everything? What were John McCain and Steve Schmidt thinking when they pulled this totally useless woman out of the hat as the one-heartbeat-away-from-the president? I'll give her due though; she was one foxy-looking lady.

George and I ventured out for a while around the city…what there was of it. The highlight of this leg of the trip was watching a Japanese man walk up to a dumpster and start taking photographs of it. I know the stereotype that these…Nips—can you believe they were called Nips and Japs during WWII?—are fond of taking pictures. But a dumpster?

George and I mulled this one over for a while. I finally reckoned the only answer was the gentleman worked for a management waste company back in Tokyo, and by taking photographs of the dumpster, he could write off the whole trip. Smart for a what? A Nipponese?

***

Ketchikan turned out to be one of those traveler money-sucking places, like Gatlinburg, Beale Street in Memphis, and any timeshare. We did enjoy the king crab at a restaurant just off the pier, but like the Cubans, was way over-priced like a two-star Michelin. Whenever we passed an inviting bar that tingled my taste buds, George would lead me forward to some shop carrying all kinds of Alaskan trinkets. Borrrring!

But things livened up shortly. As I lived and breathed, there was Jimmy Buhl, walking down the street directly toward me, playing on and off with his pecker! Serendipity.

Jimmy had glimpsed me and moved briskly right up beside me. A black lady who looked like a low-rent whore—tight, short, leopard-skin dress, blond wig, caked-on makeup, and bright red lipstick— followed shortly behind Jimmy.

Jimmy still had the look of a skinny, weasely scoundrel, his eyes moving furtively around, his hair thinning quickly to baldness. Who was the woman? His date? Companion for the night? Girlfriend? Wife (surely not)? Whoever she was, the woman pushed up closely to Jimmy and placed one arm into his. Jimmy, of course, couldn't keep his hands off of his dick, on and off, pushing and pulling. Surely, someone had let him know at some point over his miserable, corrupt life to stop this annoying

274

compulsion. Maybe the woman who was now introduced by Jimmy as Charmaine had clued him in.

"You on the same cruise as me?" Jimmy asked.

"Looks like it, Jimmy." Please, I thought, for God's sake, don't invite me for a drink.

"We need to get together for a drink and catch up on stuff," Jimmy said. "I've got a terrific stateroom with an outstanding view."

Room with a view…how nice. "Sounds good," I responded with little enthusiasm.

"Who's the fine lookin' lady," Jimmy said, pointing at George.

"Her name is George, short for Georgeanna. We are…" I searched for the right word.

"We are soulmates," George interjected, "together for life." She hit the nail on the head. I might have to spend considerable time between her legs later on, as an extra award for such an uplifting thought, or is that called a downlifting thought.

Jimmy extended his right hand toward George; she took a few steps backward and acted like she was looking for something down the street. Awkward, and the only time I had ever seen her act rudely.

Charmaine had not said even one word at this point, like a total ignoramus; she appeared to be nothing more than an ornament for Jimmy to parade around.

Jimmy glanced toward the woman and said, "Charmaine and I just got married in Vegas, and on a whim, decided to take this cruise."

Ah, true love right in front of me. We agreed to meet in his stateroom around five. No way was I inviting this creep into my room.

***

George and I sat on the veranda, lightly touching hands with our fingers and watching the ship embark from the pier. I'm really getting into the lingo—*veranda, embark, pier*. Pretty soon I'll become a perpetual cruiser, traveling around the world on six-thousand person ships. If George suggests an encore, I might be lockin,' loadin,' and firin' that Ruger right into my brain. At least George will be amply supported for the rest of her life.

As we sat drinking our delicious Diet Cokes (not! no rum, no lime, no Cuba Libre), we had our first close-to-an-argument. "That guy is such a creep, Preston. There's no way I could shake his hand. I'd be wiping slime off me for a week." She stopped to gather her thoughts and then said, "I apologize for my lack of decorum and embarrassing you in front of the man. But pleeeze, Preston, don't insist that I go with you to his stateroom. I might throw up right there on his carpet."

Trying to avoid a full-out quarrel, I tried reason. "I'd really like you to come along, so you can get a full measure of Jimmy Buhl. You know what I'm considering, and your opinion, and maybe our life together, might hinge on your judgment of my decision. Plus, you'll get the pleasure of Mrs. Charmaine's company. And thank you in advance for *never* putting together an outfit like what that woman was wearing."

George withdrew her hand, clammed up, and folded her arms together tightly against her chest like a teenage girl whose parents had just told her she couldn't hang out with her BFF and instead had to accompany them to the country club for dinner. But in the end, she went with me. Geez, I so love that woman.

***

Although George did play along to an extent, she still clung to herself as if she was harboring some secret underneath her chest. Since George had no intention of joining the conversation, and Charmaine glued herself to HDTV, apparently searching for the perfect home, the discussion would be between Jimmy and me. Jimmy poured three fingers, maybe four, of Jack Daniel's Single Barrel Select; my mouth began salivating something terrible.

George finally climbed out of her funk and began rubbing my back as if that would assuage my desire to reach down, grab the Jack Daniel's bottle, and swig the brown liquid down. One day at a time, Preston, one day at a time.

"So is this cruise your first one," I asked Jimmy.

"Nah, since I started hookin' up with Charmaine, we've done two European Viking tours, an Australian-New Zealand cruise, and multiple Caribbean ones. I enjoy the first-class luxury, the liquor packages—all you can drink, Preston!—and checking out so many places I've never seen before." The stab of alcoholism intruded again; George continued to rub, rub, rub.

"Don't all these annoying people bother the hell out of you, Jimmy?"

"No way. I just get hammered in the morning, and stay buzzed throughout the day and into the night."

Jesus, I hoped he would stop playing with himself. It's like some guy with Tourette syndrome who can't help himself, and it sent me into a paroxysm of extreme distraction.

Now to the nitty-gritty, I thought. "So Jimmy, I have some questions about our now famous...or maybe that's *infamous* case."

"Shoot," Jimmy said, as if he wanted with all his heart to spill the beans. I felt George's hand withdraw from my back, and she leaned forward intently. Charmaine must have been serious about house-hunting as she stayed glued to HDTV.

"So, first question, Jimmy. How do you pay for all these cruises on your retirement money?"

"Cause you're one helluva lawyer, Preston."

"Okay, second question. Where were you for about twenty minutes after the APD team swarmed all over the Wallace house?"

"Well, someone had to lug the four duffel bags of loot out to the alley behind their place, throw them in the trunk of a car, and drive it to a parking lot out on Fifth Street. I was the luggerman! It was a whole lotta runnin' around and about did me in."

"Whatever happened to Janard Coleman?" I then asked him.

"Gee, Preston, I have no idea," Jimmy answered, a sneer appearing across his mouth. "Whatever happened to the fucker, he deserved it. A real piece of nigger-shit. I am certain that one, or maybe more people, had it in for him."

I felt George twinge and quickly placed my arm around her before she jumped all over the ex-cop. I had one more question. "And Maurice Holloway?" I asked.

"Different result," Jimmy replied almost with conceit, as if he had pulled off a stupendous magic trick. "Wait just a minute," he said, walking toward his bedroom. George leaned in and started to speak, but I immediately touched my lips back and forth repeatedly as in zip it, zip it; she got the hint.

A few minutes later, Jimmy came back to the living room, holding a photograph. He held up the iconic picture of *Welcome to Fabulous Las Vegas, Nevada* toward my face. Underneath the sign, Maurice Holloway stood with a pie-eating grin, and in both hands, held a bunch of one-hundred dollar bills.

"Since he was in Vegas, I decided to look him up," Jimmy noted.

"I didn't know Maurice and you had ever connected in the first place," I remarked.

"Oh, yeah, we've become the best of friends going back almost ten years," Jimmy said. "Maurice moved out to Vegas; Charmaine and I had dinner with him just a few days ago. He's changed his name; don't remember what it is. Maurice must have figured out the odds at the tables because it looks like he has won a bunch!"

"Yeah, looks like it" was the only lame answer I could give. George stood up and with more contempt in her voice than I had ever heard before, said, "Check please," and wagged her finger at me to get off the sofa ASAP. As in, it's closin' time, and this party has come to an abrupt conclusion.

***

George followed me into our suite and slammed the door so hard that the room vibrated; two prints hanging on the wall fell onto the rug. George frantically paced like a nervous lioness worried about the dominant male killing her cubs, first up and down around the living room and then onto the veranda, Then, without ever saying a word to me, she grabbed her laptop and began typing in a frenzy, like a steno who couldn't keep up with her boss's dictation.

-48-

NOTE FROM ANNE HOWARD, E-MAILS BETWEEN GEORGE, ANNE, AND TONY MAY 21, 2017

NOTE FROM ANNE HOWARD: To my family and friends, the following exchanges have been deleted once again from this narrative for security and personal reasons. But you readers are so fortunate to get the real skinny!

TO: Anne Howard, Tony Nelson
FROM: Georgeanna Robards
RE: Jimmy Buhl

Good friends, I vowed to both Preston and myself to keep my happy fingers off of the laptop throughout this trip. It can be such a time-sucker.

The word sucker comes to mind because Preston and I just ran into that cocksucker, Jimmy Buhl, in Ketchikan. Jimmy and his so-called wife, who looks like she has just gone into retirement after years of prostituting herself on the streets, are on the same cruise as us. He is the most horrid example of a human being that I have ever met. Every time he opens his mouth and speaks, I get the creeps. We met the couple afterward in Jimmy's suite, and our conversation turned out to be quite revealing.

My hands are still shaking from our get-together as I write you this note. Tony, I am hopeful that your encryption app works on the high seas as it does in the lower forty-eight states.

Once I got past his disgusting, pud-rubbing, deviant habit and was able to concentrate on the discussion, I gleaned the following: first off, I now know for a fact that Buhl took the ill-gotten gains from the Wallace house and secreted it away, and second, he either killed Janard Coleman or knows who did.

But the big shocker was about Maurice Holloway. It turns out that Jimmy Buhl has known all along that Maurice lives in Las Vegas and is enjoying himself out there, high on the hog. Buhl showed us a photo of Holloway underneath the legendary Vegas sign, the old man grinning and holding wads of cash in his hands.

I haven't spoken to Preston yet; I am just now coming down off my rage about Jimmy Buhl. But I would expect that he feels like me. No one should begrudge Maurice Holloway's windfall. He was a poor, old, black man living on the eastside, and if he chose to take the money and run, so be it. From what I have learned about the criminal case, it was a loser anyway once Sam Evans testified, although Maurice's testimony might have clouded things a bit.

But Jimmy Buhl and his cohorts, Banks and Williams...well, they warrant the fullest damnation and punishment. They have never received the retribution that they have coming. So any reservations that I might have had, and there weren't a whole lot to begin with, are now erased. If you two are in all the way, count on me to help in any way possible.

BTW, other than this hiccup—well not exactly a hiccup but more like a Vesuvius eruption—the trip has been the bee's knees. Preston has been, as always, so accommodating to my needs, and yes, if you have any question in your mind, he has completely stayed off the sauce. He has gone to an AA meeting every night of the cruise, and even though I can sense that he has the desire every now and then—make that often—to drink, he stays sober.

Of course, he can't keep his motor-mouth shut, always getting into some kind of mischief. One of his tall tales at the cruise dinner table involved fighting in Vietnam, working in Nepal with the Peace Corps, playing bridge with the Lama—picture that one!—and hiking Everest. The story was so ludicrous, but a woman sitting with us bought it hook, line, and sinker. I started to laugh so hard that I had to escape the table. I guess, though, that is part of the reason I love him so much.

He just about took on an Indian man over some wild and crazy kids, but fortunately cooler heads prevailed…sorta. More on that fiasco when we come home.

Any comments, advice, whatever? I miss both of you guys a whole lot and look forward to filling you in on our trip.

Love from the-cruising-the-Alaska-seaways,
George

TO: Georgeanna Robards, Tony Nelson
FROM: Anne Howard
RE: Jimmy Buhl

How prescient that you should write to us, George. I've always wanted to use that word in an email, and wow, there it is!

Tony and I have had several luncheon meetings where we have planned, often in sotto voce to keep any snoopers from listening in, the steps necessary to administer justice to Banks, Buhl, and Williams. After much mental excruciation on Tony's part, he has agreed to jump in full throttle and help us. As Tony explained the steps necessary to carry out our plan, I have realized that without Tony, we would be unable to successfully pull off this caper.

There's a lot of stuff to consider, but this one is by far the most important. In the end, unless Dad decides to pull the trigger on the three retired cops, all of these plans will go for naught. He chickened out on the Pensacola shooting...thankfully, and I don't know if he really has the nerve to shoot those dirty cops guys in cold blood? We'll see.

I am a Nervous Nelly thinking about all of this craziness. I've never even cheated once on my tax returns, and now I am thinking about murder. Insane, isn't it? I haven't told Barry a word about what we're discussing; he would have a shit fit.

Is the omission of a material fact to your spouse a violation of the marriage vows? Do I need a ruling on this question from the minister who married us? Better not ask though because he might not give me the answer I'm looking for. LOL.

Hope you're taking oodles of pictures so I can vicariously enjoy your trip. Barry has advised me that we will take a cruise when hell freezes over. I'd debate him on this matter, except I can't imagine being around so many nutso people, sniffling kiddies, and adults who let their inhibitions go when they buy those liquor packages.

Always your buddies-in-arms,

Anne

-49-
PH'S JOURNAL MAY 21, 2018

As our cruise thankfully began to peter out today, George and I sat on out on the veranda (I like that word more than "balcony"—more fancy-pants), reliving this leg of the trip. I tried to beg off any more cruises on a ship. "George," I pleaded, "please, no more trips like this one. I for sure enjoyed every minute of your company, but oh my God, it's just too cramped with annoying people."

"Oh, what a whiney boy," she said mockingly. "But to relieve your angst, Preston, I promise no mas. We'll go the Holiday Inn route all the way for any future excursions."

"You such a nice lady," I answered in my best Chinaman voice.

"Don't tempt fate by being a wiseass; otherwise, we'll take the Miami to Lisbon cruise. Just imagine, days upon end across the Atlantic, arguing with Indian parents about their ne'er-do-well children during every dinner and having highbrow conversations with people like Jimmy and Charmaine."

"You are so mean you could be Lucifer's agent," I fired back.

George stood up from her chair, leaned over to give me a kiss filled with her tongue and parted mouth, and reached between my legs. "Please no," I told her. "There's only so much time left to see the enchanting, never-ending water." We stood up hand-in-hand and walked into the bedroom.

After a few hours of romping around in our playpen followed by a leisurely dinner with the now well-behaved, mouth-zipped Indian kiddies, we sat on the veranda again. I pulled out a paper laying out the twelve AA steps and read over it.

"I have read over the twelve steps to the point that they are imprinted in my brain forever." George stayed quiet, instinctively knowing that I wanted to talk a bit.

"It is such a burden being an alcoholic. I'm not being, as you so often like to say, a whiney boy. It's just a fact. Having to take a moral inventory of myself is scary in and of itself. I look at myself and see a loathsome man. Admitting all my wrongs. Thinking about the people whom I have wronged and making amends to them. The list just goes on and on. Like I said, a burden."

"But you're working through the steps," George said in an almost murmur. "I have been watching you closely..."

"No shit," I interrupted.

"Don't!" she reprimanded me. "You are fighting your addiction and doing a damn good job of it. And get the notion out of your head that you are loathsome. Since you sobered up, you have become a truly wonderful man whom I am proud to call the man I have always wanted to be with and whom I love to the core of my heart."

Boy, after that soliloquy, no way I could be a wiseacre and make some inane remark.

"Question," George continued. "Whom do you want to make amends to, Preston?"

"That's easy enough," I replied. "My kids, Conrad, Tony, you,"

"Good start," George continued. "Don't worry about your amends with me. You have more than made up for your extremely shitty beginning with me, in so many ways. What about Donna?"

"She's on my list too, but that will be a tough one. She has so much lingering resentment over our marriage, and I'm not sure she'll ever want to speak with me."

"But...?" George said.

"But yes, I must take that step when we return."

"Another question, Preston. You are not a godly man—as a matter of fact, far from it. And you've been mum about what represents your higher power. So how have you dealt with that rather major issue?"

I hemmed and hawed around for more than a minute, reluctant to say it. Then I mumbled the words so inaudibly into the floor that George said, "Speak up for Christ sakes!"

I gasped for air, looked up at George, and said, "You are my higher power, George. When I think about it, you became my higher power around the time of my first AA meeting."

"That's what I figured," George said quietly. "And I am proud that you put me at the center of your universe. Just so you know, though, whether it's God or me, in the end, the onus still sits right on your back."

"Got it, darling."

287

-50-
PH'S JOURNAL MAY 22-25, 2018

Back to the real world…if Canada qualifies as the real world. I wished the dude behind the Enterprise counter would have discarded his stodgy comportment, just like the other Canucks here, and say something like "Next, asshole." But noooo, he treated me like a respected customer. I would almost rather freeze my ass off in a place like Toronto with such courteous people than endure any more insanity in the country of my birth.

The break from Trump's serial absurdity has been such a relief. No attacks on the press, the FBI, Mueller, Democrats, et cetera. I still have lingering regrets about the decision to walk away from the Pensacola rally; however, the reality that faced the near-impossible task of carrying out the assassination has brought me to terms, at least a little, but not entirely, about my choice. George and I will shortly fly back into the three-ring circus, but we still have a few days of respite left.

George agreed that we should have finished up our trip in Vancouver and flown home. We were both worn out and ready to return to Austin. I told her the only reason we were exhausted was her nymphomania-like tendencies. "Tough titty, weenie boy" was her response. So we rented a car from the oh-so-polite counterman and rode the rigorous eight-hours-plus trip to Jasper.

Our decision to continue the trip eastward turned out to be worth it. The Canadian Rockies weren't up to the Hubbard Glacier but were still an extraordinary sight—colossal mountains, one after another, all along BC-5 to the north.

We stopped at the Athabasca Glacier, one of the six principal ice croppings along the Columbia Icefield. At the rest center, people could check out the vistas, even using pay-for-play telescopes. Several photographs showed that the icefield originally sat where the rest center had been built. The almost-mile recession of ice over more than one hundred years was startling, but just remember, global warming is nothing more than a Chinese hoax. We got that gem from our inquiring-minds-want-to-know president. But former veep, Al, might get on his white horse and ride to the rescue (Hi ho, Silver, away!), that is if he'd ever answer emails from his fans.

The next four days, we hung out first in Jasper—lovely town—and then drove south to Banff, another money-sucking city; although, Lake Louise was worth the look. I took a photo of the lake sitting between two looming mountains as the sun radiated out between the clouds. This picture will be framed and placed somewhere in George's condo…with her permission of course. She might decide it's not sufficiently Far Eastern.

Tomorrow, we finish up in Calgary and fly back home early the following morning to the land of the free and the brave. Hooray for the red, white, and blue!

The time is drawing nigh, and I must decide whether to take a jump into the abyss.

-51-
AUSTIN AMERICAN STATESMAN May 27, 2018

Blog by reporter Terry Palmer

June 10th is the ten-year anniversary of the controversial decision by the district attorney's office to withdraw murder and prejudice in the infamous case involving the Austin Police Department and possible corrupt dealings by three police detectives. On May 15, 2007, Detective Sergeant Willard Banks and detectives James Buhl and Theodore Williams executed a search warrant for narcotics at the home of Leroy and Shanice Wallace on 17th Street in East Austin. During the execution of the warrant, gunfire exploded in the residence; the result was the death of Leroy and Shanice Wallace and their three children, Jazmine,10; DeShawn, 8; and Tyrone, 7.

Following the shooting, the Austin Police Department and Travis County District Attorney's Office conducted a thorough investigation. The case was reviewed by a grand jury, and indictments were rendered against the three officers for criminal homicide against the entire Wallace family and numerous counts of perjury. The three officers pled not guilty to all the charges.

The case against the three Austin officers appeared ironclad going into the trial. A key witness, Maurice Holloway, observed key elements of the shooting that apparently made it clear the version of the shooting alleged by the officers was totally contradicted by Mr. Holloway's version. Further, Shanice Wallace made a dying declaration to APD sergeant, Sam Evans, at Brackenridge Hospital that fingered the three officers for killing the entire family.

One of the fascinating facets of Ms. Wallace's statement given during Sergeant Evans's testimony was the likely presence of five-million-plus dollars inside the Wallace house, never thereafter recovered. Allegations floated around that the purpose of the raid by detectives Banks, Buhl, and Williams was to snatch the money, but this particular matter was never resolved during or after the trial. When Sergeant Sam Evans shocked the courtroom by invoking the Fifth Amendment protection against self-incrimination during his cross-examination by Attorney Preston Howard, the state's case went south.

Toward the end of the trial, Judge P. I. Davis put the district attorney's office in a box, asking whether the state wanted to continue with the case, due first of all to the absence of Maurice Holloway's testimony. Second, while he ruled the tape of Shanice Wallace's dying declaration could not be admitted due to the inaudibility of the tape, Sergeant Sam Evans was permitted to testify from his notes about Ms. Wallace's statement. But it was to no avail since Sergeant Evans refused to answer questions from Defense Attorney Preston Howard on cross-examination, creating issues of credibility on Sergeant Evans's part. The state withdrew all charges against the defendants with prejudice, meaning that the charges could not be revived in the future.

Many questions still remain about this case. Did the three detectives in fact murder the five Wallace family members? Did they steal five million dollars? Whatever happened to the key witness, Maurice Holloway? Was Janard Coleman's murder—he was one of the persons on the defense witness list— somehow related to the case? Why did Sergeant Evans take the Fifth? Why were officers Banks, Buhl, and Williams permitted to retire with full back pay by the police department? There has been no transparency on the part of the APD or the district attorney's office since none of these questions have been answered to any extent by either agency.

This reporter has spent considerable time running down the principals in the case. The retired officers were all contacted and asked about their actions during the shooting and about the lost money. Mr. Banks and Buhl both refused to comment when asked these questions. Mr. Williams only stated that he was proud of his representation by Attorney Preston Howard, and justice was served by the final decision in the case. Other then this statement, Mr. Williams commented that he had nothing else to say.

Considerable time has been spent trying to run down Maurice Holloway. Unfortunately, nothing has turned up as to whether he is still alive, and if so, where he now resides.

The ADA who handled the case, Oliver Baird, has since retired. He was willing to talk on the record, although reluctantly, about the case. Mr. Baird said, "I have always believed that Banks, Buhl, and Williams were guiltier then hell. But between the disappearance of Maurice Holloway, the ruling by

Judge Davis that the tape of the Shanice Wallace's dying declaration wouldn't be admitted—a mistake in my opinion—and Sergeant Sam Evans's refusal to testify on cross-examination, my case disintegrated to nothing.

"We could have continued on with our case and might have had a shot at a guilty verdict, especially since Sergeant Evan did testify from his notes taken as Mrs. Wallace died. Unfortunately, the powers-that-be above my paygrade decided against going forward. The confluence of events that led to a dismissal of the charges against those cops was a sad result, in my opinion."

The police department has adamantly refused from the original trial until now to comment on the decisions related to why the three officers were permitted to retire and the circumstances surrounding Sam Evans's resignation following the trial.

Sam Evans now works as a bailiff for a judge up in Williamson County. When contacted, Mr. Evans refused comment.

Judge P. I. Davis could have offered some insights into the case and several of his rulings. Unfortunately, Judge Davis passed away from lung cancer more than two years ago.

The attorney who represented the three officers, Preston Howard, is now retired. He was available just before press time, having just returned from a trip. Mr. Howard said, "I especially feel bad about the death of the three children. I wonder frequently about how the lives of Jazmine and her siblings would have turned out if they had lived. There's really nothing else to say other than the wheels of justice can sometimes be perverse."

So even today, there are still no answers to what happened and why. Many people still wonder whether justice was truly served when Banks, Buhl, and Williams walked out of the courtroom free men.

-52-
PH'S JOURNAL MAY 28, 2018

Home at last! But when we arrived home, the larder had been depleted; since we didn't look forward to scooping up Poupon mustard or mayonnaise for our breakfast, we played rock, scissors, and paper to see who had to go shopping.

George's rock demolished my scissors, so I ran over to Whole Foods to pick up a few items for breakfast the next day. After picking out some eggs, multi-grain bread, and coffee (Costa Rican, for sure!), I walked to the "15 items and less" line. A lady had not one but *two* carts stuffed with food, and the cashier was scanning, scanning, scanning. "Ma'am," I noted sternly, "I am with the Grocery Police, and you have committed a blatant violation of Whole Food policy. I will have to take you to the back room for an interrogation, and it won't be pleasant; although, because of customer complaints, we no longer engage in waterboarding." The poor lady became so flummoxed that she told the cashier, "Stop scanning. I'm done." Pretty funny if you ask me.

Other than the breakfast articles, I had bought some fava beans—one of my favorite snacks—at the olive bar. The cashier scowled at me while I pulled out the items, I suppose for the Grocery Police comments. As he scanned the fava beans, I said, "When I get home, I'm gonna eat my friend's liver with these fava beans and a lovely Chianti." Then, ala Anthony Hopkins, I chomped my mouth as if even the thought of that delicious meal excited my taste buds. Now, the cashier's eyes jumped around as if he were checking out which exit he could run to first. He just didn't get the joke—even funnier, in my not-so humble opinion.

George and I have been walking around like zombies, so exhausted that when we finally hit the bed, spooning was about the best effort we could undertake. Not that spooning is such an unwelcome activity. We lay there, heated bodies touching, and quietly relived the highlights of our trip. In between reminisces, George would moan quietly...not a carnal sound but instead an indication of complete satisfaction, I suppose not only of our excursion but also with me. It was a special, loving moment, the kind that will linger in my head for a long time.

The Trump watch continues unabated. Mueller is boring down on the president and his underlings as the G-man continues his investigation into possible obstructing of justice and Russian involvement with the 2016 campaign and Trump's ties to Russia.

Whenever the man lies, it reminds me of the saying from *Alice in Wonderland* that up is down as if his many deceits are objective truth. There is absolutely no rationality to the untruths spouting out of his mouth. But the base believes his mendacity, and thus upward and onward he goes.

If I had tried to write a novel early on in his presidency based on his story, no agent would touch it and no publisher would print it. But by now, if someone like Frederick Forsyth or John Le Carre were to put pen to paper about a Russian mole in the White House, it would be instantly snapped up and displayed in bookstores like Barnes and Nobles,

Powells, and other purveyors of fine books across the country. But sadly, I'm not Forsyth or Le Carre.

I sometimes worry, though, that when Mueller finishes up, the Trumpster will squirm out of his jam, and the final result will be no there there. What a letdown if that turns to be the outcome…bummer.

Trump has gotten so far into my head that I dreamed about the sonofabitch last night. We were conversing, and he asked me, "Why don't you ever tell me what's on your mind; you know, tell me the truth." I answered, "Because if I tell you what's on my mind and the truth, you won't listen to my opinion anyway, so what's the point?" He fumed and fussed, and then to my relief, the dream dissipated.

I wondered in my waking hours if his White House lackeys have the opportunity to dodge his fury so easily as I did last night. At least the eternal battle between the Dream Police and the Beelzebub of Bourbon hasn't shown up for a couple of days.

I just read over Terry Palmer's piece in the Sunday *Statesman*. Terry has been a thorn in my side for years, a real anti-police, anti-attorney scandal-monger journalist. But for once, his reporting was reasonably balanced; he even refrained from cutting my balls off.

I can't believe that ten years have passed so quickly since the case that has eaten at my craw for all this time. If I am going to take some action that will at least to some extent right a grievous wrong, then the Ides of March has arrived.

I sent an email to Donna today, asking if we could meet for lunch this week. I took this step in some part from George's urging, but also it was a step I needed to take on my own.

Tony and my daughter Anne will be stopping by tomorrow in the afternoon for discussions about the Three Amigos. Tony and my daughter, along with George, are adamant that we need to get together STAT.

Siggy and Golda are coming to our condo tomorrow night (whatever happened to this place being only George's condo?) and then going over to the Country Line on 2222 for the best baby back ribs anywhere. I figure Siggy wants to check up on my sobriety and also lay some more corny Jewish gags on me. I actually have missed Siggy; he has been a true sponsor and friend.

He texted me several times on the cruise: "You good?" "Every day is a new day." "Reach for your higher power if need be." I sure as hell reached for my higher power often on the cruise and in many positions but not in the manner that Siggy suggested. Hardy, har, har.

Tomorrow's itinerary is filling up. At some point this week, I want to take George to dinner at the Roaring Fork—the sooner the better. She loves the food there, and we're both wondering whether this trip will be the last time we eat there.

May 30th, 31st, and June 1st will be my first Days of Atonement, followed by a visit to my sons. Not the one day Yom Kippur but the Preston Howard five-days-of misery. I have set up separate meetings with my daughter, Tony, Conrad, Dawn/Don, and if she gets back with me, Donna. That one would be a doozy; I expect some fireworks from her, but I will accept whatever she dishes out with as much aplomb as I can muster.

The Atonement Tour continues over the weekend as I fly out to visit my two New York sons. I feel bad that the two boys haven't spent much time with me; I don't know whether I'll see them again for a long time and am reluctant to tell them my plans…which might or might not happen, depending on my resolve to pull the trigger.

-53-

EMAIL BETWEEN PRESTON HOWARD AND WILLY BANKS, JIMMY BUHL, AND THE SPLENDID SPLINTER MAY 28, 2018

TO: Willy Banks, Jimmy Buhl, the Splendid Splinter
FROM: Preston Howard
RE: 10th year reunion

Hey, guys, how have you been? I just ran into Jimmy a little more than a week ago when we were both on the same Alaskan cruise. My girlfriend, George, and I had the opportunity to meet up not only with Jimmy but his delightful wife, Charmaine, as well. I've also seen Willy and Jimmy in the recent past.

Did any of you notice the article in the *Statesman* yesterday? That so-called literary-hack reporter Terry Palmer's article was nothing more than a rehash of the same old facts…absolutely nothing to worry about.

We are shortly coming up on the ten-year anniversary of our big case and victory—June 10th, only thirteen days away! I would hate to have the date slip by without some kind of ceremony. I know all three of you are busy circumventing the globe, but if you're free on that day, I would suggest that we meet up for a celebration.

To make it an especially eventful time, let's meet at Mount Bonnell and watch the sunset, which will be around 8:30. Let's all get there around eight or so. I will buy some obscenely expensive champagne for us to cheer our success ten years ago, and if any of you would prefer some more heavy-duty libation, put your order in. I'll bring a cooler with ice, flutes for the champagne, and glasses for the hard drinkers!

Since the Splendid Splinter might have trouble managing the deep steps to the top, let's meet up at the pullout about twenty-five yards north of the steps. There's a path right there and an easy walk up to the smooth rocks that overlook the Colorado below...a perfect location to watch the sunset. At this time of night, and it being Sunday, most lookie-loos will be further south of our location if they're even there, so we can enjoy our time without interference. It'll be the most beautiful vista you will ever see for the rest of your lives.

Please confirm at your earliest convenience.

Your attorney and pal,

Preston

-54-

PH'S JOURNAL MAY 29, 2018

Met with Tony, my daughter, and my redoubted companion, Tonto, for a few hours in the morning. Is George my Tonto and I'm the Lone Ranger or is it vice-versa? Either way, she has been, and is, my Rock of Gibraltar, and she always will be.

The meeting was…well, it was what it was. Whoever came up with that ridiculous saying "It is what it is"? What is this expression called? A non sequitur? A post hoc? Who gives a damn, right?

Our evening with Siggy and Golda was a pleasure. When the couple walked into the condo, Golda informed George and me that Siggy had been instructed to lay off the Jew jokes. That worked for me since he had been wearing me out with the cornball gags. Golda brought some non-alcoholic wine to celebrate our return to Texas civilization. "Can I spike this fine vintage with a little pinot noir?" I asked this assemblage of buddies. "Certainly, sweetheart," George responded with a smarty-pants laugh, "if you can find it anywhere in our place." Yuk, Yuk. I laughed my ass off.

Siggy was a little subdued, likely at Golda's urging since he couldn't try out his repertoire of Semitic jokes. George showed Golda around the condo interior, explaining her collection of Oriental curiosities. Siggy and I sat out on George's deck, away from the jabbering Percy, taking in the breathtaking views of the Hill Country; Siggy filled me in on a few of the alkies who had been backsliders and had to start back at day number one while I was gone.

I told Siggy that my Days of Atonement were coming up this week and then asked him if he needed to be on my honor roll too. "Don't be a schmuck, Preston. You've done nothing to disappoint me." He stopped for a moment and then asked like a detective questioning a suspect, "Have you?"

"C'mon Siggy. You would be the first to know if I had fallen off the wagon. In fact, George would have acted like a narco-snitch, and you would have been standing at our front door when we pulled up."

Siggy stood up, stepped toward me, and kissed me on the forehead. "For a goy," he said, "you're a helluva guy." I guess with Siggy, that comment represented as good a praise as he could give, and it meant a lot to me for sure.

We all ordered baby backs at the County Line, savoring them until not even one shred of meat was left on any plates. As we said our goodbyes in the parking lot, I suddenly realized that I might never again have the pleasure of my sponsor and good friend's company. I pulled Siggy close and held him for a full minute. When the moment passed, Siggy glanced at me quizzically, I'm sure wondering what the big hug meant. And then Golda and he were gone, likely never to be seen again.

-55-
PH'S JOURNAL MAY 30, 31 AND JUNE 1-3

I have decided to keep a progressive account of the Preston Howard Atonement Tour. My meetings with my daughter, Anne, Tony, and Conrad went as I visualized. Long conversations and reminiscences with each of them, lots of hugs, and a few tears from Anne and surprisingly, from Tony. I knew from the outset that when I started with "I have so many things to be sorry about…" that each meeting would be relaxed, like close friends who talk freely, with comfortable nostalgia about our times together.

My son/daughter Don/Dawn drove down from Arlington and we met at El Borrego on South Congress where we both ordered our favorite heart-clogging meal—a pound each of barbacoa, three fried eggs on top, and pico de gallo full of jalapeno seeds that made our brows sweat from the extra heat. Our exchange began tentatively as she—okay, I just began exclusively using the pronoun—talked about the chip on her shoulder from what she perceived as our family's rejection of her. I explained the shock many of us felt at her transition and the difficulty we had with the change. In the end, Dawn said she understood; we reminisced over her Texas Friday Night Lights games and her exceptional college football career. As she left, we embraced, shed a few tears, and Dawn told me that other than my original resistance to her transition, she felt I had always been the best of parents.

I selected Mayfield Park in near West Austin to meet Donna on Friday, a peaceful location except for the occasionally squawking peacocks. We met mid-morning, a time that I hoped would be, and as it turned out was, sparsely occupied.

We sat on a park bench, Donna sitting as far away from me as she could, her arms drawn close against her chest ala a pose that George would sometimes use when she felt bothered about something. Donna glanced away from me, looking out toward a live oak copse farther away. We sat there for at least five minutes, not saying a word to each other.

"So why are we here?" Donna started out, her words almost malicious.

"I asked to meet you, Donna," I answered, "because I need to say a few things to you."

No response. Painfully uncomfortable.

"I have made so many mistakes with you over the years," I continued, hopeful that she wouldn't numerate the grievous missteps I had taken over the years like many spouses do—reliving any and every miniscule, painful screw-up down to things that would otherwise have been forgotten. "I simply want to sincerely apologize for any and all of my many, and I do mean many, fuck-ups that wound up ruining our marriage."

Still nothing from Donna. Please say something!!

"I can't do anything other than say I am so sorry and hope that you will forgive me for making your life a living hell. You didn't deserve this kind of marriage."

Finally, Donna pulled her arms slightly away from her body and turned her face somewhat toward me. "So why now, Preston? What's the point of it? Our lives together are over, and we've moved on. I am bitter about our marriage…and over you. If you hadn't turned into a total alcoholic, we could have had such a different outcome to the last quarter of our lives."

"I was a lush," I replied, "and for certain, our marriage might have survived if I had gotten off the sauce. But that's not what happened, so here we are in different circumstances."

"Different circumstances?" Donna said. "For sure, different. As it turns out, my life has turned to shit. The guy I met when we divorced turned out to be a liar and a Don Juan, I think even worse than you. Every other guy has either been too frail and over-the-hill—doddering old men—boring, or after my money. It just sucks being into the seventies and alone. Then I find out from Anne that you are like a love-sick puppy, happy as a lark. Gee, how nice."

I refused to bite on her condemnation; it wouldn't have done a whit of difference. "I can't replay the past, Donna. It is what it is (ugh, can't believe I used that hackneyed expression). I have gotten sober and stayed that way…at least so far." I crossed my right fore and middle fingers together, for luck. "And having gotten to a point of sobriety, it's time for me to try and get things right, at least to the best of my ability."

"I've been reading up on Alcoholics Anonymous, probably much later then I should have," Donna answered. Now she faced directly toward me. "So I gather you're here to atone for the many horrible things you have done to me."

"That's the gist of it, Donna," I responded. "I'm calling it my Days of Atonement." I decided to omit the five-days-of-misery reference. "And you are highest on my list of....atonees." Ridiculously senseless choice of a word, but the best I could pull up.

After my last remark, Donna had to suppress a smile. Now she sat quietly, her hands sitting in her lap. Then she stood and gestured for me to get off the bench. She stepped toward me with her arms displayed outward and moved in to hug me. I reciprocated.

"While I still hold much bitterness, Preston," she said, starting to sniffle, "I fully accept your apology. Thank you for making the effort to meet me, which I know was as hard for you as it was for me. You are forgiven from the bottom of my heart." Donna then swiftly turned around and walked away toward the parking lot. From the back, it appeared that her body was heaving as if she might be crying.

The need to drive over to Bartlett's for a drink at the charming bar only five minutes away hit me like an ocean wave engulfing my body. I needed a dirty vodka martini. *Now!!! I'll just have to go back to day one, that's all. No problemo.*

I sat in my car for at least fifteen minutes in the restaurant parking lot, deciding between Bartlett's and George, and then walked into Bartlett's. After sitting at the bar, gazing down at the frosty, enticing dirty vodka martini holding three olives stuck on a swizzle stick for another ten minutes, I laid down cash for the drink, drove back to our condo, walked in, sat on the sofa, and began crying, telling her about this moment of my greatest crisis and weakness...how I had nearly succumbed to my addiction. George held me in her arms, alternately caressing my back and wiping away my tears and assuring me that she was there for me, always and ever.

Later, she asked me if I was too fragile to go ahead with the plan. After thinking over her question, I said, "Nope. Just a slight blip. I'll be fine by next week."

In late afternoon, I flew to Newark, rented a car, and made it up to West Point well after ten. Since no one at the base ever locks their homes (the honor code at work), I opened the door, walked in quiet as a stone without waking up the family, and went to bed. So weird, the need to turn the clock back and drink earlier today had come and gone like a wisping fog that dissipated into nothing.

My son, Preston Junior, drove up from Hell's Kitchen—not the old Hell's Kitchen but rather, the gentrified version. He and my son, Kyle, sat out on the Army-boy's side porch with me, talking quietly and watching the Hudson River flow past. When I started into my atonement routine, which at this point was getting old, they both shut me down almost simultaneously. "No need to go there, Dad," Preston interjected. "Anne alerted us to the reason for your trip up here, and you wasted your time and money...although, we both enjoy hanging out with you and listening to your many fanciful, over-the-top tales." Both of the boys guffawed over that comment. "You have been more than a terrific dad," Preston continued, "and I'm just relieved that you have stopped drinking. We've all been worried about it for the longest time. If you say you're finished with it, that's good enough for me."

All Kyle said was "Ditto. Nothing to add. Did you bring cigars, Dad?" Kyle and I have always had the similar trait of getting down to the bottom line, likely a more apt feature in the service than it was in my line of work.

"Sure did," I told them. I handed out Montecristo gigantes to each of them. As we sat smokin' away, we relived our craziest time together when we were hiking Rainier and became lost on a crevice field with fog all around us. We laughed about that experience; although, at the time, I was just about going incontinent from fear.

And that was that. The Days of Atonement had come to an end. I had made peace with everyone important to me, and life could now move forward somewhat unburdened. Well, perhaps not exactly.

-56-

PH'S JOURNAL JUNE 6, 2018

More than an hour ago, maybe around six p.m., George lounged just outside the condo against her car, a sleek, black Nissan Maxima with power to spare on the open road while I carried out several pieces of luggage that she would need for at least a week or two. Every time I would step outside with another bag, George would go, "Step on it, buster. You're a slacker; that's what you are!" And I would reply, "I'm a steppin', Massa; I be a steppin'." This silliness went back-and-forth for several trip until finally, we both started giggling like two little kids who didn't need a whole lot to be entertained.

Anne and Tony will come in tomorrow with a small Penske truck and help me lug out some of George's furniture that was important to her. She will drive down to her daughter Alexandra's home in New Braunfels for a few days prior to the confluence of events that might or might not happen.

The only piece in my condo that held any sentimental value was Buster's floor-to-ceiling, light oak bookshelf that years ago held Buster's and my great-grandfather's legal tomes. As I noted in my memoir, the bookshelf would sometimes indistinctly speak to me at night as if Buster or his father had some important message for me. We would carry out that piece to the truck as well and take them to Tony's garage for temporary safe-keeping. Tony has the ability to temporarily disable the security cameras by our condos, an important step if Tony and my daughter can insulate themselves from any involvement in this scheme. I have no idea how he pulled off this sleight of hand, like a magician reaching into his top hat and grabbing out a rabbit.

Back to the George toting chore. After I finished, we both leaned against her car and kept silent for a few moments. I noticed her gray t-shirt with green and yellow lettering for the first time; the inscription on her tee read "Hodag Country Festival."

"You're like an onion, George—more-and-more peels keep coming off, showing another part of you. I never realized you went to Rhinelander for the festival."

"Oh, you betcha," George answered with a mangled Midwestern accent. "I drove up from Chicago years ago for the event—great music and food. I stored the t-shirt away years ago and just now found it."

"I just happened to be in Rhinelander for some work there when one of the festivals opened," I told her. "I took a walk into the woods for some exercise and ran plumb into one of those Hodags; scared the livin' shit outta me. The creature was enormous, with fiery, red eyes, scary-looking horns, and claws that would have gouged me to death. The breath coming out of the Hodag reeked, kinda like…" I stopped and pointed toward her pelvic area "…only ten times worse. The Hodag scared me to death when it roared, and I ran like a son-of-a-bitch to get out of the forest. I'm lucky to be alive and able to tell you this story!"

George started twittering. "You are so beyond full of bullshit, Preston Howard. If you don't quit with these outlandish tales, I might have to turn you in for a new model…except that every now and then, you do offer some feeble entertainment…which I likely can't find with any other man. But don't ever again refer to my twat as stinky. That's just beyond disrespectful to your co-habiting mate and her luscious-tasting pussy."

We then both started laughing hard, like two friends who can't get enough of a comical moment.

After we settled down a bit, I turned into her, placed my arm around her body, and gravely said, "It's time, darling."

George began crying, her expression full of mixed emotions just like Olivia Colman—melancholy, fear, need, poutiness, and who knew what else. "I know," George began. "It will be so frightening for us to be apart, not knowing how this saga will end. I worry about you, and what you're about to do."

"You're really apprehensive that it might turn out like Pensacola, right?" I replied.

"Pensacola, yes; although, that would be okay with me so long as you get out alive." Now she began shivering uncontrollably. "And don't say it is what it is, dipshit."

"All we can hope is for the best, George. So let's just leave it alone at this point. I do have one final request of you, darling."

"What is that, sweetheart?" Her voice quavered, the fingers of both hands wiping tears from her cheeks.

"Our first kiss, right on the steps of your condo…" I pointed toward the front door "…is an unforgettable moment, stamped on my brain just like Bierstadt's *Lake Lucerne* in the National Gallery of Art stays with me forever. May we please have a repeat performance?"

"Fuck Bierstadt. Our first kiss had better be one of the best things you ever experienced," George answered as she opened her arms toward me and we locked our open mouths together for what seemed like an eternity but was really for only a minute or two.

How blessed that moment in time! Rick and Elsa would have perhaps been envious that George and I had outperformed their famous kiss.

I opened the car door, and George stepped inside ever so deliberately as if gravity was trying to push her back up to the parking lot. When finally seated, George said, "Please, please be careful, Preston. I don't want to lose you, ever, ever."

"Seeya 'round, kid," I said, trying a pathetic imitation of Rick AKA Humphrey Bogart. I carefully shut the car door. George smiled wanly up at me, flipped me the finger, which then changed to her middle finger moving back and forth as in goodbye, and drove off. That was just like George, sarcasm and love rolled up into one

My two favorite love story movies are *Groundhog Day* and *Four Weddings and a Funeral*. As good as those moves are, they in no way come close to the love story I have been living with George. I miss her already.

-57-
PH'S JOURNAL JUNE 9, 2018

Tonight will likely be my last night in Austin, in Texas, and in my country where I have lived for seventy-four years. Since George's house feels like King Tut's crypt—no furniture there, not even a mouse is stirring—I have decided to spend the night in my own condo. The wraparound deck in the back is silent tonight; the coyotes' howling and stalking prey must be somewhere further west in the Hill Country.

I have no fear or doubts about leaving the United States. The country has become afflicted with insanity; it is full of rot and uncertainty. Voices scream at each other across the political divide, and there seems to be no way for this rupture to heal anytime soon, at least not for the little time I have left on this earth.

Whatever happened to real political leaders, men (so far anyway) who could move our country in a righteous direction? Men like Abe, Teddy, FDR, even Reagan. With this president, the bar has been set so low that any Tom, Dick, or Harry could easily take the reins of power and muck things up even more.

Now for the moment of truth. Do I have the will tomorrow night to pull the trigger and set things right? I've never even hunted an animal, so what makes me think I have the resolve to kill those three men?

Anne, Tony, and George have been more than willing to play their roles in this insane plot. The only question left—am I?

-58-
AUSTIN AMERICAN STATESMAN FRONT
PAGE, JUNE 11, 2018

MURDER ON MOUNT BONNELL!
Retired Austin Cops Long Suspected of Corruption
Shot Down Last Night

Retired Austin police officers Willard Banks, James Buhl, and Theodore Williams were killed in cold blood last night on the Mount Bonnell turnout just north of the long steps there. Coincidentally, their deaths took place exactly on the ten-year anniversary of the dismissal of the murder charges against them for the deaths of Leroy Wallace and his family during a nighttime narcotics raid of the Wallace residence. Ironically, *Statesman* reporter Terry Palmer wrote a special blog about the Banks case only fourteen days ago.

The shooting, often referred to as the Banks case, became the most infamous trial in the history of Austin criminal jurisprudence. Represented by renowned attorney, Preston Howard, the three officers were indicted by a grand jury in 2007 and went on trial in May, 2008. During the trial, numerous facts came to light about alleged corruption by the three officers and also a key prosecution witness, Sergeant Sam Evans.

Judge P.I. Davis made several controversial rulings in the case, forcing the district attorney's office to dismiss charges with prejudice against the three police officers. ADA Oliver Bair, who represented the state in the case, commented in

Palmer's recent article that he felt the officers were guilty as hell. Immediately after the trial, the *Statesman* editorial board condemned the Austin Police Department, the three officers, and the incompetence of the district attorney's office and commented that justice delayed was justice denied.

As of press time, Austin Police homicide detectives and forensics civilians were out in force at Mount Bonnell scouring the crime scene. A spokesman at the scene stated that at this time, there were no suspects to the shooting.

The *Statesman* will follow up with more information about the murders in tomorrow's edition.

-59-
AUSTIN AMERICAN STATESMAN JUNE 12, 2018 BLOG BY REPORTER TERRY PALMER

CITY REELING FROM COP MURDERS!

People in Austin are still stunned by the murders of retired police officers Willard Banks, James Buhl, and Theodore Williams. The police department has been tight-lipped about the investigation and declined requests from this reporter for further information about the case.

An anonymous source inside the department has, however, been forthcoming with some juicy morsels about the murders. The three retired officers were each shot first in the back of the head, followed by shots to the front, in their forehead.

Further evidence was also recovered at the scene. Several empty bottles of champagne and flutes were found but only with fingerprints of the victims. A cooler was also located, filled with ice, Southern Comfort, and glasses; no fingerprints were located. Additionally, a photograph of Jazmine Wallace, one of the victims of the shooting ten years ago, had been placed on top of the cooler.

Two couples sitting south of the shooting above the steps at Mount Bonnell heard the shots; they all stated that precisely six shots were fired—three shots in succession, followed by three more a half-minute later. The two couples, their names as yet undisclosed, stated that they were at first apprehensive about approaching the location of the shots. Approximately fifteen minutes later, they did finally walk the trail rim northward above the Colorado River and found the three officers lying on the ground, all deceased. The witnesses stated that there was no one else present, and one of them called 911 immediately.

My source further informed me that the police department has been keeping tabs on officers Banks, Buhl, and Williams since their acquittals ten years ago and that the FBI and IRS have been conducting an investigation into possible tax fraud by the three men. Apparently, each of the officers has been living beyond what their retirements would provide, travelling throughout the world with no apparent financial means to do so.

Further reporting will be forthcoming as information develops.

-60-
AUSTIN AMERICAN STATESMAN JUNE 22, 2018 BLOG BY REPORTER TERRY PALMER

SUSPECT NAMED IN COP KILLINGS
Local Attorney Preliminarily Fingered for Murders

Austin Police Chief Alfred Abrantes and FBI agent-in-charge James Trotter conducted a joint press conference on Thursday afternoon in the APD press room, the first time the authorities have revealed any information regarding the investigation into the shocking murders of retired Austin police officers Willard Banks, James Buhl, and Theodore Williams on June 10th of this year at Mount Bonnell.

Chief Abrantes began the press conference by announcing that famous attorney, Preston Howard, has been listed as a person of interest. Chief Abrantes emphasized that while no guilt has at this point been attributed to Mr. Howard, there are certain facts that do point to his possible involvement in the murders.

The chief went on to say that police department homicide detectives executed a search warrant on Mr. Howard's condo in northwest Austin. He further said that another person, at this time only a possible witness—Georgeanna Robards—is also sought for questioning and that her condo, in the same complex as Mr. Howard's residence, was also searched pursuant to a warrant. When asked about the results of the two search warrants, Chief Abrantes declined to comment.

Later in the press conference, FBI agent-in-charge, James Trotter, said that there is now a nationwide search underway for both Mr. Howard and Ms. Robards. Agent Trotter stated that the full resources of the FBI are being used to locate these two people.

Following the press conference, this reporter contacted two different anonymous sources in the police department. The first source stated that the search of both Mr. Howard's and Ms. Robards's residences uncovered nothing substantial. No computers, laptops, cell phones, or other significant evidence was found.

Another source stated that both the police department and FBI are bewildered that no trace of Mr. Howard or Ms. Robards can be found. Apparently, efforts have been made through airlines, trains, and buses to locate the pair, to no avail.

-61-
AUSTIN AMERICAN STATESMAN JULY 18, 2018 BLOG BY REPORTER TERRY PALMER

ON-THE-RUN AUSTIN ATTORNEY DIES IN PHILLIPINES

Anne Howard held a press conference yesterday afternoon at the offices of Howard, Diamond, and McGowan to announce that her father, Attorney Preston Howard, has been killed in an automobile crash in Cebu City, Philippines, a city in the Central Visayas region of the country.

A distraught Ms. Howard, at several times during the press conference hardly able to speak through her tears, began by first stating that she has been bewildered that her father has been accused of murdering detectives Teddy Banks, Jimmy Buhl, and Ted Williams. "My dad has always been a peaceful, compassionate man, and there was no reason why he would want to kill them." Ms. Howard also stated that she was bewildered as to why her father went to the Philippines.

Ms. Howard was asked by this reporter whether she has been questioned by the authorities about her father's possible involvement in the murders and his whereabouts. "Yes, I have," she answered. "An Austin police homicide detective and FBI agent questioned me for several hours last week." She stated that she had been forthcoming with the authorities and also that she was represented during the questioning by Attorney Conrad Diamond, Mr. Howard's prior law partner.

Ms. Howard was asked how she found out about her father's death. "A police spokesman from Cebu City in the Philippines contacted me early last week to advise me that my dad died in a fiery automobile crash. His body was disfigured beyond recognition." She went on to say that fortunately her dad had her personal information among his effects, and the police in Cebu City were kind enough to send her a death certificate which she will need to probate her dad's estate. Ms. Howard stated that she turned over a copy of the death certificate to the APD and FBI.

She went on to further state that she requested her father's body be returned from the Philippines....She noted that her father had always wanted his remains cremated. She received the ashes at the same time as the death certificate, and at her father's request, scattered the ashes into the Colorado River.

This reporter's anonymous source inside the Austin Police Department leaked that homicide detectives and FBI agents are skeptical of Mr. Howard's death. Apparently, there is a thriving business in the Philippines of deaths being contrived for the purpose of suspects evading apprehension. My source further stated that no police officer in the Philippines has been identified as having telephoned Ms. Howard. The FBI has sent agents to the Philippines to look further into Mr. Howard's disappearance. Finally, my source stated that as of right now, if Mr. Howard is still alive, he has fallen off the face of the earth.

-62-
SEPTEMBER 25, 2018
NOTE TO FAMILY AND FRIENDS FROM ANNE HOWARD

Dear family and friends,

So here is the story about my dad. I am shocked and dismayed by this turn of events, as I am sure you are too. I certainly don't have any answers as to what really took place or whether my dad had any involvement in the murders of the three police officers. All I know at this point is that I miss my dad terribly and am left with more questions than answers.

Sincerely,

Anne Howard

PS: If you haven't figured out yet who slipped me Conrad Diamond's Banks file, you probably weren't paying attention!

-63-

OCTOBER 2, 2018
EPILOGUE: READERS, ONLY YOU ARE SO LUCKY TO GET TO THE BOTTOM OF THIS CRAZY TALE!

Dear Clarence,

C'mon, Dad! You couldn't come up with a more anonymous alibi than Clarence Darrow? Surely, you could have picked a better name that wouldn't be like a colossal billboard blazoned across the highways and byways of Costa Rica. At least you could have selected Richard "Racehorse" Haynes, a less celebrated attorney—although Racehorse might feel slighted by my comment. I can't believe that you picked the name Clarence Darrow or that Tony agreed to it.

Since it has been a tribulation to send this letter to you in Quepos—Tony sent it after dodging an FBI agent still on his and our trail—I'm not sure how soon another missive will be posted your way for some time. Thus, this account will be lengthy.

I still can't believe that I became ensnared in this irrational scheme, but I did, and after giving it somber thought, I'm admittedly glad I signed up for it. Justice has finally been served, and while the Bible says in one place "thou shalt not kill," in another it says "an eye for an eye." I suppose it's easy to rationalize what we've done under the "eye for an eye" premise; I, for one, have not yet felt one shred of guilt over what we have done, at least not yet.

I was actually only afraid twice after the killings, the first time being when I picked you up on the street outside your condo away from any security cameras just after you shot those three sorry cops. As I took the almost four-hour drive with you to DFW International Airport, my hands and arms trembled with dread. What if a state trooper or local Smokey the Bear stopped us for some trivial traffic violation? Jesus, I would have probably disassembled right on the spot!

Since I dropped you off a block away from the La Quinta near the airport so you could take a shuttle per Tony's admonition to me about security cameras, I missed your brilliant disguise as you went into the airport—gray wig, totally dyed gray goatee, hoot-owl glasses, silicone fake belly, Texas Ranger baseball hat pulled low over your eyes, and cane—quite a get-up—plus having a redcap push you along in a wheelchair.

I kept my fingers crossed that your initial forged passport under the name John Savage—jeez, an actor of all things—would hold up to close inspection at DFW and the Philippines. So were you like Superman out there, changing from your John Savage persona to Clarence when you got on the plane to Central America?

George left her condo and drove the car down to Alexandra's house in New Braunfels and left it there. A day before you did the deed at Mount Bonnell, Alexandra drove her back up to my house. George swore on a stack of bibles that she only told her daughter she would be gone for a little while and didn't want her car unattended.

Tony and I gave her goodbye bear hugs at my house, and then I drove George to the Stephen F.

Austin Hotel downtown where she took a cab out to Bergstrom. Wanting to outdo you, she wore a drab, blond wig, teacher shoes, a smudged, beige sunhat that looked like it had seen better days, a prosthetic nose (something you definitely didn't need with your schnozola!), and once again, silicon fatty belly and glasses that looked like Mr. Peepers, except shaded. I would never have recognized her in a million years if she had passed me on the street.

George flew to Mexico City with her new and improved passport name of Jane Brown. Gee, Dad, notice the diff between her name and your ostentatious surnames. From Mexico City, she embarked to San Jose—not sure how she got on down to Quepos, but likely by bus, which seems to be a fairly standard form of transportation there.

The second time I was a fraidy cat took place when an APD homicide detective and FBI agent insisted on interviewing (interrogating?) me shortly after the Mount Bonnell shootings. I called Conrad forthwith, and he insisted on coming with me to the meeting. I couldn't tell Conrad the real story—no reason to get anyone else beyond our little quartet in on the con; although, I somehow got the feeling that Conrad had sniffed a rat when I told him I knew *nada*.

When we walked into the interview, the FBI agent read me my rights and told me that if I lied to his agency, the falsehood constituted a crime. I could feel my bowels growling like a mad dog. But I forced myself to stay calm as a cucumber (ouch, Dad, corny…you would come up with a better metaphor, I'm sure). I just stuck to one theme—I'm shocked, I don't know, I never knew, not my Dad. When the officer and agent started getting ugly with me, accusing me of lying (you talking about *moi?*), Conrad interceded and said *no mas*, and we left. Conrad left it with the two guys that they could either charge me with something or otherwise leave me along. I finally got a taste of what it's like to be on the suspect receiving end of law enforcement...ouch!

Now to my Oscar-winning performance at the press conference in Conrad's office after the death certificate and "your ashes" arrived by Fedex ("the envelope please"). I'm certain that you paid someone to send the package, once again to avoid those prying cameras. Conrad took a copy of the birth certificate to the PD and the FEBs and told them I had thrown your ashes to the four winds into the Colorado River. The powers-that-be were, according to Conrad, exceedingly pissed at not getting their hands on those ashes. He also helped me write out some points for the press conference, which were helpful in getting me through the event.

To draw up tears and upset feelings, all I had to do was think back to the time in the eighth grade when I sneaked over to a high school senior boy's house to go swimming at his pool and where he would have presumably pressed me, too early in my childhood, to have sex. You found out where I was, scared the shit out of the boy, and grabbed me away from the pool in a rage, screaming at me the whole way to your car. I cried all the way out of the kid's home and going home as well. All I had to do at the press conference was draw that horrible moment into my head, and the tears flowed like Victoria Falls.

Without Tony, none of this plan could have been executed; he was a godsend if there ever was one. I remember you telling me that Tony worked for the CIA, and for the APD as a detective in both the homicide and organized crime units. With Tony's background, he must have had some sordid underworld types who offered services that cannot be otherwise found, guys with hook noses from the Big Apple and probably other major cities as well.

He obtained two different forged passports and driver's licenses for you so you could pull off the Philippines caper and the Clarence Darrow passport for Costa Rica. I'm still burned about that second one, just so you know. Tony pushed for you to fly out to Samoa to avoid extradition, but I am glad that you chose this hemisphere, so I will be able to see you once the laws give up. Please tell George that I now know who the Throwin' Samoan is, but I'll never be in the same league as her when it comes to obscure athletes.

Tony did the same thing for George—forged passport as noted above and also a driver's license. Tony also secured one of each for me, so at some point I can hopefully visit George and you.

Tony planned everything through and through. He disabled the condo security cameras, and speaking about security cameras, he remembered that Mount Bonnell had none, which allowed you to execute your part of the scheme. When I say "scheme," is that just a euphemism for murder? LOL

More about Tony. He carefully selected the airports for George's and your embarkations. He figured out that Houston International had just initiated a facial recognition system; whereas, both DFW and Bergstrom had not. You could have been uncovered later on by the FBI by going through Houston, so it was a real life saver.

And even more about Tony. You owe your friend bigtime for all of his shenanigans. While you were snuffing out the Three Amigos, Tony was saying goodbye to George and then wending his way in the air from DFW to Paris, and then on to Dubai. Once again, with no facial recognition at DFW, and since he had a forged passport, the authorities in Paris could only match up his passport to his face, so no problem.

Once he got to Dubai, Tony used a power of attorney under your Clarence Darrow identity to transfer your checking and saving accounts to a bank there, plus your IRA funds that were also pulled out and transferred in Dubai by Tony. Since you will be disappearing from the face of the earth, you shouldn't be too terribly concerned about the IRS consequences.

Obviously, Tony has been the subject of intense scrutiny by the APD and FBI. They immediately jumped on him since he is widely known as your closest friend. Tony went to one of those tough interviews, but he didn't need Conrad to tell the coppers that he knew nothing and don't bother him again unless they're charging him with a crime. He still has to look over his shoulder, as do I, for shadowing cops watching our every move.

Another tricky piece of the puzzle was whether to ship George and your belongings to Quepos without creating any attention. Tony and I agonized over what to do with George's and your stuff. We originally thought that right after the killings, I would haul ass in a Penske truck (rented under my forged passport and driver's license, geez, how many criminal offenses have I committed?) from Austin to Miami; meet with a representative of Complete Logistics Solutions, a company that specializes in moving personal effects throughout Central America; and at some point later, have your belongings sent on to Quepos.

But there were just too many things that might have gone wrong, including the Miami company remembering me. Thus, we stayed with the plan of putting your belongings in Tony's garage temporarily and immediately after he returned from Dubai, he moved everything to a house out in the Hill Country that his deceased father owned. Maybe at some point later on, Tony or I can send you George's stuff and Buster's library bookshelf, so Buster and your great-grandfather can continue their conversations with you. George and you will have to rent a furnished place or buy your own furniture. Sorry about that.

The decision to provide me with your power-of-attorney was helpful. I have put your condo on the market, and it should sell for a top dollar. The only fly in this ointment has been Charmaine Buhl making noises about suing you for the death of her husband. However, Conrad has advised her that if she files suit, it might very well open up questions about her finances, which will likely be tangled up with Jimmy's money. She is apparently rethinking her decision. Since your condo and your car are really the only asset you have left, I will, as your executor, place those two items into probate shortly.

I hope you haven't fallen asleep from this way too long missive. But hang with me for just a few more sentences.

Mom came by my house shortly after your connection to the murders became publicized. She was flabbergasted, but all I could do was shrug my shoulders and tell her how shocked I was as well. The same with Siggy and Golda. They just couldn't get their heads around what you *allegedly* did; once again, all I could do is say gee…it can't be true! I just don't believe it! Although Siggy did recall when you hugged him the last time; he thought it was overdramatic at the time, but later put it together with subsequent events. He wondered out loud whether it could be true. I just shrugged my shoulders.

Speaking of Siggy, I hope you are staying off the bottle. The pressure has been extreme for all of us, but I especially worry about you and how this entire spectacle might push you back to drinking. I am certain that George will keep you on the right path; she has been your salvation many times over. I did check, and there is an AA in Quepos, which you are hopefully attending.

Terry Palmer has been driving me nuts. He calls me two or three times a week like a Nosy Parker. I figure that at some point, he will tire of me telling him, "No news, Terry."

The only thing I regret is that my relationship with Barry has been tarnished, and I feel so guilty about it. He knows in his heart-of-hearts that I am up to my eyeballs in trouble. And yet, he won't come out and accuse me, I suppose, because he is such a decent man. At some point further down the road, I will maybe fess up and tell him what happened, maybe whenever you leave this earth for whatever lies beyond. Hopefully though, not any time soon.

Make certain to let George know that Alexandra is taking good care of Percy and Zsa Zsa. She drove up to Austin a few weeks ago to report on how the Quaker parrots have fared in their new digs. Alexandra says that the birds have acclimated to the Germanic ways in New Braunfels; although, she is attempting to disabuse Percy from continuing to shriek "Eat me!" I got the impression that she knows at least a little bit about what happened and that George is alive and well. I didn't bite, however, on giving out any of the ugliness that has taken place recently.

I relive these recent events quite often, turning them around in my head, wondering whether I will be punished either on this earth or whatever lies beyond for the many transgressions I have committed. Like I said earlier in this letter, Banks, Buhl, and Williams deserved what they got; it's just, should I have taken part in their deaths? I hope I never regret my decision.

Please give George many hugs from me. I care for her so much...for her tenacity and the wonderful affect she has had on you.

I love you so much, Dad. Best of luck, Clarence!

ACKNOWLEDGEMENTS BY PRESTON AND ANNE HOWARD

1.   Our editor, Jeff LaFerney, has as always kept me on the right path toward making this book more readable. He answered all the key grammatical issues: comma or not, semi-colon or something else like an ellipsis, and so on. One of these days, we might make Jeff proud of us and complete a draft with no mistakes...not! Any writer who needs a top-flight editor should use Jeff; he is the best!

2.   Fellow Arkansan and author, Ashley Fontainne, has once again been generous with her time and advice that has made it possible for this book to be finalized and published. It could never have been accomplished without her assistance. She has always been available to help us with our writing, even at the expense of her own terrific books. Also, Ashley designed the attractive book cover.

3.   We owe much gratitude to Susan Gay from Vermont. Sue and I (Preston Howard) grew up together in the sheltered town of Madison, New Jersey. She claims that we used to dance together during middle school lunch periods; I have no recollection of that particular endeavor, which is a good thing since the spirit of Fred Astaire never favored me. Susan helped us immensely with the many chapters in the book related to alcohol addiction, which helped us to accurately express the disease of alcoholism and the ways to deal with it. Due to her assistance, these chapters came to life; they were realistic and powerful depictions of what

alcoholics face every day of their lives. Any errors we have made on this subject are entirely ours.

4.   We could never have successfully completed the chapters related to the Banks file and capital murder trial without the knowledge and skill of good friend and colleague, Austin attorney, Greg Zaney. Greg represented criminal defendants in Texas over many years, and he pointed out the many dumb errors we wrote in the first draft. He actually made it look like we knew what we were writing about! Once again, if we missed something in Greg's translation, it was entirely our fault.

5.   Our friend, Anthony Nelson, Austin detective extraordinaire, filled us in on the many misconceptions we had about how homicide investigations proceed. Without Anthony's voluminous knowledge, based on his many years of working murder cases, we would have been whistling in the dark. Thank you, Anthony, and if we messed up on any of the finer points, just laugh us off as a bunch of wanna-be cops!

6.   Once again, a shout-out to Texas labor attorney Ron DeLord for his contributions in Chapter 2 related to the Ice-T and Capitol media room stories. Exciting stuff!

7.   A thanks to Jim Parks and Tim Clark (sadly, now deceased) for their hilarious story in Chapter 2 about the cow stuck in a culvert.

8.   As always, we wish to thank Blair Johnson, my (Anne's) husband and my (Preston's) son-in-law. He has been supportive of our work and offered many suggestions to improve the final result.

ABOUT THE AUTHORS

Preston Howard still lives in Hot Springs, Arkansas, where, since his retirement, he continues with his passion for writing. As Preston completed his 2018 taxes, he wondered whether the IRS would permit a write-off for use of his deck overlooking scenic Lake Hamilton where he does most of his work, but then thought better of it; no sense risking an audit by the vigilant tax man.

After his debut novel, "The Sheltering Palms," his daughter Anne Howard and Preston have enjoyed completing this noir thriller, which include more farcical stories and adventures. Early in this new book, the debate continues about the adequacy of Preston's college and law school education. Readers: as Anne Howard wrote her parts of the story, think about how she figuratively rolled her eyes at her father's preposterous antics and pranks

Connect with Preston and Anne:

Facebook.com/prestonhowardauthor; or send them email: an authorprestonhoward@gmail.com

www.ingramcontent.com/pod-product-compliance
Lightning Source LLC
Chambersburg PA
CBHW030920260626
47169CB00002B/342